Oliver Optic

A Young Knight-Errant

Or Cruising in the West Indies

Oliver Optic

A Young Knight-Errant
Or Cruising in the West Indies

ISBN/EAN: 9783337280642

Printed in Europe, USA, Canada, Australia, Japan

Cover: Foto ©Andreas Hilbeck / pixelio.de

More available books at **www.hansebooks.com**

A YOUNG KNIGHT-ERRANT

OR

CRUISING IN THE WEST INDIES

BY

OLIVER OPTIC

AUTHOR OF "THE ARMY AND NAVY SERIES" "YOUNG AMERICA ABROAD"
FIRST AND SECOND SERIES "THE GREAT WESTERN SERIES" "THE WOOD-
VILLE STORIES" "THE STARRY FLAG SERIES" "THE BOAT-CLUB
STORIES" "THE ONWARD AND UPWARD SERIES" "THE YACHT-CLUB
SERIES" "THE RIVERDALE STORIES" "THE BOAT-BUILDER
SERIES" "TAKEN BY THE ENEMY" "WITHIN THE ENEMY'S
LINES" "ON THE BLOCKADE" "STAND BY THE
UNION" "FIGHTING FOR THE RIGHT"
"A MISSING MILLION" "A MIL-
LIONAIRE AT SIXTEEN" ETC.

BOSTON
LEE AND SHEPARD PUBLISHERS
10 MILK STREET
1893

A YOUNG KNIGHT-ERRANT

TYPE-SETTING AND ELECTROTYPING BY
C. J. PETERS & SON, BOSTON

S. J. PARKHILL & CO., PRINTERS, BOSTON

TO

PREFACE.

"A Young Knight-Errant" is the third volume of the "All-Over-the-World" series; and while it contains a completed story which may be read without reference to its predecessors, it is a continuation of the adventures of Louis Belgrave, introduced in the initial story of the set, and to some extent of all the cabin party sailing in the Guardian-Mother, the magnificent steam-yacht of the "Millionaire at Sixteen." The young gentleman makes no display of his wealth, for he handles it himself only to a very limited extent, and is as modest as one in his position ought to be, though his surroundings are calculated to inflate his vanity.

Louis is as honest, respectful, and considerate as when he was practically and comparatively a poor boy. Above all, he is as thoroughly devoted to his mother as when they lived together in the old house at Von Blonk Park. The whole family, reinforced by the presence of several others, have made a new home on board of the steamer, and the hero is still surrounded by all the hallowing influences of his boyhood's fireside.

The principal title of the volume is not intended to convey the idea that Louis Belgrave is a sort of Don Quixote on shipboard, punching wine-sacks and tilting at windmills with a kitchen spit for a lancé and a barber's basin for a helmet, or that he indulges in extravagant feats of arms, or without arms, though unfortunately he has occasion to use a weapon in one instance, and would have done so in another if he had not been robbed of his revolver. He did not "win his spurs" in any imaginary encounters, and his designation is not given him on account of his prowess in the field, or even on board of the steamer of which he is the sole owner. Uncle Moses, his trustee, is inclined to indulge in humor, and insists that the young man is thirsting for adventures, for he certainly is engaged in many of them, and gives him his title as "Sir Louis," though he and the captain are about the only ones who ever make use of it; and then only as a pleasantry. But it is shown that, though Louis is very frequently the chief personage in an adventure, not one of them is of his own seeking, as is the case with those to whom the name was properly given.

The Guardian-Mother makes her voyage among the Bahama Islands, and circumnavigates Cuba, visiting the principal cities; but the volume is not intended as a guide-book, or even as a record of travel, though incidental descriptions are given of some notable events and places. The volumes are all devoted to stories, while they are believed to contain much useful information in geography as well as manners and customs.

WILLIAM T. ADAMS.

DORCHESTER, September 10, 1892.

CONTENTS

CHAPTER IX

CHAPTER X

CHAPTER XI

CHAPTER XII

CHAPTER XIII

CHAPTER XIV

CHAPTER XV

CHAPTER XVI

CHAPTER XVII

CHAPTER XVIII

CHAPTER XIX

CONTENTS

ix

CHAPTER XXXI

CHAPTER XXXII

CHAPTER XXXIII

CHAPTER XXXIV

CHAPTER XXXV

CHAPTER XXXVI

A YOUNG KNIGHT-ERRANT

CHAPTER I

A PLEASANT EXCURSION

"Faix, ye're the quarest millionaire Oi iver heard of in the whole coorse of me loif, Louis Belgrave!" exclaimed Felix McGavonty to his friend who sat by his side in a car on a train going from Von Blonk Park to New York City.

"What do you mean by that, Flix?" asked Louis, looking into the face of his seat-mate.

"Is is phwat do Oi mane? Sure yere altogedther different from all the odther millionaires Oi iver looked on in me loif. That's joost phwat Oi mane. Have ye's talked so mooch Frinch that ye's can't understhand English?" demanded Felix.

"I may be able to understand English; but I am not sure that I can always understand Irish," replied Louis, laughing at his friend's speech, as he was quite in the habit of doing, for Felix's brogue was not always the same thing, and he delighted in introducing new varieties of the Milesian dialect.

"It isn't Oirish at all at all that I spake, but English," protested Felix. "Sure, the Oirish is one of the ancient and classikle languages, loik the Latin, Grake, and Haybrew."

"I dare say it is, Flix; and as you never went to college you never learned it."

"Niver a wurrud of it; though me modther, long loif to her, though she's been dead since Oi was a small bit of a b'y — sure you know she doid whin I was nodthin' but a babby — me modther shpoke the Oirish language better than she could Grake and Haybrew."

"I have no doubt of it. Perhaps she could speak it better than you do English," suggested Louis.

"Oi donno; I niver heard her shpake it at all at all."

"Don't you think you could contrive, by the most tremendous effort of your lifetime, to speak your English without a brogue?" asked Louis.

"Don't I know I can shpake it as well as you can, Louis Belgrave?" answered Felix. "But sure, that woould niver do."

"And why not, I should like to know?"

"Is it why not? Sure, you kin shpake the Frinch language as well as ye's kin the English."

"Not quite, Flix; I wish I could."

"The professor says ye's kin; and phwat's the rayson ye's kape studyin' it, and shpakin' it, and gitt'n' crazy over it. Sure, ye'd rather talk Frinch with the professor than ate raw paraties."

"On the question of good looks, so far as you and I are concerned, I have not a word to say; but do you consider me a respectable-looking young man ?"

"Certainly I do.   Who could think otherwise ?"

"Am I dressed well enough ?"

"No; you are not !" exclaimed Felix stoutly.   "You look respectable, and that is all that can be said about it.   A coat of whitewash would do you good."

"Indeed!   But you say I present a respectable appearance."

"I would go on the stand, so far as that is concerned."

"You present quite as respectable an appearance as I do, Flix.   You are as well dressed as I am, and you know how to behave yourself as well as I do."

"The court admits the evidence."

"My point is this : it must be astonishing to people like the gentlemen behind us, to hear a good-looking and well-dressed young man break out in his language with a brogue which would sound all right in a hod-carrier, but not in a gentleman in appearance."

"That's what is the matter, is it, Louis ?" asked Felix, laughing.

"You attracted the attention of two persons by your brogue, and I don't know how many more.   Now, Flix, I am going to ask you to shut down on your brogue in public places, and as much as you can in other places."

"Not another wurrud of brogue !" exclaimed Felix. "But I thought it amused you."

"So it does, and at proper times and in proper

places I do not object to it.   You began to say that I was queer about something when we branched off on the subject of language."

"I said you were the queerest millionaire I ever heard of in my life; and I will say it again if you insist upon it, Louis," replied Felix, looking his companion in the face.

"May I ask why I am a queer millionaire?" asked the other in a very low tone, for he did not care to have it known that he had any more money than his friend.

"You don't dress like one, to begin with.   You have your clothes made by that cheap tailor at Von Blonk Park when you ought to go to the most fashionable one in New York, and have a suit made that would cost at least a hundred dollars."

"I prefer to dress about as I do now, for I don't believe that fine clothes make the man," said Louis, laughing at what he regarded as the folly of his crony.

"Your Sunday clothes are not much better than those you have on now.   You don't wear a single diamond on your shirt front, when you ought to have one as big as your fist."

"Diamonds don't make the man either; and when I see one with a big gem in his shirt I begin to think he is a hotel clerk, or a sporting man.   I see what you are driving at, Flix; and I utterly and entirely disagree with you.   I have no inclination to dress any better than I do now," said Louis very decidedly.

"You carry that old silver watch still when you ought to have a gold one worth five hundred dollars," persisted Felix.

"If I carried a time-keeper as valuable as that I should want a policeman to go about with me to prevent me from being robbed of it. If I had such a plaything the fear of losing or injuring it would worry me all the time, and I should have no peace."

"You could buy another if it were lost or spoiled."

"That is not my style, Flix. I don't believe that because a fellow is a millionaire, he ought to waste his money on follies and frivolities. He had better give it to the poor and needy than do that."

"Such frivolities as a hundred - thousand - dollar steam-yacht," said Felix slyly.

"You know very well that the Guardian-Mother was purchased to save my mother from the custody of a villain," replied Louis with energy.

"Of course it was, and I was only joking," added Felix, aware that he had said something that was not proper. "You saved me, too, with it."

By this time the train had arrived at Jersey City, and then they moved to another part of the car, where Uncle Moses Scarburn and Mrs. Belgrave were seated. They got out, and walked to the ferry-boat. On their arrival in New York, Louis called a carriage.

"You don't often order a carriage, Louis, for you either walk or ride in a horse-car, which is hardly becoming in a millionaire," said Felix, as they went for the vehicle.

"Because I prefer to walk or ride in a horse-car; and I am more accustomed to a horse-car than I am to a carriage, and feel more at home in a car than in a carriage," replied Louis, who saw that his crony needed a great deal of training on the subject of millionaires.

The party were seated in the carriage, and they were driven to the foot of West Twenty-Third Street, where they found the barge of the Guardian-Mother awaiting them. The magnificent steam-yacht was at anchor off the pier. Another party had just embarked, consisting of Mr. Woolridge and all the members of his family, and Captain Alcorn, the sailing-master of the Blanche.

In a few minutes Louis's party were on board of the steamer, exchanging salutations with the party of the magnate of the Fifth Avenue, as the owner of the Guardian-Mother had been in the habit of calling him. Louis and his mother had frequently been the guests of Mr. Woolridge on board of the Blanche, and on his return from the Bermudas he had taken the earliest opportunity to reciprocate the kind attentions bestowed upon the Belgraves.

The steamer was soon under way, and during the day she made what proved to be a very pleasant excursion to Fire Island, where a bountiful lunch was furnished. Captain Ringgold, the commander of the steamer, had made all the arrangements at the request of the owner. It was half-past five in the afternoon when the Guardian-Mother returned to her berth in the river; but the festivities were not yet ended, for the guests had been invited to dine in the state cabin after the steamer came to anchor, so that there should be no excuse for sea-sickness.

CHAPTER II

THE DINNER IN THE STATE CABIN

THE dinner provided on board of the Guardian-Mother was a very elaborate affair, and Monsieur Odervie, the chief cook, found in the occasion the opportunity he had desired since he came on board to distinguish himself. The steam-yacht had not been in commission more than two weeks, during which time she had made a voyage to the Bermudas, and had proved herself to be not only a very fast vessel, but also an excellent sea-boat.

She had been fitted up by Colonel Singfield, a wealthy gentleman, for his own use; but his sudden death had rendered her sale necessary in the settlement of his estate. Louis Belgrave had inherited over a million dollars from his grandfather, though he had to dig it out from under the house before he came into possession of the fortune. Squire Moses Scarburn, a very good-natured gentleman whose avoirdupois exceeded two hundred pounds, was the trustee of this wealth, and had so carefully invested it that it produced an income of seventy thousand dollars a year.

Louis had been a great favorite with Uncle Moses,

as the boys who knew him always called him. Felix McGavonty was the squire's office boy, and had been brought up by him, for he was an orphan from his early childhood, and the good man was a widower with no children. He was a lawyer more in favor for his soundness and common sense than for his brilliancy. He was inclined to be a humorist, and Felix had amused him greatly as a child, and each was very much devoted to the other. The orphan had been sent to school from the time he wore short clothes until he was sixteen, which was the age of the two boys, who had been cronies from their first meeting, so that it seemed to be a case of "love at first sight."

Louis's father, Paul Belgrave, had been severely wounded in the war of the Rebellion, and had died. His mother had contracted a second marriage, but the husband proved to be a thief, a swindler, and embezzler, who had grossly deceived her, and married her under an assumed name. This man, who called himself Wade Farrongate, though his real name was John Scoble, had in some manner discovered that Louis's grandfather had concealed his large fortune, all in gold, under the chimney of his house where his grandson had found it.

Scoble was a vicious and reckless man. Louis was the sole heir of the property by his father's will, and in case of his death before he became of age, his mother was to inherit it. The boy's step-father hated him intensely from the time of his marriage, and it was evident to those who understood the situation that he desired to get rid of him, so that his wife might come into possession of the fortune.   He had attempted to convey his wife and her son to England; but the boy would not go, and succeeded in convincing his mother that Scoble was a villain, and she repudiated him.

But the vicious husband would not abandon his purpose to obtain the fortune.   Receiving a considerable sum of money at the death of an uncle in India, he crossed the Atlantic in a schooner he called a yacht, and by resorting to trickery enticed his wife and her son on board of his vessel, which the young man desired to purchase if she suited him and his mother.

Louis had invited Captain Royal Ringgold, a wealthy, retired shipmaster, to visit the vessel as an expert; and Felix had obtained permission to join the party.   The schooner sailed as soon as the visitors were on board on the pretence of showing her sailing qualities.   By more trickery, Scoble contrived to get rid of Captain Ringgold and Louis, and, after various adventures, sailed with his wife and Felix for Bermuda.

Louis dreaded the influence of her repudiated husband upon her, and did all that he could to restore his mother to his home.   The worthy shipmaster had become greatly interested in the affair, and perhaps in the lady also, and he assisted the son to the best of his ability.   In fact, Louis and the captain became very warm friends.   He had advised the young man to persuade his trustee to purchase a steam-yacht for him ; but the young man would not entertain the idea of such an expensive craft. He changed his mind when the possession of the steamer appeared to be the only means of recovering his mother.

Uncle Moses, under the complicated circumstances of the case, readily assented to the purchase of the vessel, to which Louis had given the name of the "Guardian-Mother," in honor of Mrs. Belgrave, as she chose to call herself after the repudiation of her unworthy husband. The young man loved his mother ardently, and was enthusiastically devoted to her in all things, and in his thought of her he had long before associated that rather odd name for a steamer with her.

In the Guardian-Mother, under the command of Captain Ringgold, Scoble's schooner had been pursued to the Bermudas, where it was wrecked ; but Mrs. Belgrave, with all on board of the vessel, had been rescued by the crew of the steamer. Though Scoble threatened to pursue his former step-son all over the world in order to recover his wife, the party left him at the islands, and steamed back to New York. Neither Louis nor the commander of the Guardian-Mother had any fear of the villain who had shown himself so much in earnest in a bad cause.

Mr. Woolridge had befriended Louis in his troubles, and rendered him very valuable assistance. He was the owner of a beautiful sailing-yacht, the Blanche, in which he had frequently invited the Belgraves to excursions, treating Louis and his mother with the greatest kindness and consideration before the discovery of "The Missing Million" had made them wealthy.

Mr. Woolridge had a son of thirteen and a daughter fifteen. Blanche was a very beautiful girl, and Louis could not help admiring her pretty face and graceful form. Before the boy became a millionaire at sixteen, Mrs. Belgrave had been very much afraid that her son would get into some entangling relations with the young lady; but the million and a half made them equals, and she said no more, though Louis claimed that he treated her no better than he did her mother. But the young people certainly had no serious intentions, and Louis was not in the slightest degree "spooney."

"Well, Louis, I am of the opinion that you have the finest yacht that sails out of New York," said Mr. Woolridge, who was seated next to the youthful owner of the Guardian-Mother.

"Captain Ringgold thinks so as well as yourself," replied Louis.

"He is a competent authority on such a subject. By the way, my boy, you are extremely fortunate to obtain such a gentleman to command your yacht," continued the owner of the Blanche. "I have inquired about him, and I find that he is highly esteemed by all who know him. They say he is worth at least half a million, and it isn't every gentleman of means who can obtain a wealthy man to command his yacht."

"I should not have thought of such a thing as asking my trustee to buy such a magnificent steamer as this one if it had not been for him. All I was thinking about at the time was to get my mother back to the Park; but the captain enlarged upon this idea, and proposed to make the steamer my college, from which I am to be graduated after a voyage all over the world."

"It is a capital idea if one has the means to pay the expenses, for it makes a very costly education."

"But this little joker is able to stand it," interposed Uncle Moses, who was seated on the other side of the table. "After I had invested the young gentleman's fortune to my own satisfaction, I was not a little perplexed to ascertain how he was to spend his income; but Louis plucked up his courage and came to my relief by asking me to buy this steamer for him."

"But he wanted her simply to enable him to go in search of his mother," suggested the magnate of the Fifth Avenue.

"He would have given his million and a half to find her if it had been necessary. Now, his mother's only fear is that the money will spoil her son; but I don't think there is any danger of that, for the boy has a level head, and has no vices of any kind. I look upon him as a model young man, though he is fond of adventure; in fact, he is as much a knight-errant as though he had been dubbed a knight by some competent authority of the ancient time."

"All boys of any spirit are fond of adventure," added the magnate.

"I am no more a knight-errant than Uncle Moses himself," protested Louis.

"Don't deny it, Sir Louis; the finding and bringing back of your mother were just the sort of things that suited you," said the corpulent lawyer, shaking his fat sides with laughter. "Felix McGavonty is to be his esquire, and when you hear from the party that sail over the world in the Guardian-Mother, you will hear of islands captured, lions, tigers, and crocodiles killed."

"But Sir Louis informs me that the steam-yacht is to be his college," said Mr. Woolridge. "Wild adventures are not exactly consistent with hard study."

"Well, I hope he will not study too hard," laughed Uncle Moses. "But I am going with the party as ballast; and I think I can do duty in that capacity better than any other. But my special business is to see that the owner of the steamer does not study too hard; that is, I shall be a sort of moral ballast."

"I trust you will not be worked too hard in this capacity," added the magnate. "But where are you going, Sir Louis?"

"Captain Ringgold refuses to lay down the programme of the entire trip, declaring that a man is a fool to become a slave to any routine of cruising laid out beforehand. We are going to the Bermudas first, for we did not go ashore there last week; and then we go to Nassau, and perhaps to some other of the

Bahama Islands. During the coming winter we shall go around the island of Cuba, visiting the principal cities."

"That will make a very interesting voyage, and I should like to go with you," said Mr. Woolridge.

"I should be glad to have you go with us, with all your family," replied Louis earnestly.

"It is useless for me to think of such a thing, for it would be impossible for me to do so; and Blanche and Morris must attend to their studies."

"We are to have a college on board, as I said before," interposed Louis.

"I am afraid I should have to work too hard to keep my son and daughter from wearing themselves out with too much study," said the magnate with a hearty laugh.

"Then you would be able to sympathize with me, Mr. Woolridge," suggested Uncle Moses. "Sir Louis will reduce my flesh about ten pounds a month; but I am willing to be wasted in any good cause."

"I will endeavor not to overwork you, Uncle Moses," said Louis, as the party rose from the table.

"Then I shall have to be a sort of Sancho Panza, and curb the spirit of knight-errantry in Sir Louis, or he will be tipping over all the windmills, and punching all the wine-skins that fall in his path."

"I am afraid I shall have to become a knight-errant, or an adventurer of some kind, in order to verify some of your predictions," replied Louis as they went on deck.

The party had thoroughly examined the steamer during the excursion. It was about sunset, and for an hour they walked the deck, or passed the time in the boudoir. Miss Blanche played the piano, and everybody was happy. Just as they were getting into the boat to go on shore, Felix called Louis, and walked with him to the forward part of the vessel. There he pointed out a man with a dark skin and a twisted visage. The owner of the steamer could not remember that he had ever seen the person before; but he remained on board when the rest of the party went ashore.

CHAPTER III

AN AGENT OF THE ENEMY.

THE person to whom Felix called the attention of Louis was dressed in good clothes, though there was nothing genteel in his appearance, and he would not have been taken by any one as a Fifth Avenue resident. He might have been the mate of a vessel, a shopkeeper, or even a book agent. He was not a mulatto in the shape of his features, though he was dark enough in complexion to be one. The twist in his visage seemed to be given to it by the circumstance that his mouth was turned to the left side, so that he talked out of this side of it.

He was speaking to Spokes, one of the quartermasters, with whom he seemed to be acquainted, and the observer had abundant opportunity to see the peculiar working of his mouth as he conversed with his companion. Louis studied his face very attentively, and walked backward and forward several times in order to get a view of him from several points. The stranger took no notice of him, though Spokes must have told him that the young gentleman was the sole owner of the steam-yacht. Louis felt confident that, if he had ever seen the man before, he should be able to recall a face so utterly peculiar.

As he continued to observe the stranger at the constant urging of Felix, he thought he had a great deal of difficulty in managing his mouth in talking, for he spoke with evident labor. Louis concluded that he must have been partially paralyzed in his head, which might have caused the turning of his mouth to the left side. He was a person whom almost any one who saw him engaged in conversation could hardly help noticing.

"Do you know him, Sir Louis?" asked Felix, as they entered the pilot-house together.

"No, I do not; I never saw him before in my life, Sancho Panza," replied Louis, laughing when he saw that his crony had adopted the title given him by Uncle Moses. "Any one who ever saw a man with such a mug as that, would know him again, even if he met him in the middle of the Desert of Sahara."

"Are you sure you never saw him before?" demanded Felix, too much absorbed in the matter between them to heed the appellation his friend had bestowed upon him in retaliation for knighting him.

"I don't know that I should be willing to swear to it; but to the best of my knowledge and belief, I never set eyes on him before. How could a fellow ever forget a face in which the lips seemed to be trying to make the acquaintance of the left ear?"

"When I come to think of it, you have not seen so much of it as I have; but if you should turn down his shirt, you would find near his right shoulder the scar of a wound there made by the ball from a revolver," continued Felix, when he had assured himself that no one was within hearing distance of them.

"What do you mean by that, Felix?" asked Louis no wiser than he had been before. "What has the scar to do with me?"

"Nothing," replied Felix, who thought his crony was not as sharp in his perception as usual. "Nothing, only you gave him the wound of which that scar is the mark."

This explanation was enough to convince him of the meaning of his friend's blind statement. But he was unwilling to accept the conclusion at which Felix had arrived in regard to the identity of the man, for he was still confident that he had never seen the stranger before, much less that he had ever put a bullet into his shoulder.

"Do you mean to say that this man is Ovid Kimpton?" he asked.

"That is precisely what I mean to say, and do say," replied Felix very decidedly. "I was on board of the Maud nearly a week with him; and I believe he is the greatest scalliwag that ever went unhung."

"But Kimpton's face was not twisted like this man's," protested Louis.

"And Kimpton's complexion was five shades lighter than this fellow's," suggested the Milesian. "His face and hands are painted, and I would wager a pint of molasses against a fried sausage that I could knock that twist out of his mouth with one crack of my fist."

"It looks to me as though he had been paralyzed in the side of his face."

"If he had been, it would have knocked the cheek out of him, and he has it all there. When I first saw this fellow he was watching you very closely. You were walking the deck with the siffle."

"The what ? "

"The siffle," replied Felix gravely. "I mean Miss Blanche."

"My mother called Miss Woolridge the sylph; but I am sure she never applied such a word as you use to her. Never mind that. This fellow was watching me; but he would not look at me while I was observing him."

"He knows better than to attract your attention. That man is Ovid Kimpton as sure as you live, and I live to watch over you and protect you from the wiles of your great enemy."

"Prove to me that this man is Kimpton, and I will believe you."

"In the first place, I know his voice, for it is a cross between the croaking of a bullfrog and the crowing of a rooster. He can't utter two sentences in the same key, for one will be bass and the other tenor."

"I noticed that peculiarity in the fellow. He was trying to make Baldy Bickling go on board of the Maud, had knocked him down, and was trying to tie his hands when I interfered. He warned me to keep off, and pointed a revolver at me. He talked to Bickling in the tenor key, and to me in the bass. When I saw his weapon I fired at him, and disabled him in the right shoulder."

"Settled on the voice. I got a view down the back of his neck, and he is as white below his collar as Kimpton was."

"He is certainly of the same height and build as Scoble's agent. I am willing to believe that the fellow is Kimpton. Now, what is he here for?"

"That is more than I know."

"But how could he get here so soon?"

"Easily enough, for there is a steamer every two weeks, and he must have hit one of them."

"I thought you had gone ashore, Mr. Belgrave," said Captain Ringgold, coming into the pilot-house at this moment.

"No, sir; Flix had something to tell me, and I came forward with him. He has discovered that one of the agents of John Scoble is at this moment on board of the Guardian-Mother," replied Louis.

"One of the agents of Scoble!" exclaimed the commander, starting back in his astonishment. "How do you know that?"

"We have both seen him, and identified him. You remember that I had occasion, when my life was threatened at Dolphin Bay, to put a ball into the shoulder of Scoble's agent."

"I was not there, but I remember your report of the affair."

"It was the same fellow that set fire to the Phantom, causing her entire destruction, and thus preventing us from keeping the Maud in the bay."

"I remember him very well, for he was saved from the wreck of the Maud with the others. You say he is on board of the steamer at this moment?" demanded the captain with some excitement in his manner.

"He was talking with Quartermaster Spokes a little while ago."

"Show me the man, and there shall be one less of Scoble's agents loose in the world, for I will have him indicted for burning the steamer," added the captain with energy, as he led the way to the deck.

Louis and Felix began a vigorous search for the man with the twisted mouth; but they were unable to find him. There were some visitors who had been permitted to come on board to see the steamer still on the deck, but Kimpton was not among them.

"What sort of a man is Spokes, captain?" asked Louis.

"He is a good wheelman; and that is really all I know about him," replied the commander. "Do you think he is an agent of Scoble?"

"I do not suspect it, and I only asked the question about him because he was talking some time with Kimpton, and seemed to be acquainted with him. You can judge a person to some extent by the company he keeps."

"Knott," called the captain to a man who passed

them at this moment, "pass the word for Spokes, and tell him to come to the pilot-house."

"Spokes has gone to the city, sir; the first officer gave him liberty to spend the evening on shore," replied Knott.

"Did you see him when he left the ship, Knott?"

"I did, sir."

"What boat did he go in?"

"In a shore boat, sir. Some friend of his came on board, and he went ashore with him."

"Did you see Spokes's friend, Knott?"

"I did, sir; and he was a mighty queer-looking man, with his mouth almost under his left ear," replied the seaman, laughing at the deformity of the stranger.

"They cannot have been gone long. Mount the rail, Knott, and see if you can make out the boat in which Spokes went on shore. Report to me as soon as possible in the pilot-house," said Captain Ringgold in brusque tones, as he led the way from the deck.

"It looks as though Spokes was pretty well acquainted with this fellow, or he would not have gone ashore with him," suggested Louis, as they seated themselves on the divan abaft the wheel.

"But I do not think there is anything to be feared from this fellow, either to you or your mother, Louis," added the commander thoughtfully. "I have no doubt Scoble is still in the Bermudas, and Kimpton can do nothing without him."

"I am not so sure of that, captain," replied Louis.

"He is an utterly unscrupulous man, desperate enough to do 'a deed without a name.'"

"I make out the boat, sir, with Spokes and the other man in it; and it is about half way to the shore," Knott reported.

"Show me the boat," said the captain hastily, as he rushed out of the pilot-house, followed by the seaman.

Both of them mounted the rail, and the sailor pointed out the boat; but it was so near the shore that it was useless to attempt to overtake it before it reached the pier it was approaching.

"I shall sleep on board to-night," said the captain, who appeared to be somewhat troubled by this visit of the satellite of John Scoble, though he tried to conceal it from Louis. "I will see Spokes when he comes on board to-night. If he knows anything about this fellow, I will get it out of him."

"I was to stay on board also to-night, as Captain Ringgold had arranged with me," added Felix. "As he has done me the honor to appoint me captain's clerk, I was to learn something about my new duties."

As Felix was to make the cruise all over the world in the Guardian-Mother, Uncle Moses thought he ought to have some position on board, if there was one he was competent to fill, for he did not believe in permitting him to be an idler, for he was not a mil-lionaire, like his crony. He had suggested the idea to the commander, who had consulted his owner in regard to the matter. Louis consented when the cap-tain assured him that there would be plenty of work for him to do, though the amount of it would vary at different times.

"I don't quite like to have you go on shore, and to the Park alone, Louis, my darling," said Felix anxiously. "Since I saw that blackguard of a Kimpton, things look squally to me; and I am a bit afraid that Spokes is a mule of the same color."

"Nonsense, Flix!" exclaimed Louis. "Do you not think I am as able to take care of myself as you are to take care of me? I shall give the captain the order to retain you on board, and have you attend to your work if necessary. You can go home by the late train with the captain."

Felix remained on board, and the owner's barge conveyed Louis to the shore; he went from the pier to the ferry, and crossed the river; but he did not get much farther that night.

CHAPTER IV

A DISAGREEABLE ADVENTURE

It was quite dark when Louis Belgrave reached the Jersey-City side of the ferry. As usual, there was a vast multitude of passengers at this hour in the day. As he was walking to his train the cry of a "Man overboard!" was raised in the station, and, as is always the case, everybody rushed to the water, many of them doubtless with the desire to render assistance, but most of them from mere curiosity.

It is really wonderful how an accident, or an alarm of any kind, will attract the attention of the multitude in the street or elsewhere. If anything happens, a crowd is immediately gathered. If a man should stop in the street and gaze in a given direction fixedly for a minute or two, he would soon gather a crowd of people around him, all staring in the same way as himself.

It is not likely that any one knew where to look for the man overboard; but the passenger from the ferry-boat ran in the direction of the water, which could be approached only between a couple of buildings near the drop. Louis happened to be abreast of this opening when the alarm was given, and he followed several men who ran in this direction. It led to a pier, upon which there were hardly a dozen people when he reached it.

It was light enough for him to see that a yacht had just come up into the wind off this wharf, and a man appeared to be struggling in the water about half way between the vessel and the shore.

" Who knows how to row ?   I want a man to help me pull the boat," said a man on the edge of the pier who held the painter of a craft of some sort in his hand.

He was standing at some steps used by people in getting into a boat, and Louis was one of the first to come within speaking distance of him. Several volunteered to render the required service, the young millionaire among the number.

" You look like a stout young fellow," said the man holding the painter. " You will do ; get into the boat in a hurry, or the man in the water may drown before we get to him ! "

Louis hastened down the steps, seized one of the oars, and placed himself on the forward thwart. The person in charge of the boat followed him closely, pushing off the craft as he stepped into it. He had his oar in the water in another moment, and both of them began to pull together."

" Can you see the man overboard ? " asked the man at the stroke oar, as he began to give way.

" I cannot," replied Louis. " Don't you know where he is ? "

"I did know a minute ago, but I have lost him now," said the man, looking behind him.

"We shall gain nothing by hurrying if we don't know where the man is," said Louis, standing up in the boat, and looking earnestly out into the darkness.

"Help! Help!" shouted the person in peril; and Louis discovered him in the water, a short distance from the yacht, which seemed to be doing nothing to save him.

"I see him!" exclaimed Louis. "He is directly ahead of us. Keep the boat as she is, and we are all right."

They pulled together again for a couple of minutes, and Louis looked behind him frequently to make sure that the boat was still going in the right direction.

"Don't run over me!" called the man in the water; and he seemed to be very cool and self-possessed in his peril.

"Way enough!" said Louis, when he saw that the boat was close upon the swimmer, for that was what he was, and the bow oarsman wondered that he had not reached the yacht by this time, for that seemed to be the nearest point of safety.

The man swam very well and with a strong stroke. Possibly he had "lost his head" in his danger, but Louis thought it would have been an easy thing for him to swim to the yacht if he had his wits about him. He reached over the bow of the boat with both hands, and the man grasped them with desperate energy. It was more than a straw to which he clung, and aided by his own efforts he dragged him into the boat. The rescued person did not seem to be exhausted, and seated himself on the fore thwart. He had on only a shirt and trousers, and his feet were bare, as though he had prepared himself for the bath he had taken.

"All right!" exclaimed the man at the stroke oar.

Precisely what the speaker meant by this exclamation Louis did not know, for it did not seem to him to be exactly in place at that moment. But what attracted his attention still more was a certain familiarity in the sound of the voice. He thought that he had heard that voice before, though he could not place it at once. The man had spoken to him on the pier; but his mind had been occupied with the condition of the sufferer in the water, and he had not noticed it.

"You have had a cool swim," said Louis, turning to the rescued person. "Did you fall overboard?"

"No; but the swash of that ferry-boat nearly drowned me, so that I could not swim in it," replied the man who had been drawn from the water. "I belong to that yacht; our tender broke adrift, and I was swimming after it."

"Where is it now?" asked Louis, looking about him.

"This is it," replied the swimmer; and there was something like a chuckle in his tones.

"You see the boat was forced up to the pier by the

swash from the ferry-boat, when I heard that man cry for help," added the stroke oarsman; and there was also something like a chuckle in his tones. "I got hold of the painter, and called for some one to help me row her."

"Now, if you will put me on board of the yacht, I shall be all right, and the boat will be all right," said the rescued person.

"But I should like to be put on the pier before you go to the yacht," suggested Louis; and he was beginning to think there was something wrong about the affair, though everything appeared to have occurred in a perfectly natural manner.

"The yacht is going directly to the next pier to the ferry, and we will land you both in a few minutes," replied the man from the water.

"In that case I shall lose my train," added Louis.

It was too dark for the young millionaire to look over his companions in the boat, and he could not make out what they were; but it struck him that the one he had pulled out of the water was very ungracious in his manners, for he had not taken the trouble to thank his deliverers for their services. The fellow took the oar Louis had abandoned, and he and the one at the stern began to row. In a few minutes the boat was alongside the yacht.

The pleasure-craft was a vessel of twenty-five tons, rigged as a schooner, and appeared to be quite a stylish affair. There were only two men on board of her, who assisted Louis to the standing-room, where he seated himself. One of the men went to the wheel, and another attended to the jib-sheet. The yacht came about, and, though the wind was fair for the shore, she was headed down the river. Not one of the men spoke a word.

Louis did not know what to make of the situation. It was too dark for him to see the faces of his companions ; but he began to foster the suspicion that all was not right. Of course, the knowledge that Ovid Kimpton had been on board of the Guardian-Mother, and had left her with Spokes, the quartermaster, increased his doubts, and seemed to form a substantial foundation for grave fears.

He had asked Captain Ringgold about the character of the quartermaster ; but the commander only knew that he was a good wheelman. The steamer had been in commission only about two weeks, and in that time had made her voyage to the Bermudas. He had not had much time to become acquainted with his men. Louis had often seen Spokes at the wheel, and had talked with him, as he did to many of them.

Louis concluded when the yacht filled away to wait a little while before he said anything, in order to ascertain whether or not the party on board intended to land him at the pier, as one of them had promised to do. It did not require many minutes for him to decide that the man at the wheel, and whom he took to be the skipper of the craft, had no intention of putting him on shore. In fact, he regarded himself as a prisoner on board of the yacht.

At first he was not a little cast down when he realized that he was again in the hands of the enemy; but he soon rallied from this depression, and if Uncle Moses had been near enough to speak to him, he would have said with a chuckle that "Sir Louis had embarked in another adventure," and that he was once more in his element. But if the worthy squire had said so, it would have been no truer than similar remarks on former occasions had been. It was certainly an adventure; but he had been forced into it without any desire or intention on his own part.

He could not well avoid connecting the affair with the departure together from the steamer of Kimpton and Spokes, and he even reached the conclusion that the former had been the person in the water, and the latter the one in the boat. Of course, he could not fail to comprehend that the "Man overboard!" had been a contrived plan; and Spokes, if his supposition that it was he was correct, had followed him over from the pier where he had landed from the steam-yacht, and raised the alarm in the ferry-house.

Louis had seated himself in a corner of the standing-room, next to the open door of the cabin. After the jib had filled, and the yacht had laid her course down the river, the other three men had taken seats near the skipper. The schooner passed various other craft, though there were not so many as may be seen in the daytime.

The prisoner was faithfully considering what he should do. Four men directly in front of him were rather a formidable obstacle to doing anything. He thought of hailing a steam-tug, for he saw several of them near him; but he was absolutely sure that if he did so, the three men not just then employed would proceed to violence.

It would be madness for him to attempt to resist such an overwhelming force, though he had a revolver in his right hip pocket, and a box of cartridges in the left one. Whether his captors were similarly armed he had no means of knowing. He carried the weapon in his pocket since he first began to apprehend that the presence of John Scoble threatened him with violence. He had practised with the arm in a shooting-gallery under competent instructors, and taken lessons in the manly art of self-defence, though he had no taste for pugilism for itself. He had had occasion to use his skill either with his fists or with his revolver.

"You don't seem to be headed for the pier at Jersey City," said Louis, after he had considered the situation for a time, addressing his remark to the skipper.

"Not just yet," replied the man at the wheel.

"I have lost one train, and I hope you will not compel me to lose the next one," added Louis.

"I think you might as well give it up," interposed one of the others, with the same chuckle he had heard in the boat.

That was undoubtedly the voice of Ovid Kimpton, for he recognized the two different keys. The villain chuckled over the success which had attended his vicious scheme. It was not difficult to conjecture that John Scoble had sent him from the Bermudas to make him a prisoner. His late step-father was now a rich man, and could afford to pay a couple of villains a thousand dollars apiece or more to get the son of Mrs. Belgrave out of the way.

Doubtless the yacht was bound to some obscure place on the Jersey coast, where he could be effectually disposed of, and Louis decided to do something very soon.

CHAPTER V

A WOUNDED CONSPIRATOR

Louis Belgrave regarded Ovid Kimpton as the most dangerous of his enemies in the boat with him, for the simple reason that he considered him the wickedest and the most unscrupulous. Spokes had always seemed to him on board of the steamer to be a pleasant fellow, and perhaps he had talked with him more than with others for this reason, and because the owner spent much of his time on the voyage in the pilot-house.

Kimpton had proved to him that he was a desperate fellow, and Louis had been compelled to put a bullet into his shoulder to save his own life. He was convinced that he was the man against whom he would be called to act, for all the others were evidently his employees. Probably he had corrupted Spokes with the promise of a considerable sum of money, but the prisoner did not believe that the quartermaster would take part in anything like a flagrant crime.

"Don't you intend to put me on shore so that I can take my train for home? for my mother will be very much worried if I should not return to-night," said Louis in a quiet and pleasant tone.

"No train for you to-night, my little cockchaffer," replied Ovid, in a rallying tone, as though he was in the heartiest enjoyment of the victim's situation.

"What do you mean, Ovid? This does not seem to be precisely the art of love that you are practising," continued Louis, who did not intend to give the enemy even a moral advantage over him by manifesting anything like depression of spirits.

"It seems that you know me, even in the dark," replied Kimpton. "Although my name is Ovid, I don't deal in soft stuff."

"I am well aware of it; and I hope you have recovered from that bad twist in your mouth which impeded your speech this afternoon."

"Entirely recovered from that, and you can see that my speech is as polished as your own."

"The last I saw of you before to-day was when you where landed on the Island of St. George in the Bermudas. How do you happen to be here?"

"I don't happen to be here; and it is not by accident that you and I meet again. I am here on a mission, as fellows of your sort would say."

"A mission for your friend and fellow-scorpion, John Scoble, for there is a hole in that millstone."

"Exactly so; and I mean to earn the money I am to be paid for it."

"I have no doubt of it; and you ought to pay Spokes well too, for there will be a vacancy of one quartermaster when he goes on board of the Guardian-Mother next time," added Louis, as he glanced at the man he took to be Spokes.

"But I had nothing to do with this matter, Mr Belgrave," protested the man at whom he looked, as he sprang to his feet.

"No lies will help your case, Spokes," replied Louis in a severe tone.

"That is just what I told you, Mr. Kimpton!" exclaimed Spokes, plainly indicating that he was disgusted with the affair, for the words of the prisoner showed that he was to lose his place on board of the steamer; doubtless he had not expected to be recognized.

"You are all right, Ethan," Kimpton interposed. "It is not eight in the evening, and in a couple of hours more you can go on board of the steamer, and nobody will be the wiser for what you have done."

"But the owner of the Guardian-Mother has already recognized me," argued the quartermaster.

"What of it? He is not going on board of that steam-yacht any more."

"Then there will be no place for officers or seamen on board of her," Spokes returned. "This thing will be the ruin of me, and to gain five hundred dollars I have thrown myself out of a place which promised to lead me in time into the position of second officer. I was a fool to have anything to do with it!"

"That's so, Spokes. Captain Ringgold knows very well who and what Kimpton is, in spite of the ugly mug into which he twisted his mouth; and he knows that you went ashore with him in the boat in which he came off!"

"Do you hear that, Mr. Kimpton?" demanded Spokes indignantly.

"I hear it, and I have heard enough of it," replied the chief actor in the outrage, as he picked up a heavy stick which seemed to have been placed on the seat for his use. "Now, Mr. Belgrave," he continued in a supercilious tone, "you and I will adjourn to the cabin, where our conversation will not be interrupted. Skipper, strike a light below, so that this fine gentleman may see that I am as handsome as he is."

"It is hardly a question of beauty just now," added Louis for the sake of saying something.

"I should say not!" sneered the ruffian.

"See here, Ovid Kimpton, if you intend to do Mr. Belgrave any harm, I want to be in the cabin also," Spokes interposed. "You told me this was to be a harmless frolic, which the young gentleman would enjoy as much as any of us. If you offer to do him any injury, I shall be on his side, and willing to fight for him."

This made the affair look a little more hopeful to the prisoner, for, with the assistance of the quartermaster, it might be possible to overcome the principal ruffian. As he was waiting for the light in the cabin, Kimpton took something from under the seat in the standing-room, and the victim discovered that he had a pair of handcuffs in one hand, while he held the club in the other.

"I suppose you will not object to the use of these things, Spokes, for I spoke to you about them beforehand," said the ruffian, as he held up the manacles.

"I suppose they will not hurt him," replied Spokes tamely.

"Now, Ethan, if you turn traitor to me just in the nick of the time, I will shoot you like a dog!" exclaimed Kimpton. "I have paid you one hundred dollars on account, and you shall not go back on me at this stage of the performance. Now, Mr. Belgrave, will you do me the favor to go down into the cabin; and I will say, for your information and that of Ethan Spokes, that I desire to talk over matters with this fine gentleman, and, if possible, come to an arrangement with him in behalf of my friend and employer, whom this young rascal has injured and outraged in his tenderest feelings."

Louis realized that a refusal to comply with the request of Kimpton was likely to be followed by a blow with the club. He had considered his situation, and he had not only decided to act, but how to act. He descended the three steps to the cabin, which had been lighted, and was followed by the chief ruffian. Kimpton stopped as he entered, closed and locked the two doors.

"Now, my dear Mr. Belgrave, sole owner of the magnificent steam-yacht Guardian-Mother, I shall be under the painful necessity of fitting these bracelets to your wrists, so that in the conference we are to have in this cabin you may not be tempted to do anything that would lead to unpleasant consequences," said Kimpton, as he turned from the doors, with the handcuffs in one hand and the club still in the other, and approached his prisoner.

Louis realized that if the handcuffs were once put on his wrists, he would be deprived of all power to do anything in his own defence. He had his right hand on the revolver in his pocket, and when the villain had taken half a dozen steps, he pointed it at him. As soon as he saw it, he dropped the club, and put his hand behind him with the evident purpose of drawing his revolver, and the critical moment had come for decided action.

Louis fired.

His practice had given him the ability to take his aim as quick as a flash. He had done just what he had intended to do, and he was as cool and self-possessed after the shot as though he had not put a bullet into the body of the desperado.

Louis had not intended to kill him, or give him what would prove to be a very dangerous wound. He aimed at his right shoulder, and the instant he fired, the right arm of the villain dropped to his side, and his revolver fell to the cabin floor. Either on account of the shock of the wound, or in an attempt to recover his weapon, he fell at full length in the middle of the apartment.

The moment of peril to the prisoner had not passed, for the desperado, rendered furious by his wound, could pour all the shots in his revolver into his victim.

Louis fully realized that the situation had become desperate for him, and he threw himself upon the prostrate form of Kimpton before he had time to rise. He clutched him by the inside of his shirt collar, and turned him over on his face.

The wretch howled like a mad wolf, and vented some of his wrath in a torrent of oaths. Louis put his right foot on the small of his back and held him down till he could pick up the handcuffs the fallen man had dropped. Drawing the two arms of his conquered enemy behind him, he sprang them upon his wrists, and Kimpton was powerless to harm him. The defeated wretch writhed with the pain of his wound, and doubtless his conqueror had hurt him severely when he twisted his arm around so that he could adjust the handcuffs.

The wounded man howled and swore in the most shocking manner; but he could do nothing to harm the other occupant of the cabin. Louis picked up the revolver of his victim, and put it in his pocket. The blood was flowing inside of the sufferer's shirt, and the hole made in his vest could be plainly seen. It was clear that the ball had passed through the shoulder near its junction with the arm.

"Open the door!" shouted a voice which Louis recognized as that of Spokes. "What is the matter there?"

At the same time the speaker outside kicked and pounded upon the doors which opened into the stand-ing-room so that they could not be forced in. This shouting and pounding had been continued from the time of the firing of the shot till the victor had secured his foe. He then went to the doors and opened them.

Kimpton still lay upon the floor, rolling and squirming with pain, when Spokes came in. He stood aghast when he saw the fallen man, and looked inquiringly at the young millionaire. He was soon followed by the skipper, who had given the helm to his assistant.

"Here is a pretty row to be settled in the court!" exclaimed the captain, as he gazed at the wounded man. "Is this your work?" he demanded, turning savagely to the young man, who was the coolest person in the cabin.

"That is my work," replied Louis, as sternly as the skipper had spoken.

"You have a fair chance of being hung for it, if you are a millionaire," added the captain.

"That will be my lookout. Now, as you are the captain of this craft, you will take your orders from me, and you will put me on board of the steam-yacht Guardian-Mother, which lies off the foot of Twenty-third Street."

"I don't obey any such order!" exclaimed the captain. "You have got up a pretty scrape for this yacht to work out of! Do you think I am going to put myself in a place where the police can pounce upon me, and take my boat away from me?"

"Don't get mad, Captain Jeffers," interposed Spokes.

"I am not going near that steam-yacht, to be taken up by the police."

"Captain Jeffers, you and your boat have been used in a ruffianly outrage, and you have more to fear for that than for the wound this villain has received. I fired upon him in self-defence, and any court will justify the shooting. Now, my man, you will put me on board of the Guardian-Mother, or there may be another wounded man on board of your yacht."

Louis drew both of his revolvers, taking a place where he could defend himself from an attack.

CHAPTER VI

AN IMPERATIVE ORDER

IF Louis Belgrave was not a knight-errant, as
Uncle Moses playfully asserted that he was, he certainly had obtained an unusual degree of experience
for one of his age in just such adventures as that in
which he was engaged on board of Captain Jeffers's
yacht.   But, unlike the wandering knight who went
forth seeking the occasion to break a lance with a
real or imaginary foe, the young millionaire had never
wilfully thrust himself into any such affair; and
therein he was not entitled to the handle his trustee
applied to his name.

In the cabin of the yacht the young man had certainly "taken the bull by the horns," for he had fired
the first shot in the conflict.   To allow his enemy to
reduce him to the condition of a manacled prisoner
was to abandon himself to whatever fate John Scoble
and his agents had doomed him.   Mrs. Belgrave's
late husband evidently believed, judging from his ac-
tions as well as from what he had said, that he could
win back his wife if her son were not in the way;
and therefore he had a double motive in getting him

out of the way. Louis felt that he was fighting for his life with desperate and unscrupulous men.

With a revolver in each hand he menaced the skipper of the yacht; and with the writhing wretch on the cabin floor before him, he could not help realizing that Louis meant "shoot;" and doubtless he had it in his eye. Captain Jeffers must be an unreliable and vicious man, or he would not have been engaged in such an enterprise as that for which Ovid Kimpton had employed him, and the young man had no respect or consideration for him.

The skipper looked at the two weapons pointed at him, and he plainly did not regard the prospect as a pleasing one. Spokes stood by his side, but he had neither said nor done anything. The only person on board was the man at the helm, who seemed to constitute the crew of the little vessel. Louis did not anticipate any action on the part of the quartermaster, unless it were upon his side of the question, for the seaman was clearly disgusted with the result of the enterprise.

"Mr. Belgrave, if you will agree" — Captain Jeffers began in a more subdued and submissive tone than he had used before; but the young man would permit him to proceed no farther.

"I will agree to nothing; I will promise nothing!" exclaimed Louis, interrupting him. "My order is plainly and simply that you run your schooner alongside the Guardian-Mother; and if you do not obey the order, I will fire at you, and I don't miss my aim!"

"But you can see for yourself, Mr. Belgrave, that " —

"I can't see anything for myself, but I can see for you that you are making things worse for yourself with every moment you waste," said Louis, breaking in upon him in a very severe manner for one usually so mild and peaceable. "I shall not talk about it all night either. Now is the time for action, and will you obey my order at once ? "

"I don't see that I can help myself," muttered the fellow, confronting the two revolvers.

"I don't see that you can," added Louis. "You have no right to ask anything of me. You have led me into a trap in which my life or liberty is at stake, and I am not inclined to concede anything to you. I shall turn you over to the commander of the Guardian-Mother, and you may make any terms you can with him."

"I should like to talk the matter over with you, for I had no idea what this man on the floor was going to do," pleaded Captain Jeffers.

"No talk! Not another word! Come about and stand up the river, or I will end the whole matter in five seconds by putting you alongside of Kimpton on the floor," said Louis in a loud and menacing tone.

The skipper turned on his heels and went out of the cabin. His involuntary passenger followed him to the door; and he took occasion to assure him that any indication of treachery would invite a shot from one of the revolvers. Captain Jeffers went to the wheel, and took it from the hands of his assistant.

"Ready about!" said he.   "Go forward, and stand by the jib-sheets!"

These orders showed that the skipper intended to carry out the command of the imperative young millionaire, who appeared to have wiped out his enemies, in spite of their greater number and heavier weight. Neither the skipper nor the quartermaster was armed; and the possession of a revolver in the hands of one who has the decision and skill to use it effectively, gives him an absolute advantage, as Louis had abundantly demonstrated.

Firearms are dangerous playthings, and Uncle Moses had lectured both of his *protégés* by the hour on the subject of carrying concealed weapons; and under any ordinary circumstances he would not have permitted the boys to do so; but Louis was in constant peril, and he had conceded the point to this fact alone. He had practically procured the permission of the authorities of Von Blonk Park and New York for him to do so; but Felix McGavonty carried his weapon without any permit.

"What is going to be the end of this thing, Mr. Belgrave?" asked Spokes, in a tone quite as subdued as that of the skipper had been when he retired from the cabin.

"I don't know, Spokes," replied Louis, unwilling to discuss the question.

"I did not understand what Kimpton was about, sir," pleaded the quartermaster.

"Then you were an idiot, but more probably you are a liar. I have nothing more to say about it," replied Louis very decidedly. "Captain Ringgold will settle the matter."

Louis, returning one of the revolvers to his pocket, and retaining the other in his hand, walked up and down the cabin, passing the form of the wounded conspirator on the floor several times. Kimpton had, in some measure, abated his wrath; but he was still howling and groaning with the pain of his wound, which appeared to be much more serious than the one he had received from the same weapon about two weeks before. Spokes was in a serious frame of mind, as well he might be after confronting the failure of his principal to carry out his purpose. He had seated himself on the transom, and fixed his gaze on the floor.

"I am in terrible pain, Louis Belgrave!" groaned Kimpton.

"I have no doubt of it; but you have only yourself to blame for it," replied Louis, roughly for him.

"You have twisted my shoulder out of joint, I believe, and made the wound ten times as painful as it need be," howled the sufferer. "I wouldn't let a dog suffer as I do."

"I can do nothing for you," replied Louis.

"Yes, you can!" exclaimed the wounded man angrily; and the pain seemed to increase his wrath again. "You can take the bracelet off my right arm, and that would relieve me."

"I shall not do it, for I cannot trust you with the use of even your wounded arm."

"Will you sit there, Spokes, and see a fellow-creature suffer as I do?" demanded Kimpton, turning his head towards his fellow-conspirator against the life or liberty of the young millionaire.

"No, I won't," replied the quartermaster, rising from the transom. "I will go out into the standing-room."

"No, you will not! Stay where you are, Spokes!" Louis interposed, demonstrating towards him with his weapon. "I don't care to lose sight of you for a moment."

"You are rather rough on me, Mr. Belgrave," said Spokes with a sort of pleading look at the owner of the Guardian-Mother.

"I am not half so rough on you as you have been on me," replied Louis sternly. "If I had supposed there was a single man on board of the steamer who would accept blood-money, and join a conspiracy against me, I should have been apt to have him sent on shore, even on suspicion."

"But I did not understand this thing, and I declare upon my honor as a man that I had no intention to do you any harm," protested Spokes.

"You know very well that you do not speak the truth. You followed me over on the ferry-boat, and it was you who sounded the cry of 'A man overboard!' It was you who got the yacht's tender at the steps, and selected me of all others to be your companion in the boat. It was all a contrived plan."

"That's so!" exclaimed Kimpton, evidently dissatisfied with his fellow-conspirator because he rendered him no assistance.

The quartermaster could make no progress in shielding himself from the obloquy cast upon him, and even his principal seemed to join with the intended victim of the plot. He said no more, and Louis went to the door again to take an observation of the surroundings, in order to ascertain if the skipper was acting in obedience to his order; but he was careful to keep one eye on the quartermaster. He could make out the ocean steamships lying at the wharves of Hoboken, which were about a mile from the berth of the Guardian-Mother, and he saw that the schooner's course lay about half a mile from the piers on the New York side of the river. Captain Jeffers was so far acting in good faith.

A little later he ran the yacht alongside the steamer. With his weapon still in his hand, Louis left the cabin, and mounted the trunk of the little vessel. The captain shouted to his man forward to lower the jib, while he secured the mainsail himself.

"Guardian-Mother, ahoy!" shouted the owner of that magnificent steamer at the top of his lungs.

"On board the schooner!" returned a man on the rail of the ship.

"Is Captain Ringgold on board?" asked Louis.

"Who's there?" called the commander himself;

and the owner promptly recognized his voice. "Who is it?"

"Louis Belgrave," responded the young millionaire.

"Is it you, Mr. Belgrave?" demanded the captain, who seemed to have some difficulty in believing his owner could be on board of a sailing-yacht in the river after he had seen him depart from the steamer for his home about two hours before, for the clocks of the great city were then striking nine.

"Is it yourself, me darlint?" shouted Felix.

"It is myself, Flix."

"What has happened, Mr. Belgrave?" demanded Captain Ringgold, beginning to descend the accommodation steps, at which the skipper had hauled up his yacht.

"Send half a dozen men on board of this schooner, if you please, captain. I have brought Spokes on board."

The commander gave the order for the men to board the yacht, and continued on his way down the ladder.

"What under the canopy does all this mean, Mr. Belgrave?" asked the captain as he grasped the hand of the owner.

"I have been the victim of a conspiracy; but I have fought my way out of it," replied Louis.

"Bad luck to me for a spalpeen as I was, that didn't go home wid ye's and spread the mantle of me protiction over ye's!" exclaimed Felix, who had followed the commander down the steps.

"I don't believe the mantle of your protection would have done me any good; but I thank you for your good intentions all the same," replied Louis, taking the hand of his crony, and laughing at the Irish gush of the young man. "I am all right now, and a good deal better off than some of the conspirators."

"But who were the conspirators?" asked Captain Ringgold, his tones full of the anxiety which had taken possession of him.

"Spokes and his companion with the twisted mouth, Ovid Kimpton," replied Louis. "But come into the cabin, captain."

The commander followed the owner into the cabin of the yacht.

CHAPTER VII

THE OUTCOME OF THE CONSPIRACY

THE six men for whom Louis had asked hastened on board of the yacht, and halted in the standing-room for orders.

"Pass the word for Mr. Boulong," said the captain.

"And don't let any one leave the schooner, Captain Ringgold," added Louis; and the order to this effect was given.

The commander followed his owner into the cabin, where Ovid Kimpton still lay upon the floor, groaning and writhing in his agony.

"What is this, Mr. Belgrave?" asked the astonished captain, as he looked down on the miserable wretch on the floor. "Who is this man?"

"That is Ovid Kimpton, the friend of Quartermaster Spokes, who sits on the transom," replied Louis, pointing to the latter.

"I saw this fellow; but he does not seem to have the crooked mouth he wore this afternoon."

"He has got over that."

"But what is the matter with him?"

"In self-defence, when he was about to put me in irons, I was compelled to shoot him; but I took especial care not to give him a mortal wound, and I put the bullet through his shoulder," replied Louis very quietly, though the commander was somewhat excited.

"On board, captain," said Mr. Boulong, the first officer of the steamer, reporting his presence.

"Take the first cutter, and pull to the shore as speedily as possible. Go to the nearest police precinct, and bring off a surgeon and three or four officers, for this man seems to be badly wounded, and it looks like a serious affair," said Captain Ringgold to the first officer, who hastened on board of the steamer to execute the order.

"Is Spokes wounded too?" asked the commander.

"He is not; but he is one of the conspirators against me, and took an active part in the first part of the proceedings."

"What were the proceedings of which you speak, Mr. Belgrave?"

Louis related all the events of the evening from the time he had left the steamer till his return to her in actual possession of the yacht, while all on board of her were practically his prisoners. He detailed the particulars of the shooting very minutely, and gave his reasons for the extreme step he had taken in putting a ball into the shoulder of the wretch on the floor.

"You did precisely right, Mr. Belgrave; and if you had not fired the shot when you did, I know not what your fate might have been, for of course this villain is an agent of John Scoble," said Captain Ringgold as he grasped the hand of his owner.

"I did the only thing I could do when I saw Kimpton draw his revolver; and if I had not fired when I did, it would have been all over with me."

"You can bet your life on that!" howled the wounded conspirator, with intense hate in his tones.

At this moment the first cutter of the steamer dashed alongside, and Mr. Boulong leaped into the standing-room of the yacht. He was followed by four policemen, and a gentleman with a case of instruments under his arm who proved to be the surgeon. Captain Ringgold asked the officers to be seated in the stern of the schooner while he conducted the doctor to his patient. Then he directed Louis to repeat his account of the conspiracy to the policemen, one of whom appeared to be a sergeant or lieutenant.

The conspiracy could not be understood by his auditors without the earlier history of the affairs of the Belgrave family, which Louis narrated as fully as the occasion seemed to require. He had not proceeded far before the listeners were intensely interested, for they knew all about the robbery and absconding of John Scoble, *alias* Wade Farrongate. Besides, the young fellow who talked so fluently was a millionaire, and possibly this fact increased their interest in the case.

It took him over half an hour even to tell the story as baldly as the truth would permit. On the details of the outrage perpetrated upon him that evening he was very minute, and took care that the officers should understand the case perfectly.

In the mean time Captain Ringgold had conducted the surgeon to the cabin. He directed Mr. Boulong to send Spokes into the standing-room, with a couple of the hands to see that he did not attempt to escape. Calling two seamen into his presence, he attended to the examination of the patient, whom the two men had placed on the cabin table by direction of the surgeon; but he seemed to be in no haste to begin upon his work, though he ordered the seaman to remove the handcuff from his right wrist.

"I haven't the pleasure of your acquaintance, sir," said the doctor, very politely, as he turned to the captain. "I am Dr. Brookburn."

"And I am Captain Ringgold, commander of the steam-yacht Guardian-Mother, alongside of which this yacht lies; and I am very happy to know you, Dr. Brookburn," replied the captain as he presented his hand to the surgeon.

"Ah, indeed, Captain Ringgold! I am very glad to meet you. Your steamer has been the admiration of all my friends who are interested in nautical matters, as I am to a considerable extent myself," continued the doctor very cordially. "I have been told that a young millionaire not more than sixteen years old is the sole owner of this beautiful vessel."

"That is quite true, sir; and the young man who left the cabin after you came in is the owner himself," added the captain. "I shall be happy to introduce you to him, for he fired the shot that wounded the man on the table, and he will be anxious to know how badly he is injured."

Dr. Brookburn pulled off his gloves, and opened his case of instruments, placing them on the table by the side of his patient. He asked one of the seamen to bring him a bowl of water and some towels, and Sparks was sent for to provide these articles. The doctor could see where the wound was located, and he proceeded with the help of a sailor to remove the shirt of the sufferer. While he was thus employed he continued to talk about the beautiful steam-yacht, and he was sure the owner must be a happy young fellow.

"Is it a very bad wound, doctor?" asked the captain, after he had been at work for some time upon the patient, talking all the time about the steamer, regardless of the yells of pain which Kimpton could not suppress.

"It is a bad wound, and it will lay the patient up for a couple of months perhaps; but there is nothing dangerous about it with proper care in the hospital," replied the surgeon, who immediately continued his conversation in regard to the Guardian-Mother, in which he seemed to be more interested than in his patient.

"I am glad that it is no worse," added the captain.

Doctor Brookburn had probed the wound and extracted the ball, which he gave to the commander, and proceeded to dress the injury. The nautical gentleman had been in the navy, and he saw that the operator was a skilful surgeon, and certainly he was not at all affeeted by the sufferings of his patient. Kimpton was placed on a berthsack upon the transom and made as comfortable as his condition would permit.

"Captain Ringgold, this is Lieutenant Bardoff," said Louis, entering the cabin at this moment, followed by the chief of the officers. "I have finished my yarn; Spokes and the skipper have been examined, and this gentleman is ready to take the next step."

"It is plain enough that an outrage has been committed upon Mr. Belgrave by these men, of whom the wounded man appears to be the prime mover. I shall arrest Ovid Kimpton on two charges: the first for incendiarism, for which a requisition must come from the State of New Jersey; and the second for this outrage, in which Ethan Spokes is also a principal. Captain Jeffers is an accomplice, and let his boat for the purpose his employers used her for. His assistant seems to be a cipher in the business. This man will have to go to the hospital. Is he in condition to be removed to New Jersey, Dr. Brookburn?"

"If he is not, he will be in a day or two," replied the surgeon.

The first cutter was ready to convey the officers and their prisoners to the shore, and the assistant on board of the yacht was directed to sail her to her usual berth. Ovid Kimpton, who had listened to all that had been said, was furious when he heard what was to be done with him. He howled, roared, and swore like a pirate ; for the wretch did not seem to be aware that he had committed any crime in the burning of the Phantom on the New Jersey shore, or in the outrage he had committed in the capture of Louis.

"Well, me darlint, wasn't it a powerful pity I didn't go wid ye's when ye's left the ship ? " said Felix when they returned to the deck of the steamer after the business had all been disposed of, and the cutter had started for the shore with the officers and their prisoners.

"What could you have done if you had been with me, Flix ? Not a thing. I did not know Spokes in the darkness, and he was the one who asked me to pull an oar in the boat ; and I could not refuse when a man was drowning near the pier, and you would not have known him any better than I did. Even if I had known him, I could not have declined to help him in such a case. It was Kimpton who was paddling about in the water, pretending to be in danger of drowning," replied Louis. "But mother will be worrying her life out of her because I do not come home, and I must be off at once."

"Faix, I'll go wid ye's this time," added Felix very decidedly.

"And I shall go also," said the commander, who had just ordered out the owner's barge.

"But I am not afraid of anything, captain, and it

is not necessary for you to go with me," protested Louis. "I have the feeling that I can take care of myself."

"You have assuredly been very fortunate, Sir Louis in getting out of the dilemmas into which you have been forced; but you may not always be so lucky as you have been this evening," answered Captain Ringgold. "But I am not going especially for your protection, Mr. Belgrave. You and I both have business in New Jersey to-morrow, and this time we will make sure that this rascally Kimpton is under lock and key in strong stone walls for the next five or seven years; and Captain Brisbane, whose steamer he burned, will not be sorry to look at him through the bars."

The business of this story with the conspirators may as well be finished at this point as at a later period. Ovid Kimpton, before he recovered from the wound in his shoulder, was sentenced to five years in the State prison, with the affair of the outrage still hanging over him. Ethan Spokes got two years, for he had no malice; and Captain Jeffers was subjected to a fine that spoiled all his profits at boating for that year. Uncle Moses, Louis, and Captain Ringgold had to employ a considerable portion of their time for the next two months in serving as witnesses.

As her son had apprehended, Mrs. Belgrave was very much worried at his non-appearance at a reasonable hour on the evening after the excursion; and it was two o'clock in the morning when the story of his adventure had been told and commented upon. The poor woman hugged her boy just as though he had not been a millionaire after she learned the peril from which he had escaped.

"Sir Louis Belgrave must have a body-guard after this," said Uncle Moses, as they were about to retire to their chambers.

"Haven't I proved that I am able to take care of myself?" demanded Louis with something of triumph in his tones.

"But the conspirator may fire first next time," suggested the squire.

"I declare, Louis, I shall not be willing to let you go out of the house after this," added Mrs. Belgrave, wiping a flood of tears from her eyes.

"We shall sail for the Bermudas in about two months. Suppose Louis should live on board of the Guardian-Mother during that time?" the captain proposed. "Of course you can be with him, madam."

This plan was adopted with some modifications.

CHAPTER VIII

PREPARATIONS FOR THE FUTURE

THE situation as indicated by the conspiracy against the liberty, if not the life, of Louis Belgrave was extremely uncomfortable even to the young knight-errant, brilliant as it made the prospect for future adventures ; and Squire Scarburn still insisted that the young millionaire was intent upon something of this kind. "It was in vain that Louis declared he had no desire to engage in adventures; that he had no wish to expose himself to any perils for the sake of escaping from them ; and that everything in the guise of an exploit had been forced upon him.

Probably if Uncle Moses had been called upon by circumstances to speak very seriously, he would have admitted the truth of his young friend's assertions ; but the worthy lawyer was inclined to be a humorist, and the fancy that Louis was a sort of Don Quixote amused him, and did not annoy the young man, though he took the pains to show that he had never voluntarily engaged in any perilous adventure.

The situation was certainly serious, and Uncle Moses treated it as such generally. Louis had mortally offended John Scoble in his efforts to save his mother from consorting with a villain, a thief, if not a would-be assassin ; and he had won his mother over to his views to such a degree that she regarded her former husband with even greater detestation than did her son.

The wretch had sworn that he would be revenged upon the young man, and that he would follow him all over the world if necessary to accomplish his wicked purpose.   Little attention had been given to his profane declaration when it was made; but the appearance of Ovid Kimpton on board of the Guardian-Mother, and the conspiracy in which he had engaged, assured all concerned that Scoble had not abandoned his evil intentions.

Kimpton had undoubtedly been sent by the first steamer from the Bermudas to entrap Louis, though the object of the capture was not apparent in detail. This agent had been effectually disposed of, and he was likely to look through prison bars for the next five years.   John Scoble had been provided by nature with an abundant stock of impudence and assurance; and in the face of all the overwhelming defeats to which he had been subjected, he still believed that he possessed power, influence, and magnetism enough to conciliate Mrs. Belgrave, and induce her to renew her matrimonial relations with him.

It appeared from the inquiries made during the late visit of the Guardian-Mother to the Bermudas that Scoble had succeeded by will to the ill-gotten gains of his brother, which placed him in possession of over half a million of dollars. That was a sufficient fortune for a modest man, and he had no occasion to pursue the million of his former step-son. But he had become infatuated with the idea of obtaining it, and he was determined to secure it. With avarice, hatred, and revenge to spur him on, he was likely to be a thorn in the path of Louis and his mother in the future, as he had been in the past, especially as he had now abundant means at his command to carry out his vicious intentions.

The party at the house of Uncle Moses had considered the subject in this light. Mrs. Belgrave wept and trembled for the safety of her son, the squire laughed and made funny remarks, as he was apt to do even in the midst of serious scenes. Captain Ringgold admitted the peril to which the young millionaire might be continually exposed, and Louis still insisted that he was abundantly able to protect himself, as he had done on several former occasions.

"As I said before, the steam-yacht is the safest place for Louis," said Captain Ringgold.

"Perhaps it is, captain; but it strikes me that it was on board of the steam-yacht the conspirator worked up his plans," suggested Uncle Moses, with one of his convulsive chuckles which shook his ponderous body.

"We learn wisdom from our former errors, Squire Scarburn," replied the commander of the Guardian-Mother. "It was a mistake of mine to allow visitors to come on board of the ship, I admit."

"Do you believe the conspiracy was hatched up on board of the ship?" asked the trustee.

"I believe Kimpton made the acquaintance of Ethan Spokes on shore, and only came on board of the steamer to notify his fellow-conspirator that the time had come to carry out the plan as soon as he saw that the excursion party had gone ashore, leaving Sir Louis behind."

"It looks as though that were a correct view of the matter. With the precautions I shall be able to use in the future, with a full understanding of the situation, I still believe that the ship will be the safest place for Louis," the commander insisted.

"That plan would exactly suit me," added the owner of the steam-yacht.

"Any place will suit me where I can be assured that Louis is safe," added the fond mother. "I am ready to take up my residence on board of the steam-yacht."

"I think the question has settled itself," continued Captain Ringgold.

The next day Mrs. Belgrave and Louis, accompanied by Mrs. Blossom, for the squire had procured another housekeeper, went on board of the Guardian-Mother. In the course of the day all their clothing and such other articles as they desired to have were in place in the cabins and staterooms of the ship, and they had actually gone to housekeeping precisely as they would have taken up their quarters at a first-class hotel. Captain Ringgold had gone on board earlier than the cabin party, and they all seated themselves in the boudoir.

"There is a man forward who has just come on board, sir, who wants to see the captain," said Twist, the remaining quartermaster, presenting himself at the door of the boudoir.

"I can't see him just now," replied the commander. "Ask Mr. Boulong if he will please to come to the boudoir."

"You have a visitor, Captain Ringgold," said Mrs. Belgrave with a look of anxiety on her face.

"And I have sent for the first officer," replied the commander with a meaning smile. "I do not think there is any danger of another conspiracy now that our eyes have been opened."

"I hope not; but after what has occurred, it appears that there may be enemies and conspirators on board of the steamer," suggested Mrs. Belgrave.

"I certainly always regarded Spokes as a good man, and one that could be trusted," answered the captain. "It appears that he was capable of being bribed. But I believe I can explain how he happened to fall from grace. When I took command formally, I called all hands, and after telling the entire ship's company what I expected of them, I stated most explicitly that I would discharge any man — officer, seaman, fireman, or waiter — if he came on board under the influence of liquor."

"An excellent regulation, captain," added Mrs. Belgrave warmly.

"I was on board nearly all the time while we were fitting out, and I watched the hands very closely. The men had plenty of liberty on shore, and Spokes was the only one who ever seemed to have drunk anything at all. I talked to him, and he offered to take the pledge. He was not intoxicated, and I did not discharge him. I am sorry now that I did not; but he had had time to get over the effect of his cups to some extent."

"Do you think he had been drinking when he took part in the conspiracy?" asked the owner's mother.

"I don't know that he had, for I was in the cabin during the dinner yesterday. It is possible that Kimpton brought off liquor to him. My theory is that the agent of Scoble watched for the hands from the steamer, and followed Spokes into a saloon, treated him, and thus got acquainted with him. It was in such a place that he was corrupted, for he was a good man, and the liquor and the money led him astray."

"I know that he had been drinking when I saw him in the cabin of the yacht, for his breath was as strong of whiskey as though he had been steeped in that fluid," added Louis.

The appearance of Mr. Boulong, who entered the boudoir, cap in hand, and saluted the ladies, with whom he had become a favorite, changed the conversation.

"Twist has just informed me that a man has come on board who wants to see me, Mr. Boulong," said the captain.

"I have seen no such person, Captain Ringgold," added the first officer.

"After the events of last evening I find it necessary to exclude all visitors not invited or vouched for by the owner's party or the officers of the ship," continued the commander. "Hereafter no person will be permitted to come on board except under these conditions. You will station a reliable man at the gangway, let him report the visitor to an officer, who will see that the person is all right before he is allowed on board."

"I will enforce the order at once," replied Mr. Boulong, as he retired from the boudoir.

"Will that order afford you any greater feeling of security, Mrs. Belgrave?" asked the captain.

"I am sure it will; in fact, it has already done so, captain," replied the lady.

"But it seems rather humiliating to me to have all these precautions taken for me," interposed Louis. "I suppose I am nothing but a spring chicken, and, as Uncle Moses suggested, that I ought to have a body-guard."

"But I believe that you are really in peril; and if it were my own case, I would use the same precaution that I do for you," replied the captain.

"That is enough, and I am satisfied," replied the owner, laughing. "If it would not humiliate you, it ought not to affect me."

"Sparks," called the commander; and when the cabin steward appeared he proceeded: "Ask Mr. Sage if he will please come to the boudoir."

Mr. Melancthon Sage, whose parents appeared to have given him a long first name to compensate for the shortness of the surname, was the chief steward of the Guardian-Mother. He had occupied a similar position in a first-class hotel, in a celebrated restaurant, and on board of a steamer, and it had required the inducement of a handsome salary to obtain his valuable services on board of the steam-yacht.

"At your service, Captain Ringgold," said Mr. Sage, as he presented himself in the boudoir.

"I wish to inform you, Mr. Sage, that Mr. Belgrave, Mrs. Belgrave, his mother, and Mrs. Blossom will live on board of the steamer, and, of course, you will do all you can to make them comfortable and happy," said the captain. "I have sent for you that they may give you any instruction they may desire in regard to their manner of living."

"I think I shall be able to please them, for I have the New York market on one side of me, and I have as good a cook as can be found in this country," replied the chief steward, rubbing his hands as though he was delighted with the prospect before him, for he had been as much pleased with the party in the cabin as he could wish them to be with him. "I engaged a stewardess the other day, and she came on board this morning. Her name is Chloe, and she has had plenty of experience on board an ocean steamer."

"I have no doubt she will be satisfactory, Mr. Sage," said Mrs. Belgrave. "We may occasionally have dinners on board which will call forth your skill; but I wish to say that for our party we desire no elaborate meals, for we are all accustomed to simple living."

"But what you have you wish should be very good, both in the material and the cooking, do you not?"

"Certainly; we go as far as that with you; but I do not wish my son to become a dyspeptic from too high living."

Mr. Sage retired with the politest of bows, and the captain went to see his visitor.

CHAPTER IX

THE NEW QUARTERMASTER

CAPTAIN RINGGOLD's visitor was seated near the door of the engine-room with Mr. Sentrick, the second engineer, with whom he had been in conversation for half an hour. In fact, the chief officer had placed the stranger under the supervision of the latter to make sure that he did not drop a dynamite bomb through the skylight of the state cabin, or corrupt any of the ship's company.

The visitor was a man of at least forty-five years of age, well dressed, though there was nothing genteel about him. He was inclined to be rather stout, his complexion was somewhat sallow, and he had the appearance of being a person in ill health. But his eyes were piercing and brilliant, and he seemed to look through Mr. Sentrick every time he glanced at him.

"That is the captain," said the engineer as the commander passed near them on his way forward.

"Is that the captain?" asked the stranger, apparently somewhat surprised. "I have seen him before."

When Captain Ringgold heard the voices he halted,

and the visitor stepped forward, taking a letter from his pocket as he did so, which he tendered to the commander, politely raising his hat as he did so, proving that he was not unfamiliar with the forms of good society.

"Introducing Mr. W. Penn Sharp," the captain read from the face of the letter. "I am happy to see you, Mr. Sharp," he added, giving his hand to his visitor.

"I am glad to see you, Captain Ringgold; but I am only an applicant for any position on board of this elegant steamer which you may be able and willing to give me," returned the visitor.

"I am afraid I shall not be able to do anything for you," added the commander as he opened the letter. "From my old friend Captain Buttrick," he added, as he read the signature of the writer.

He read the letter through, and then looked at the bearer of it. He could not fail to notice the brilliant and piercing pair of eyes which had impressed the second engineer, for they were about all that one could see in glancing at his face.

"Captain Buttrick informs me that you sailed with him many years ago, and for your skill as a seaman and your fidelity as a man, he made you his second mate," continued the commander. "He intended that you should be his first officer if you had not insisted upon abandoning the sea."

"Yes, sir; I took a fancy to go into other business, which I have followed for twenty years."

"As a detective, it appears from Buttrick's letter."

"Yes, sir; I had a cousin in that calling who was sure that I should make a success of it, for I had had a little experience of it with him before I went to sea."

"And you did make a success of it."

"I did fairly well at it," replied Mr. Sharp modestly.

Captain Ringgold invited him to take an arm-chair near the door of his cabin, and taking another himself he conversed with the applicant for a position for half an hour, and Mr. Sharp mentioned some of the "cases" in which he had been engaged. Among them was that of the Maud on her first visit to New York harbor, when he had been employed by Mr. Woolridge to watch her. He had been to Von Blonk Park in the discharge of his duty, and had seen the commander, though he had never spoken with him.

"Why do you abandon this calling in which you have been so successful?" asked the captain.

"On account of my health. I have not been exactly an invalid, but I have not been very well for a year; and I am confident that a voyage or two would build me up and make me as good as new," replied Mr. Sharp.

"The Guardian-Mother will sail in about two months for the West Indies, and she will probably go round the world before she returns. Perhaps this would be a longer voyage than you care to take," suggested the commander.

"It is just about the one I thought of taking. I like the sea, and should never have left it if my cousin had not teased me into doing so. I am not a rich man, and not precisely a poor one. I could live comfortably if I gave up business altogether."

"Then your calling has been a profitable one," said the captain, with a smile which the other could not fail to understand.

"I know that men in our business are looked upon as little if any better than the rogues they are employed to hunt down," replied Sharp, fixing his keen gaze upon the face of the commander. "But I assure you there are honest detectives, and I claim to be one of them myself;" and he straightened up his figure like one who realizes an inborn dignity in his character, keeping his sharp eyes fixed upon the captain.

"Oh, I do not doubt it in the least!" exclaimed Captain Ringgold, impressed by the words and the appearance of the applicant. "I have known such myself."

"I am forty-seven years old; and I can say that I never engaged in a dishonest transaction in all my life, and I can say the same of my cousin. I always saved the money I honestly earned, and I engaged with my humble capital in a couple of enterprises, more honest than stock-gambling, which proved to be very profitable. There is not a dollar of my little fortune that is in bad odor."

"If you are so well off in this world's goods, why don't you go to sea as a passenger, Mr. Sharp?" asked the captain.

"I could do so, and am able to do so; but that would not serve my turn. I must be employed; I must have an object before me. I might as well be on shore as go to sea as a passenger."

"That is precisely my own case, and I can understand you," replied the commander. "Of course you have no intention to go to sea before the mast, for that would be an immense let-down from the position you have been occupying during the last twenty years."

"If I cannot obtain any better place I shall go to sea before the mast, for I should like to rough it."

"I am very sorry that I have not such a position as you are competent to fill. My first and second officers are entirely satisfactory to me, and I could not displace them."

"Have you any position, Captain Ringgold?" asked the applicant with a great deal of earnestness.

"The only vacancy in the sailing department of the ship is that of quartermaster; and that is not up to your qualifications."

"But that is a place that would exactly suit me," answered Sharp, with not a little eagerness in his manner. "I know all about that vacancy, and how it was created. Spokes's place is the very one I had in my mind when I came on board."

"Then the place is yours, Sharp; but perhaps I ought to say that we can make no distinction between one quartermaster and the other for the reason that he is the proprietor of a fortune, small or large," added the captain. "We cannot call you 'mister' because you have a bank account."

"I neither expect nor desire anything of the kind, captain. I expect to be treated only as a common sailor, sir; and I know precisely what that means, for I have been there myself."

"Then we understand each other perfectly. Every man on board of the Guardian-Mother will be well treated, and the two quartermasters have a room forward by themselves. I allow no profanity or other evil speech on board, and a drinking man will be discharged at once. Our owner is a young millionaire of high moral tone, and the ship is to be a sort of college for his instruction."

"I know all about him, captain, and I have met him twice in connection with the Scoble business. Mr. Woolridge told me all about it. In regard to my own habits, I do not drink, smoke, or chew, and I have been a member of the Methodist church for over ten years, if I am a detective."

"But I wish to employ you in a double capacity," added the commander.

"In a double capacity?" queried the applicant, opening wide his bright eyes.

"Both as a quartermaster and a detective," replied the captain with a smile. "You know something of the affairs of Louis Belgrave, and we know that his life or liberty is menaced all the time; and they are likely to be during our long voyage. Your wages"—

"Never mind the wages, if you please, Captain

Ringgold. I will accept only the pay of a quarter-master; but I will do everything in my power to protect the young gentleman in precisely the same manner as though I were employed as a detective and liberally paid as such. I consider myself extremely fortunate to obtain the place you have given me on board of such an elegant steam-yacht, and I would have taken a lay as a common sailor."

"If anything should occur to make a better position for you, Sharp, I shall not forget you, though I acknowledge that I should prefer to have you mess with the hands forward so that you can inform yourself in regard to them for the reason that you can deduce from the affair of last evening."

"I ask for no better position, captain; and I am not sure that I should accept it if it were offered to me, for I am a little rusty after twenty years on shore, and I should not care to serve as a watch officer at first," replied Sharp.

Captain Ringgold then conducted the new quarter-master to his cabin, where he talked over the affairs of Louis Belgrave for a couple of hours, and Sharp was fully informed in regard to the past and the possible dangers in the future. The new hand took his leave with the promise to report for duty the next morning.

The cabin party adjourned from the boudoir to the state apartment, and passed the remainder of the day in arranging their clothing and other articles to their satisfaction. At one o'clock they were called to lunch. The table was elegantly decorated with flowers; but the dishes were hardly as simple as Mrs. Belgrave desired.

"Mother, I have been missing something since I came on board this morning," said Louis, as they rose from the table.

"What have you missed, my son?" asked the lady, looking at him with some anxiety in her expression.

"Flix," he replied.

"Perhaps you might be able to get along a day or two without him; and it is his brogue that you have missed," added Mrs. Belgrave, her fair face brightening up so that it made the eyes of Captain Ringgold sparkle.

"I do miss his brogue, though I asked him to hang it up when we are in public. But we have overlooked him in this new arrangement of the men on the checkerboard. Flix is one of the best fellows that ever lived, and he must not be ignored."

"I have no desire to ignore him, for he was my knight-errant when you were not with me on the voyage to the Bermudas in the Maud, my son."

"But not a word was said about him last night when we agreed to live on board for the next two months; and I am going out to the Park to rectify the mistake. Uncle Moses sent him into the country early this morning to attend to some business; but he has procured another office boy, and does not need him, especially as the squire's new partner has taken

his place in his office. I am going out to the Park
now."

"No, my son; you must not leave the ship!"
protested his mother; and she looked as anxious as
though he were already in deadly peril.

"Not leave the ship, mother? Am I to be a prisoner in this gilded cabin, like a canary bird in a cage
hung up in a drawing-room ?" demanded Louis.

But when he looked at the expression on his
mother's face he abandoned his intention at once.
She would suffer in his absence; that was enough.

CHAPTER X

AN OPENING FOR A KNIGHT-ERRANT

Louis looked upon the fears of his mother in regard to him as rather childish; but he could not give her pain. The principal cabin of the Guardian-Mother had four staterooms on each side. The two forward ones were much larger than the others, and were fully equal in every respect but size to a suit of apartments in the highest-toned hotel. Connected with it was a bathroom with every convenience. The berth — for there was only one — had the semblance of a bedstead, and all the furnishings were of the richest description. Something very much less elaborate and ornamental would have suited the present owner just as well; but he had to make the most of things as he found them.

Among the articles of furniture was a desk abundantly supplied with drawers and pigeon-holes, with a bookcase over it, and the occupant of the room was more interested in this piece than in any other. After the conversation at the table Louis went to his room, not for a siesta, for he had not yet acquired any such luxurious habit, but to write a letter to Uncle Moses in relation to Felix McGavonty. He insisted that his crony should live on board with the family during the two months before the steamer sailed on her long voyage. He hoped also that the squire would spend all the time his business in closing up his affairs would permit on board of the ship. A boat was sent on shore with this letter and some others which the ladies had written.

During the forenoon of the next day Uncle Moses came on board for a visit, and Felix came to take up his quarters in the cabin. He was quite contented to take one of the smaller rooms, and declared that it was a palatial apartment. Louis's apartment was the forward one on the starboard side, and the one next aft had been assigned to Uncle Moses. The forward room on the port side had been occupied by Mrs. Belgrave on the passage from the Bermudas, and she still retained it; and it was like that of her son in every respect.

The wind blew a fresh gale when the owner's barge in charge of Mr. Gaskette brought off the worthy trustee and his assistant, as he called Felix, and both of them had been well drenched by the floods of spray that broke over the boat. They were taken to the galley to dry themselves, and in half an hour they were all right again.

"Now, Uncle Moses, I will show you your room," said Louis when the squire declared that he was quite comfortable.

"My room, Sir Louis? I was not aware that I had a room on board of this ark," replied the trustee.

"Of course you have a room, for you belong on board of the Guardian-Mother henceforth and forevermore as long as any of us belong on board of her. Besides, Noah took into the Ark with him two of every kind, and we haven't even one of your kind, for I am quite sure that no one connected with the ship carries about with him anything like two hundred pounds avoirdupois. If you call the steam-yacht an ark, where shall we look for your mate?" said Louis as they entered the boudoir on their way to the cabin.

"In the dime museums. As you say, Sir Louis, I ought to have a mate, for I might upset the ship," chuckled the squire.

"Upset the ship? How could that be?"

"I have somewhere read a story of the movement of a small steamer with a man of my size and weight on board of her. By the way, Sir Louis, where do you keep the chain-box?"

"We do not keep any such thing on board; and I don't know that I ever heard of such a thing," protested Louis.

"Why, a big chest on wheels, filled with chains and other heavy things, to be moved from one side to the other of the steamer to keep her on an even keel."

"Oh, I know what you mean! But those are used on paddle-wheel steamers so as to dip both wheels to the same depth. This is a screw-steamer, and we don't need any such thing."

"In the story, every time the fat man changed his position, the order came down from the pilot-box "—

"The pilot-house, Uncle Moses. You must be nautical now that you are going to sea," interposed the owner.

"Do you not know where charity begins, Sir Louis ? "

"At home."

" Sometimes ; but it always begins at C."

"Very good, Uncle Moses ; and original of course."

"If good at all, it is just as good borrowed as original. The moral is that you are not to pick at me because I don't comprehend nautical slang, for I don't know the spanker smoke-stack from the main top-gallant hatchway. I will struggle to learn the diction of sheate."

"But you did not finish your story, Uncle Moses. 'Every time the fat man changed his position,'"—

"The order came down from the pilot-house — I mean the main royal pilot-house — to shift the chain-box. The story was very funny. Now, if you will get another fat man, I will draw up a bond that when I am on one side of the ship, he shall keep on the other side ; and that will make an even thing of it, and we shall not tip the vessel over. When I am on the port-starboard side he is to be on the other."

"Then he should be on the starboard-port side. I shall find the man, and you had better have the bond ready to sign."

Louis threw open the door of No. 2, and invited

Uncle Moses to take possession of the room. He pointed out the desk in the room, and displayed its draws and pigeon-holes, and suggested that he should write out the bond he had mentioned.

"It will be time enough to write the bond after you have found the fat man, and he has been weighed," replied Uncle Moses. "I came off to-day bringing with me the captain's clerk."

This was the office to which Felix McGavonty had already been appointed, but he had been forgotten in the arrangement for the family to live on board of the steamer. Felix had remained on board till a late hour, and had then gone home with the captain. He was to come on board occasionally, and attend to the ship's accounts ; but his actual work would require very little of his time.

"But the main point is that you shall permit him to live on board with me," said Louis.

"In any such matter as that I am not a free agent," chuckled the squire. "Of course I must permit him to live on board ; I have no option."

"Don't consent if you are not perfectly willing to do so, Uncle Moses," protested Louis.

"Why, Sir Louis, I should as soon think of taking you away from your mother as of taking Flix away from you. Besides, he is your squire ; and you can not do without him any more than I can do without my shadow when the sun shines. He may live on board."

"Thank you, Uncle Moses ; I am very much

obliged to you. But you are to be my Sancho Panza:
no small potatoes about me."

"When you go to the coast of Africa or Asia, and
go to hunting lions and tigers, I have no doubt Flix
could get about more rapidly than I could; but I
should make a fuller meal for the king of beasts or a
royal Bengal tiger than he would," said the squire,
shaking himself like a pot of freshly made jelly with
his laughter. "I see that you are looking out for
the larder of the beasts, Sir Knight."

"I hope you don't think, Uncle Moses, that I
would let any beast eat my squire. No, sir! I
should have too much regard for the animal's diges-
tion."

"You ought to join the Society for the Prevention
of Cruelty to Animals, Sir Louis. You have a kindly
nature — for the beasts."

"I have given Flix No. 3, next to you; and I
think I ought to have two squires when I have so
much material at hand for this service."

"Well, I shall furnish most of the material and
Flix can do the running. On an emergency I shall
be willing to wrestle with an elephant if he is a good-
sized one."

"You are very obliging, Uncle Moses. There
seems to be something exciting on deck," said Louis,
as an unusual noise was heard over their heads. "I
must see what that means;" and he rushed up the
grand staircase as though everything depended upon
his immediate presence on deck.

"All the second cutters, in the boat!" shouted Boatswain Biggs as Louis came out of the boudoir.

It was evident to the owner that something extraordinary was taking place, and Louis rushed to the gangway. As he leaped to the rail he discovered a yacht of about forty feet in length in the very act of going to the bottom. Half a dozen men were clinging to her, but she soon dropped out from under them, and they were left on the top of the water struggling for their lives.

The crew of the second cutter, which had been kept in the water, ran down the steps and took their places in the boat almost in the twinkling of an eye. The young knight-errant could not help following them. Captain Ringgold had gone on shore to attend to some business of his own, and Mr. Boulong was in command. He had taken his place on the bridge where he could better see the condition of the sinking yacht.

"Take charge of the boat, Biggs!" shouted the first officer.

The boatswain was close to the gangway, and he hastened to obey the order; but before he could descend the steps Louis had taken a place in the stern sheets of the cutter. Biggs raised no objection to his presence, for he seemed to think that the owner had a right to do as he pleased.

"Shove off, lively, my lads!" shouted Biggs before he was fairly in the boat. "Give way, and bend your oars!"

"THE BOAT HAD REACHED THE STOUT GENTLEMAN." Page 89.

The cutter shot away from the gangway like an arrow, and it seemed to be hardly a minute before the boat was in the midst of the struggling men. One of the party was a very fat man, and if Louis had not left him in the cabin of the steamer he would have supposed it was Uncle Moses, for he could see only his head. The crew of the cutter immediately began to haul in the persons nearest to them, and, as usual, they were the ones who had the least need of help, for they had swam away from the scene of the disaster.

The stout man had seized hold of a plank that had floated from the deck of the yacht, and seemed to be doing very well for the moment. But there was another gentleman who could not swim, judging from his struggles, who appeared to be in imminent peril. He wore a pair of gold spectacles, and it was evident to Louis, who concentrated all his attention upon him, that he had lost all control of himself. The water on his glasses must have prevented him from seeing anything.

The boat had reached the stout gentleman after the men had drawn in three of the party, and the bow oarsmen were making an effort to pull him into the cutter; but it looked as though he would swamp her if he got as far as the gunwale. The sixth man was swimming with all his might towards a tug that was approaching him.

"Let me alone now, and go to the assistance of the professor!" said the counterpart of Uncle Moses.

"I will hold on to the boat, and I shall be all right."

The stout gentleman puffed and blowed like a por-poise, and doubtless his mouth and throat were full of salt water, and it was very difficult to understand what he said. The bowmen did not appear to com-prehend what he meant, for they continued their efforts to draw him into the boat. Louis's attention had been turned but a moment to the scene at the for-ward part of the cutter; but when he looked again at the one who wore the glasses, he was in the very act of sinking.

The young millionaire could endure the scene no longer in inaction. In the twinkling of an eye he had taken off his coat, kicked off his shoes, and dived over the stern of the cutter.

CHAPTER XI

THE OBESE DOCTOR AND HIS PATIENT

THE boatswain in charge and the four seamen who formed the crew of the second cutter were absorbed in the struggle to get the corpulent gentleman into the boat. The one who wore the gold spectacles had drifted away from the spot where the yacht had now gone to the bottom, and for the moment he appeared to have escaped the attention of all except Louis Belgrave. He had watched the encounter between physical strength and over two hundred pounds of obesity with interest, and if the lives of the two gentlemen had not been in peril it would have been amusing.

The cutter was single-banked, and therefore rather long for its breadth of beam, and the muscular seamen had not a very stable foundation upon which to exert themselves. The boat slipped away from under them every time the zealous tars seemed to be on the point of achieving a victory over the rebellious avoirdupois of the monstrosity. Biggs gave frequent orders to his crew, but they seemed to confuse the men rather than assist them.

Louis did not feel at liberty to interfere with the

operations of those in the cutter with him ; but it was plain to him that the gentleman whom his companion in the yacht called "the professor" was actually drowning, and he could not remain inactive any longer. He was strongly inclined to all innocent athletic sports, and he had given no little attention to the art of swimming in a school of natation. Biggs had risen from his seat in the stern sheets and moved forward, where he could better observe the operations of the men, so that he had not noticed the owner of the steamer when he divested himself of his coat and shoes.

He heard the splash when Louis made his vigorous plunge into the rough water of the river. This act of one whom all the ship's company had been instructed to regard with the utmost respect was even more exciting to him than the contention with the bulk of the nearer victim of the accident. If he should permit the owner of the Guardian-Mother to drown in his chivalrous attempt to save the professor, it would be ruin to him and to all the fine prospects of the magnificent steam-yacht. If his heart did not mount to his throat, there was a stuffy feeling in his gorge of something that did not belong there.

When last seen the professor was not more than a boat's length from the stern of the cutter, and Louis accomplished this distance in a very short space of time. He had not "lost his head," but still carried it very firmly set above his shoulders. As usual when he was going to do anything, he had considered how it was to be accomplished before he set about it. He knew where he was all the time, and when he reached the locality where he had last seen the professor, he turned a sort of forward somerset, and darted down towards the bottom.

"Idiots!" growled the stout gentleman when he had been nearly exhausted by the struggles of the seamen to pull him into the boats. " I am safe enough now, and the professor is drowning!"

"Are you all right, sir ?" asked Biggs.

" I have hold of the boat, and I can hold on for a month," puffed the stout gentleman. "For Heaven's sake save the professor!"

"Stern all! Back her!" continued the boatswain, more alarmed about the safety of the owner than of the professor.

The two after oarsmen had been retained in their places, for not more than two could get hold of the obese gentleman at a time, and they backed water very vigorously, for they could not help sharing the feelings of the boatswain. Bangs, one of the men in the fore-sheets, and one who had proved himself to be a bold, brave fellow at the wreck of the Maud, threw off his shoes the moment he saw Louis in the water, and he kept his eyes fixed on the spot where he had disappeared under the tide.

"Come aft, Bangs! Look out for the gentleman in the water, Williams!" said the boatswain, seeing that one of the bowmen was all ready to make a dive when the occasion should require.

The stern of the cutter had hardly receded a boat's length before the action of the water indicated a movement below its surface, and Biggs directed the two men to cease rowing. He had hardly uttered the words before the head of Louis rose on a long wave almost within reach of those in the stern sheets. His right arm was clasped around the form of the professor, and he was swimming with his left and his feet. The boatswain directed the action of the two oarsmen so that the stern of the cutter was brought near enough for Louis to lay hold of the gunwale.

As soon as he obtained the air the sufferer began to struggle again, and Louis had a difficult task to retain his embrace of him; but he held on with all his remaining might, for he was nearly exhausted by his efforts. Bangs sprang to a point where he could reach the professor, and with the aid of the boatswain he was jerked into the boat as though he had been only a babe. Louis was assisted into the boat and dropped exhausted on the after thwart.

The professor, in spite of his struggles in the water, which had doubtless been involuntary, was now as inanimate as a log of wood. He was laid on the floor of the stern sheets on his back. The stout gentleman had made himself reasonably comfortable under the circumstances, and had observed the rescue of his companion with the most intense interest and solicitude, lifting himself up from time to time so that he could see over and into the boat.

"That won't do!" shouted the stout gentleman

with energy when he observed the position in which the boatswain had placed the sufferer. "I am a physician. Turn him over, and let his head rest on his left arm!"

"Ay, ay, doctor!" replied Biggs, glad to have some one at hand who understood better than himself the restoration of an asphyxiated person, and he placed the professor in the position indicated.

"Now open his mouth and draw his tongue forward," continued the doctor when he saw that his first direction had been carried out.

Biggs had been the master of a coaster, and had had some experience in caring for the victims of accidents. He obeyed the order of the physician with great care and with some skill.

"Now, roll him gently over to the left till he is flat on his face," continued the doctor. "All right! Now, roll him back again till he could see the stars if his eyes were open and there were any stars to see," added the corpulent practitioner, with something of the chuckle of his counterpart then on board of the steamer.

Biggs, assisted by Bangs, followed the direction very carefully, and the first result was the discharge of a considerable quantity of salt water from the mouth of the patient.

"Bravo, my men! I will recommend you both as nurses in the hospital. Now keep doing the same thing without any hurrying," said the doctor. "But I think we might be going somewhere at the same time."

By the time the prescription of the physician had been followed half a dozen times, Louis had recovered his breath, and felt that he was in condition to do something, and he asked the boatswain what he could do to assist.

"I think you have done enough, Mr. Belgrave, for this man would surely have been drowned if you had not brought him up," replied Biggs.

"Never mind that; what can I do?" demanded Louis rather impatiently.

"We haven't room enough to pull four oars, sir, and if you will take the tiller-lines, we can work three oars," added Biggs.

The stroke oarsman had been obliged to abandon his place on the after thwart when the drowning man was drawn into the boat. Three of the men were then placed on the other thwarts, and Louis took his place behind the back-board as cockswain. The men gave way, and the boat moved slowly towards the steamer, for the doctor, whatever he had been before, was now an impediment to her speed. Biggs and Bangs still kept up the treatment of the patient, closely watched by the physician, who bobbed up and down like a buoy in a swell in his efforts to observe what was done in the stern sheets.

It was but a short pull to the ship, and Louis stood up in his place to make sure that the bulky incumbrance at the bow of the cutter was not crushed between the boat and the landing of the gangway. Mr. Boulong and several hands were on the platform awaiting the arrival of the cutter. The acting cockswain was thinking of his mother, who would be very anxious about him, even if the danger was all over, and he looked for her; but she was not to be seen.

As the boat approached the platform the doctor lifted himself as much as he could in the water, and seemed to be perfectly at home, though it must have been a very unusual experience for him. He was even inclined to be jolly, and not to be greatly annoyed at the bath in which he had been indulging for the last ten minutes, for hardly more time than that had elapsed since the cutter left the ship.

"Way enough!" said the acting cockswain when the boat came within a length of the platform. "Stern, all!"

He brought the bow up to the platform without striking it, and he could hardly have done it better if he had been the real cockswain.

"Good!" called the doctor. "Now, go ahead another foot!"

Another light stroke of the oars brought the cutter up to the platform so that the doctor, who had hoisted himself as far as he could, sat down upon it as though he had been in his own office. The bow of the boat lifted itself as it was relieved of the two hundred pounds or more it had been carrying. Mr. Boulong and the seamen on the landing stood ready to set him up on his feet.

"The water is rather moist out there," puffed the doctor, as he turned his attention to the patient in the boat.

"Won't you go on deck, sir?" said the first officer.

"No, I thank you; not just yet. I have a patient in the boat who is forty-seven feet and six inches worse off than I am. He is not in condition to paddle up those steps just now, and you will greatly oblige me, captain, if you will have him carried up to a place where I can look him over," replied the physician.

"Certainly, sir; it shall be done at once," added Mr. Boulong.

"There comes the first cutter with the captain," said Twist.

The professor was carefully lifted from his bed in the bottom of the boat and borne to the deck, closely attended by the first officer. The doctor was carefully climbing the gangway stairs; but he made good progress for one of his bulk and weight, and Louis could not help thinking that he was just the person to sign the bond with Uncle Moses to keep the Guardian-Mother on an even keel.

The bulky doctor had hardly disappeared over the rail before the first cutter came alongside the platform, and Captain Ringgold stepped upon it. Louis had been waiting for it since it was announced that it was in sight, for he thought his good friend would be needed to pacify his mother, and he was glad to see him, as he always was.

"What's going on here?" demanded the commander, as he turned to Louis.

"A yacht upset and sank off here about a quarter of an hour ago, and the second cutter has just returned from picking up the passengers and crew," replied the owner, quietly enough.

"But what has Uncle Moses to do with it?" asked the captain, very much puzzled.

"Nothing at all, Captain," answered Louis with a smile.

"Yet I saw him going up the gangway like a mud-turtle climbing a tree."

"No, sir; that was not Uncle Moses; it was one of the persons picked up after the sinking of the yacht."

"Why, Mr. Belgrave, you are as soaked as a wet hen in a thunder-shower!" exclaimed the captain. "What does this mean? More knight-errantry! But let us go on board, Sir Louis."

They mounted the gangway, and found the obese doctor at work on his patient, spread out on the deck.

CHAPTER XII

BROTHER AVOIRDUPOIS

THE first thing that Louis Belgrave did as he leaped down from the rail to the deck was to look all about him for his mother, but she was not to be seen. He went to the door of the boudoir, but the apartment was empty, though he could hear the cheerful voices of the ladies in conversation with Uncle Moses. If Mrs. Belgrave was not in a flurry about her son on such an occasion, it was a novel experience for her and for him.

Captain Ringgold had gone directly to the quarter-deck, where the professor had been placed upon the planks by order of the doctor, and the treatment began in the cutter was continued, the boatswain and Bangs still operating. The first person that Louis encountered as he left the boudoir was the first officer.

"Have you seen my mother, Mr. Boulong?" he asked.

"I have not; I was on the bridge till I saw the second cutter approaching, and I am confident she has not been on deck," replied the officer.

"Not been on deck?" queried Louis. "Didn't she hear the rumpus on deck?"

"There has been no rumpus, Mr. Belgrave; everything has been as quiet as Sunday in a church."

"But I heard it myself in the cabin, and came on deck to ascertain what was the matter."

"Your ear is quicker than that of others in the cabin, and you were able to detect the meaning of the sounds you heard, as the others were not. I am satisfied that no one in the cabin has the slightest knowledge of what has happened."

"I am very glad of it, for my mother would have had a fit if she had known I had gone in the boat," replied Louis, as he went aft to ascertain the condition of the patient.

When Captain Ringgold went to the quarter-deck the doctor was examining his patient. He waited in silence till he had completed his diagnosis, and had set the volunteer nurses at work again. He had recognized the physician at the first sight of him, and as soon as he rose from his recumbent posture he addressed him.

"I am glad to see you, Dr. Hawkes," said the commander, extending his hand to him.

"Why, Captain Ringgold! Is this steamer the Guardian-Mother, of which I have heard you speak with great enthusiasm?" demanded the doctor as he grasped the captain's offered hand.

"This is the Guardian-Mother, Doctor; and this young gentleman, Mr. Belgrave, is her sole owner," replied the commander, as Louis joined the party around the patient.

"Then he is the millionaire at sixteen!" exclaimed the medical gentleman, seizing the hand of Louis with as much enthusiasm as a corpulent person, wet to the skin, could manifest. "The gifts of fortune are not always worthily bestowed; but in this instance the blind goddess has acted just as though she had her eyes wide open when she distributed her favor. Mr. Belgrave, I am very, very glad to make your acquaintance, for you have proved yourself to be a noble young fellow to-day, if you never did before."

"He is as good as he is rich, and that is his way of doing things," added the commander.

"*Et tu, Brute?* I can stand a little of this sort of thing from the doctor, for he is in a wet and irresponsible condition; but I did not expect it from you, Captain," said Louis, blushing like a school girl.

"I assure you, Dr. Hawkes, that he is as modest as he is good, brave, and rich," continued the captain.

"I must go and see my mother," replied Louis as he began to move off.

"Blessed be the mother of such a boy!" exclaimed the doctor, as he laid violent hands on the young man, and actually hugged him in spite of his very spirited resistance. "You saved the life of my best friend, for I know he would have been drowned if you had not dived for him, and brought him up as a duck does a worm in a puddle. You must pardon me if I gush a little, for I can't help it on this occasion."

"I will excuse you with the greatest pleasure, Doctor, if you will let up just where you are now," replied Louis, breaking away from him. "I thought you were Uncle Moses when I first saw you in the water."

"Pray, who is Uncle Moses?" asked the doctor.

"Here he comes, sir."

It appeared that Mr. Sage had been on deck since the return of the party, and had learned from the second engineer all about the disaster and the rescue, and carried the news down into the cabin, to the great consternation of Mrs. Belgrave, and hardly less of the rest of the party. The lady had hastened on deck, followed by all the rest of the company.

"Where is Louis?" demanded the frightened mother, as she hurried towards the group on the quarter-deck.

"Here I am, mother dear, guardian-mother, sound as a new dollar, and as fresh as a spring robin," replied the son, taking her in his arms, and bearing her back to the boudoir, for he dreaded a scene. "I am all right, light of my eyes and inspiration of my heart and soul. Now, dearest mother, do not make a fuss;" and he kissed and fondled her as though she had been a sweetheart instead of his mother.

"But you have been in the water, my boy!" she exclaimed as she hugged him frantically.

"But I have come out of it; and it is only the person who stays under water too long that suffers any harm from it. Now, don't make a scene, mamma, for all these people will be laughing at me," added Louis.

It required a little time to pacify her; but she soon became very reasonable. He consented to go to his room and change his clothes: but before he could leave the boudoir, Felix rushed in, and was quite as wild as his mother had been.

"Sorra one word of it I heard till this minute!" he exclaimed as he grasped the two hands of his crony. "I was keep'n the ship's books, and I didn't git a taste of it. Why in the wurruld didn't ye's sind for me to go wid ye's, me darlint?"

"Send for you, Flix? We had help enough, and too much till a tug came along and took off the men we had picked up," replied Louis, laughing at the earnestness of his friend, who appeared to think he had been abused because he had not been called to take part in the adventure.

"Ain't I your shquire?"

"If you are a squire at all, it is because you are a lawyer. What possible good could you have done if you had been in the boat?"

"I could protict and defind you from the inemies forninst ye's, and I can shwim like a pollywog. I ought to been there, and it breaks me heart that I wasn't," rattled Felix. "Sure your modther'd felt better if I'd only been wid ye's."

"I think I should," added Mrs. Belgrave, evidently to mollify the poor squire.

"Perhaps I had an enemy near me that no one but myself knew," added Louis. "The yacht was the very one in which Kimpton attempted to carry me

off, and Captain Jeffers was the man who swam for
the tug rather than for the steamer's cutter. The
craft has found its way to the bottom, though there
will be no difficulty in raising her."

"Bad luck to her! I wish she'd catch afoire down
there, and burn to ashes!" said Felix with a good
deal of vim.

"We are all right now, mother; and I hope you
will not think of the matter any more. Jack's best
friend up aloft is looking out for me, and will keep
me safely every time," continued the young millionaire as he reverently looked upwards.

"But, Louis, I want you to promise me that you will
not engage in such dangerous enterprises," pleaded
his mother, putting her arm around his neck again.

"But Jack's friend up aloft expects me to do my
duty, my dear mother. I don't like to take any credit
to myself for what I have done, but I believe the
gentleman they are at work upon would have been
drowned if I had not reached him when I did. I
could not be quiet while he was perishing, mother."

"And promise me, me darlint, to sind for me before ye's doive the next toime," added Felix.

"Must I let a man drown while I send for you,
Flix? Be reasonable, my boy. But I must go and
see how the professor is getting on," replied Louis
as he moved aft, followed by his mother and Felix.

They had raised the sufferer, and placed him in an
arm-chair. He had come to his senses, and was looking about him with a very languid air, while Dr.

Hawkes held his hand, and was telling him he would be all right again.

"This gentleman had a very narrow escape, Mrs. Belgrave," said Captain Ringgold as the lady came upon the quarter-deck.

At these words the doctor turned from his patient, and glanced at Mrs. Belgrave, to whom the commander immediately presented him.

"Happy mother of such a son!" exclaimed he, after he had taken her offered hand. "My friend there would have been cold and stiff at this moment if your son had not been a hero!"

"I wish you would take a dose of your own medicines, Dr. Hawkes," interposed Louis, laughing.

"What?" asked the physician, opening his mouth very wide as if he were ready to take it in.

"An astringent to dry you up on one subject at least," replied the owner, laughing.

"No, no!" exclaimed the doctor, intercepting his patient, who had risen from the chair and was staggering towards Louis. "That won't do, Professor Giroud;" and he forced him back to his seat.

"That is the young gentleman who saved me, and I must thank him!" replied the patient in feeble tones.

He spoke English perfectly, but it was evident to Louis from his name and from his looks that he was a Frenchman, and he hastened to his side. He spoke to him in his own language, and begged him to be very calm and quiet. Then the professor poured out his gratitude in French, and he was eloquent, though no one but the owner could understand him. As usual, Louis disclaimed any credit for what he had done ; but the most he said was to quiet the gentleman, and he left him as soon as he had reduced him to a submissive attitude.

The doctor then said that his patient must be put to bed, and he was conveyed to the guest-chamber, as the ladies had already learned to call the double stateroom, No. 7, next to that of Mrs. Belgrave. He was carried in his arm-chair by Biggs and Bangs and the physician intimated that he had further need of their services. As the doctor turned to follow the patient he saw Uncle Moses for the first time.

"I beg your pardon, Brother Avoirdupois, but you are a man after my own heart, and also after my own body, and I must felicitate myself on this joyful rencontre," said the bulky physician, rushing up to the squire, and measuring him with his eyes from head to foot.

"Allow me to introduce Moses Scarburn, Esq., a legal gentleman in high repute, and the trustee of Sir Louis Belgrave's million and a half, and holding the Guardian-Mother in trust for her owner," said the commander.

"Squire Scarburn, I am delighted to know you ; and if you are in high repute, you must also have an all-round reputation," replied Dr. Hawkes as the two fat right hands were clasped.

"There ought to be a big fellow-feeling between

us," replied Uncle Moses. "There is enough of us both to get up a good deal of that sort of thing."

"You are right; how much do you weigh, Brother Avoirdupois ?"

"Two twenty-six and a half."

"Go you a quarter better," replied the doctor. "But I must see my patient." And he hastened to the cabin.

CHAPTER XIII

THE SURGEON OF THE GUARDIAN-MOTHER

UNCLE MOSES was as much interested in Dr. Hawkes as the physician was in him, evidently on account of the similarity of their obesity. The commander led the way to the cabin, closely followed by the doctor, while Uncle Moses shuffled after them both, apparently determined not to lose sight of the twin monstrosity. Both of them were rather short men; at least, they were not more than five feet six and a half inches in height; and this lack in the perpendicular seemed to exaggerate their rotundity, for two hundred and twenty-five pounds and a half would not have been an excessive weight in men two inches taller.

"There it is," said Dr. Hawkes, drawing a small card automatically cast out by one of the public weighing-machines so common in hotels and railroad stations, and passing it to the squire. "I took account of my adipose stock as I was going to dinner to-day."

"It comes very near two twenty-seven," replied Uncle Moses, as he glanced at the card and took a similar one from his own vest pocket, and gave it to the physician.

"Yours is nearer the middle of the space between the two figuers, and my corporosity contains about four ounces more adipose matter than yours, from which it appears that I am that much your superior," replied Dr. Hawkes, chuckling in concert with the squire.

"You shall take the leather medal, doctor, but we are near enough of a weight to be twins," added Uncle Moses, his gross frame shaking with the ripples of his mirth. "But I will see you again when you are not so much occupied."

"With all my heart," replied the doctor as he went into the room to which his patient had been conveyed.

Captain Ringgold followed him into the room, called Mr. Sage, and directed that everything the physician required should be procured for him. A warm bath was provided for the patient, and the two seamen rubbed him under the eye of the medical adviser. He was then put to bed; Biggs and Banks were dismissed, and Mrs. Blossom was installed as nurse. Room No. 5 had been set apart for the surgeon of the ship when one should be appointed, and connected with it was the dispensary. Dr. Hawkes made himself at home there by request of the commander, and prepared such medicines as his patient required. The professor had taken some tea and toast at the hands of his nurse, and the potions were left for her to administer.

"Now we are at liberty to look out for our own adipose tissue," said the doctor, seating himself by the side of Uncle Moses on the divan around the mainmast, the rest of the cabin party being near him.

"Hereafter I shall look upon you as my twin brother, my dear Adipose Tissue, for only a quarter of a pound of healthy fat separates us," replied the squire, shaking all over again.

"Healthy fat hardly applies to my case, though it may to yours," added the doctor more seriously. "I am not a well man; but I do not think my superabundant adipose tissue is the result of any malady; and my fellow practitioners concur with me in opinion. I have been overworked, and that is all that ails me."

"I should think you might have overtaxed your strength from what I know of the enormous practice you have built up by your skill and devotion to your profession," said the commander.

"For more than a year my associates in the profession, and especially Dr. Sunders, my partner, have advised me to go to Europe for a year or more, or to take a rest in some other way at a distance from New York; but I can hardly get away from my practice, and I have taken to sailing in the harbor and down the bay as a sort of substitute for the voyage."

"You must get away from your business, doctor," suggested Captain Ringgold, "and be entirely free from care."

"That is precisely what I need; I know it as well as though the whole medical fraternity had voted on the question. Professor Giroud is my patient, and he is literally in the same boat with me. He has been doing twice as much work as any one man ought to do. He is my patient, and I have taken him with me on my nautical excursions during the summer."

"Is he a professor of his native language?" asked Louis, who had listened with interest to the conversation.

"Not at all; he taught French, German, and Italian when he first came to the United States; but he is a great scholar, — a remarkable scholar, the learned men of the city say, — and he lectures in various celebrated institutions on half a dozen different subjects. From my patient he became my best friend, and he has helped me more even professionally than any other man with a medical degree."

"It is a pity that his health should fail him," said Uncle Moses.

"I believe you are a bachelor, doctor?" queried the captain.

"Both of Arts and socially; I have never had time to get married," laughed the physician.

"Poor man!" sighed Mrs. Belgrave.

"But if I had met you when I had only half of my present obesity, and you and the Fates had been propitious, I should surely have found time to attend to that important social matter."

The widow Belgrave blushed, and did not venture to say anything more.

"And is the professor equally unencumbered?" asked the commander, who seemed to have a purpose in his questions.

"He would not think you as polite as a Frenchman always is if you applied that word to his family relations, for he has a lovely wife and three as pretty children as the good Lord ever sent to the earth," replied the doctor.

"Excuse me for a few moments," interposed the commander, as he beckoned Uncle Moses to follow him, and retired to the owner's stateroom. They had a consultation which did not last more than five minutes, and then returned to the cabin.

"Do you find that your yacht excursions benefit you and your patient very materially, Dr. Hawkes?" asked Captain Ringgold as he resumed the seat he had left, and took up the conversation at the point where it had been left.

"Not materially, and certainly not very materially, as you put the question, captain. I think all the good we get out of them is in the time we are away from work," replied the physician. "They give us a little rest; that is all."

"That is something."

"But not enough; and I had about made up my mind to take the advice of my friends and spend a year or two, as long as I find it necessary to do so, in Europe and the East," added the doctor. "The professor has almost consented to go with me, and his wife entreats me to take him, at all events. She is not a selfish woman, and it is not practicable to take the three children along."

"Doctor Hawkes, my owner and Mrs. Belgrave

are going all over the world in the Guardian-Mother, and I do not think it is prudent to take such a voyage without a surgeon attached to the ship," said Captain Ringgold, rising from his seat, more animated than usual. "Can you recommend a competent person for this position ? "

"I can," replied the physician, lifting his avoirdupois from the divan and with considerable excitement in his manner. "I can recommend one who will go with you for a year or two without any salary but his board and lodging; and the medical society shall pass upon his qualifications if you desire such an indorsement."

"What is his name ? " asked the captain.

"Here is his card," replied the doctor, taking it from his case, and presenting it to the commander.

"'Philip Hawkes, M.D., Physician and Surgeon,'" read Captain Ringgold from the card. "The candidate is abundantly satisfactory, and we gratefully accept his services, conditionally."

"What is the condition ? " asked the doctor, surprised at the use of the adverb.

"I have already consulted Squire Scarburn, the trustee of my owner, and arranged what the salary of the surgeon should be, and " —

"No salary about it, Captain !" protested the doctor, very vigorously; and he had the reputation of being worth at least half a million.

"We will leave that question open for future consideration," added the commander. "The only condition is that my owner and his mother consent to the appointment; and fortunately they are here to speak for themselves."

"But I do not wish to force my services upon them in this capacity, and perhaps I have to offer a condition myself," interposed the doctor. "Let the lady and her son consider the matter for a week or a month."

"I do not need a moment to consider it, Dr. Hawkes," added Mrs. Belgrave. "I should be delighted to have you appointed, for I know enough about you to save me from a single doubt; and the obligation will be all on our side."

"Thank you, madam," replied the surgeon, bowing very politely to her.

"I am not a lunatic, and I consider it an immense streak of luck which enables us to obtain the services of such an eminently skilful physician," added Louis. "I don't expect to overwork you in attending to me, but I shall be happy in having you on board, even if only as the twin brother of Uncle Moses, who is to be a passenger."

"Mr. Belgrave, it is not polite to wear one's hat in the cabin, but if I had mine on, I should take it off to you: I thank you for the confidence you manifest in such an humble son of Æsculapius as I am," replied the doctor.

"But what is your condition, Dr. Hawkes?" asked the captain.

"That I am able to get away from my friend and patient, Professor Giroud."

"But we want him also, if he can leave his family even for a year," answered the commander, as much to the surprise of Louis and his mother as of Dr. Hawkes.

"You want the professor!" exclaimed the latter. "But I warn you that he is not a professor of rope-yarns and splices, and I don't believe he knows any more about nautical ologies, if you have them, than I do."

"We don't want a professor in that department, for Biggs, the boatswain, is all-sufficient in seamanship."

"But what under the canopy of the lovely moon do you want of a professor of languages and sciences on board of a steam-yacht. I can understand why you should need a doctor, for Mr. Belgrave may have the stomach-ache, or madam, his mother, may have hysterics over his malady."

"My stomach will be all right as long as I can keep it well filled," added Louis; but he thought the surgeon had hit his mother's complaint nearer than his own.

"This vessel is the steamer Guardian-Mother, as you may have heard before, Doctor; but if we called her the College of the Guardian-Mother it would fit the situation just as well, for Mr. Belgrave will pursue his studies on board during the voyage instead of going to Columbia College. Possibly his crony and squire may also have occasion for the services of the professor."

"Not much!" almost shouted Felix, who had been an attentive listener to all that had been said. "My business is to keep the ship's books, and not to study any others."

"It is an admirable compromise you have made in the education of the young gentleman, and if the professor will go with us, he will have the best instructor in the United States," added the doctor. "Of course I cannot say he will accept the position, or that he can afford to do so."

"His salary shall be sufficient for the support of his family."

The surgeon of the Guardian-Mother went then to see his patient.

CHAPTER XIV

THE DEPARTURE OF THE STEAM-YACHT

DR. HAWKES reported his patient as improving, and he was even able to come out of his room and join the party at lunch. In the afternoon he was much better, and the arrangement proposed by Captain Ringgold was mentioned to him. He was delighted with the idea of the voyage, but he was unable to give an answer on the moment, for he was supremely devoted to his family, and he could not at once decide to leave it for a year or more.

"But I would go to the end of the world to serve the young gentleman to whom I owe my life," said he with enthusiasm. "I will consult my wife."

"I will consult her also," added the surgeon with a significant smile; and as he knew the solicitude of the lady for the health of her husband, he was confidant that the Frenchman would become the professor of the steamer.

About four o'clock in the afternoon Professor Giroud was in condition to go on shore, and the barge was ordered to the gangway. The surgeon was afraid the busy reporters had picked up the item of the disaster to the yacht, and published the name of his friend, which would give his wife a great deal of anxiety. Uncle Moses was obliged to return to the Park, and desired to take passage in the boat.

"Brother Adipose Tissue, do you think it will be prudent for both of us to embark in the same boat?" chuckled the squire as they met on the gangway.

"Chemically considered, Brother Avoirdupois, I see not the slightest difficulty in doing so, so far as you and I are concerned. Paradoxically, the heaviest bodies become the lightest under certain circumstances, for grease, oil, fat, float on the top of the water, as any Milesian dish-washer knows, and we shall be perfectly safe," replied the surgeon. "After we have saved the professor once, I should be sorry to drown him in the end. But I must refer the matter to Captain Ringgold."

The commander declared that he had entire confidence in the buoyant character of the barge, and he was willing to guarantee the safty of both the lean and the fat. The party for the shore took their places in the boat, and the eight oars gave way with a will. The captain went with them, for he had more to say to the doctor and the professor in regard to the long voyage.

Louis had a long talk with his mother and Felix after the departure of the barge, and then the owner went on deck to take a little exercise before dinner, for he was rather cramped for the want of space on board of the ship. He passed the pilot-house, and as soon as Penn Sharp, who had come on board in the morning, saw him, he went out to speak to him, for he had not yet met him. The ex-detective was dressed in a nautical suit of blue, and he looked as much like a sailor as any other person on board.

"Good-afternoon, Mr. Belgrave," said he, politely raising his cap as he approached the owner.

"Good-afternoon, sir," returned Louis as politely. "I do not remember that I have met you before, though your face looks quite familiar to me."

"I was employed in looking after the Maud in the spring, and I had occasion to go out to Von Blonk Park to see you. My name is Sharp, sir," continued the new quartermaster.

"I remember you very well, Mr. Sharp," added Louis, giving the other his hand.

"I ought to say that you needn't mister me any more, for I am now one of the ship's company and in a very humble position," said the quartermaster, laughing at the familiarity of the owner.

"Indeed?" interrogated Louis.

"I am rated as a quartermaster, and I take the place of Ethan Spokes, who served you an ill turn day before yesterday."

Louis asked him a great many questions, and he found that the new hand knew all about his affairs and those of his mother, for the captain had given him all the information he did not possess in regard to the past history of the family. But Sharp did not inform the owner that he was shipped in a double capacity, for as a detective he had an instinct for secrecy, and he did not know how much the commander had communicated to him.

Louis was pleased with Sharp, for he took a great deal of pains to make himself agreeable. Possibly if he had known that the new quartermaster was to look out for his safety on the long voyage, he might not have been so favorably impressed in regard to him. When the captain returned he saw the owner and Sharp talking together; and he knew that Louis was very sensitive about having any one police his movements, for he was of the opinion that he was abundantly able to take care of himself, and his pride revolted at anything like espionage over him. But the commander had already told Mrs. Belgrave what he had done.

Captain Ringgold was afraid that Sharp had told Louis of the double capacity in which he was engaged; and his first business when he saw them together was to hasten to Mrs. Belgrave and seal her lips. As soon as he found the opportunity, he talked with the quartermaster, and found that he had been entirely discreet.

"You have been more thoughtful than I have, Sharp," said the captain. "Mr. Belgrave is as proud as Lucifer, and if he knew that you were employed, even as a subsidiary duty, to look out for his safety, I am afraid he would resent it. Therefore it is just as well that we say nothing to him. I have told his mother about it, for it will do something to quiet and comfort her. No other person knows anything about the matter."

"And nobody will know anything about it so far as I am concerned," replied Sharp.

In one of his visits to the shore Captain Ringgold, with the concurrence of Louis and his mother, had arranged an excursion in the steamer complimentary to Dr. Hawkes, for whom he had a profound respect and regard. Several families were invited by the surgeon, of course including that of the professor; and the occasion was relied upon to some extent to lead the Frenchman to a final decision on the acceptance of the offer which had been made to him.

It is not necessary to follow the excursion party to Fire Island, or to report the details of the lunch and the dinner that were a part of the festivities. Madame Giroud and her children were delighted with the affair, and in the end she was as enthusiastic for her husband's acceptance of the position of professor on board as was Dr. Hawkes, and the decision was finally made before the party separated.

If the professor could go to sea with such delightful people as were to be gathered for the voyage on board of the Guardian-Mother, it would be selfish, mean, and cruel for her to object, and she could not do so. It was a question of her husband's health, perhaps his very life, for he had been running down hill physically for more than a year.

The organization of the ship's company of the steamer was thus completed to the entire satisfaction of the owner and the captain, as well as of Mrs. Belgrave and Uncle Moses. At a meeting in the cabin the day after the excursion those interested voted that nothing could be better, and no happier family ever embarked on a steamer, or even stayed at home. Professor Giroud came on board occasionally, and the course of study for his pupil was arranged.

It was decided, at the suggestion of the commander, that the after cabin be fitted up as a schoolroom. Four of the eight staterooms it contained were removed, and a library and cases for apparatus were put in their place. Dr. Hawkes, the professor, and Louis supplied most of the volumes, though a considerable number were purchased in addition. The millionaire student did not wait for the sailing of the steamer to begin his course of study. The Guardian-Mother would pass the winter in the West Indies, and it was evident that the Spanish language would be a desirable acquisition.

Professor Giroud was busy on shore arranging his affairs for his absence, and Louis called in the second officer, Mr. Gaskette, to assist him, for he was fluent in several languages. For the next two months the young millionaire studied Spanish as though he had been compelled to learn it in order to obtain his daily bread. He was an enthusiast in almost any enterprise in which he engaged, and he devoted himself to the study with all his might and main. Before the steamer heaved up her anchor he was able to converse with his temporary instructor in a small way; and even what he had already learned would have been of essential service to him in any Spanish-speaking country.

On the first day of December the Guardian-Mother was ready to go to sea. Captain Ringgold had made the most careful and elaborate preparations for the comfort and enjoyment of the occupants of the cabin. Mrs. Belgrave was asked to suggest anything in addition to what had already been provided; but she was unable to do so. Dr. Hawkes had been *fêted* with three complimentary dinners, and the professor with two, at all of which the captain and Louis were invited to be present.

Uncle Moses had arranged his own and Louis's affairs so that they should not suffer in his absence. The new house for Louis and his mother was to be completed under the supervision of Mr. Sanger, the squire's friend and now his law partner; and when finished it was to be closed to await the return of its future occupants. But Louis wondered if he and his mother would ever move into it, for the steam-yacht had proved to be a very delightful residence to him, and hardly less so to his mother; and he thought then that he should never be willing to exchange it even for a palace.

The Guardian-Mother was to sail after lunch on the first day of the month. The ship was handsomely decorated with the flags of all nations, and her deck and cabins were crowded by the friends of those who were to sail in her. It seemed as though about half of the population of Von Blonk Park were on board, with no end of prominent physicians and professors. A steamer of considerable size was to attend her as an escort and to convey the returning guests to the city again.

The visitors examined the ship with eager curiosity, and were enthusiastic in their praise of her accommodations. They congratulated those who were to sail in her, and wished they were of the number. At two o'clock the anchor had been hove short, the two guns on the forecastle discharged, and the vessel got under way. As she moved down the river every steam-craft she encountered saluted her with noisy whistles, and she replied in the same manner to the compliments.

The sea was a little lumpy outside of the harbor, and it was not advisable to stir up the stomachs of the guests. The steamer's screw was stopped, and the escort craft signalled to come alongside. Then came the parting scene. The most affecting was between the professor and his wife and children; but the lady had been a heroine in the sacrifice she had made, and she did not break down in the trying ordeal. If the right hand of Louis and his mother did not ache after the last of the visitors had left the ship, it was because they were proof against the consequences of excessive hand-shaking.

The screw of the steam-yacht was started when the captain rang a stroke on the gong bell, and she began to move again. Then all the gentlemen on board of the shore steamer cheered most lustily, and the ship's company were directed to return the salute, which they did in the most vigorous manner, assisted by Louis, Felix, Uncle Moses, and the professional gentlemen. In an hour's time the shore could hardly be seen. The sea was somewhat uneven; but all on board had been inured to the motion of the waves.

The voyage had actually commenced; and after the departure of the visitors, those on board in the cabin settled down to recover from the fatigue of the excitement they had just passed through. In a few hours more everything proceeded in a quiet and orderly manner, as at home.

CHAPTER XV

AN UNEXPECTED RENCONTRE

THERE was a great fracas on the ocean during the passage to Bermuda, where the Guardian-Mother was bound; but we should not get to these sunny islands if we attempted to give the details of all the daily life of the party during the voyage. There was no friction about anything. The ladies attended to their sewing. their reading. the games that were provided, and the professional gentlemen assisted them so far as they were competent to do so.

Louis attended to his studies in mathematics. logic. and philosophy, besides giving a great deal of time to Spanish. in which Professor Giroud was an accomplished scholar. The after cabin. as a library and study room. was a very popular locality with him. Felix attended to the ship's books. which required very little of his time. and then he amused himself in learning seamanship, even to knotting and splicing. and he was likely to be competent to " hand. reef. and steer " before the ship got out of the West Indies.

Brother Adipose Tissue and Brother Avoirdupois. as they insisted upon calling each other. had nothing to do but amuse themselves, and they found enough to occupy them in the novelty of the scene, for neither of them had ever before been out of sight of land, except when they went below to sleep on a shore steamer. They amused themselves, but they amused others still more. In fact, they sank the dignity of their respective positions, and behaved very much like two fat boys turned loose for a vacation.

Penn Sharp proved himself to be an able seaman and a very agreeable person besides; but not a word was said about his double mission on the voyage. Felix took a decided fancy to him, which was reciprocated by the quartermaster, who gave him most of his instruction in seamanship. The Milesian became even a greater favorite than Louis with the crew, who enjoyed the Irish wit he had inherited, and Felix was in greater danger of forgetting the English language than that of the Green Isle.

The steamer was not driven on her passage, for the captain was of an economical turn of mind within reasonable limits, and he spared the coal in the bunkers of the ship. In four days the Guardian-Mother passed through the selvage of reefs which nearly surrounds the Bermudas, and with a pilot on board came to anchor in the harbor of Hamilton.

"What is that steamer, Pilot?" asked the captain, as the ship rounded to at the anchorage, pointing to a very trim-looking screw propellor moored off the island.

"I really don't know, Captain," replied the pilot.

"This is the first time I ever saw her, for I have just returned from a fishing-trip for pleasure."

"She seems to be a fine vessel," added the commander as he turned away.

The steamer looked as though she might be a steam-yacht, and she was "quite English, you know." Captain Ringgold bestowed no further attention upon the vessel, though she was handsome enough to challenge the admiration of an accomplished nautical gentleman like himself. The anchor was let go, and the Guardian-Mother was at rest for the first time since she sailed from New York.

The ladies had gone into ecstasies as they gazed upon the bright green trees in passing near the shores of the islands, for the last they had seen of the country in New Jersey had afforded them only a view of leafless trees, frozen streams, and a flurry of snow, for it had been unusually cold during the last of November. Trees, plants, and flowers were new to them, and they were excusable for the moderate gushing in which they indulged.

Lunch was served almost as soon as the anchor touched the bottom. The party were somewhat excited at the prospect which the beautiful region around them promised, and they began to express themselves very decidedly in favor of going ashore at once.

"You will have plenty of time to see all there is to be seen, and we could exhaust the islands in three days, though you could enjoy yourselves here for a month," replied the captain. "But you shall go on shore immediately, for I have ordered the barge to be ready for you."

"How long shall we stay here, Captain Ringgold ?" asked Mrs. Belgrave.

"That is for you to say, and not for me," replied the commander with a smile. "I run the steamer as I am directed by my owner."

"We will stay as long as we desire after we have tried it a while," added Louis, who sat on the captain's right at table. "When you are ready to leave, mother, the ship will weigh anchor and proceed to Nassau."

"I shall not counsel you to live on shore while you are here ; but you ought not to leave without going to The Hamilton, at least to dine, for it is an English Hotel, though it caters largely to American people. If you like, we will dine there this afternoon, and give you a little change from sea-fare."

When the party left the table, they embarked in the barge, and were soon landed on Front Street. They walked to the hotel named, attended by Penn Sharp and the captain, the former assisting the ladies by carrying their bags. Near the shore the place looked like a suburban city, with trees in the gardens of most of the houses after they had passed out of the main business street. Most of them had never seen a palm of any kind, at least outside of a conservatory, and the view was so novel that every plant excited their attention.

They entered the hotel, which was hardly open for the season, and there were but few guests in the parlors. Places at dinner were secured, and the commander suggested a walk in the rear of the hotel in Victoria Park, for he was quite familiar with the locality. The semi-tropical verdure and the strange trees and plants kept them busy all the time. The surgeon of the ship was a botanist, and he was quite as much interested as the ladies. The whole afternoon was delightfully passed away in viewing the scenes at the town, and they returned to the hotel in season for the dinner at six o'clock.

The party consisted of eight persons besides Penn Sharp, who dined at the same table, but was not seated with the others. With three adult gentlemen and two who were men in all but age and stature, the ladies received abundant attention. Both of them were of about the same age, and both of them were very attractive women. Louis declined to take his place at the head of the table, as he had uniformly done on board of the steamer, and Captain Ringgold assumed the position. He escorted Mrs. Blossom to the table, and seated her at his left, while Dr. Hawkes rendered the same service to Mrs. Belgrave, placing her at the right of the commander, in the position of honor.

The others seated themselves just as it happened. Professor Giroud was at the left of Mrs. Blossom and opposite the surgeon, so that there were five of the party on one side of the table and only two on the other. The other guests of the hotel occupied the other end of the table, and the three seats on the left of the professor were left vacant. A lively conversation was immediately initiated. Both the surgeon and the lawyer were funny in the highest degree.

The soup had hardly been served before another guest appeared, and, seeing the three vacant places near the head of the table, he walked towards them. He seemed to be absorbed in thought, and kept his eyes fixed on the floor. He was well dressed, and in outward appearance at least he was a gentleman. He drew back the chair next but one to the professor with the intention of occupying it. As he did so he seemed to raise his eyes involuntarily from the floor, and glanced at the party near him. Then he started back as though he had received a powerful shock of electricity.

At the same moment Mrs. Belgrave drew a long sigh which amounted to a gasp, and all her strength seemed to desert her. But she presently realized that she was at a public table, and she made a tremendous effort to assume an outward appearance of tranquillity, though her heart was bounding with emotion. Louis sat directly opposite the last comer at the table, and though he was less moved than his mother, he was visibly affected by the appearance of the gentleman.

The person who had come late was John Scoble.

The only persons of the party who did not recognize him were Dr. Hawkes and Professor Giroud, and the

situation at once became very embarrassing. But Captain Ringgold appeared to be determined that the appearance of Scoble should not mar the festivities of his party, and he suddenly became filled with life and animation. He even perpetrated a joke, which was an uncommon thing for him to do. He looked at Mrs. Belgrave, and his expression seemed to plead with her not to allow herself to be upset by this unfortunate rencontre.

"Mrs. Belgrave, I hope you have not lost your appetite. If you have, I am afraid I have found it," said the captain with a very enlarged smile on his countenance.

"Oh, no, Captain; I was never in better condition in my life for a good dinner," replied the lady with a struggle, for the appealing look from the head of the table had had its effect upon her.

"These islands are rather famous for their excellent fish," continued Captain Ringgold, after the soup plates had been removed. " I see by the bill of fare that we have grouper on the present occasion, and the fish will be a new experience to you."

"Not exactly, for we had grouper when we were here two months ago; and I thought it was very good," added Mrs. Belgrave, who behaved much better than Louis feared she would, for he had kept one eye on her from the moment he identified the person opposite to him.

"I hope you are not indisposed, madam," added Dr. Hawkes when he found an opportunity to put in a word, for the commander kept the lady very busy, as he found it necessary to do so to distract her attention from the pestilent last arrival at the table.

"Oh, no, doctor; I am quite well," replied she, in a louder tone than usual, for she seemed to have taken it upon herself to make it appear to Scoble that she was not moved by his presence, and she spoke so that he could not help hearing her.

"I am very glad to hear it, for I did not know but you had determined to get up a conspiracy to rob me of a portion of my adipose tissue by getting sick, and overworking me as your medical attendant," chuckled the surgeon. "Don't do it, if you please, for I should be fearfully mortified to fall in weight below that of Brother Avoirdupois, my twin fellow-passenger."

"Give yourself no uneasiness, Dr. Hawkes: I was never in better health in my life, and you can see that I have devoured all the liberal portion of grouper brought to me," said the lady with a merry laugh which the exigencies of the occasion seemed to require of her.

"Bravo, madam! I shall watch your appetite with the most intense interest, for if you or your son should get sick under my administration of the sanitary department of the ship, I am afraid my friend Captain Ringgold would send me home as unfit for the position, and employ a medical student in my place."

"There is no danger that the son will go back on

you, doctor," added Louis, who had been watching his mother as closely as his place would permit.

"We are getting beautiful weather in the Bermudas, Mr. Belgrave," said Scoble with a pleasant smile on his sinister face.

"I am very glad of it, and I am sure our party will enjoy it," replied Louis, astonished that Scoble should speak to him, and more astonished that he should address him so pleasantly.

"I hope they will, and I should be happy to assist in promoting their enjoyment," added the late guest. "I have a fine steam-yacht at anchor off the town, and I shall place her at your disposition."

John Scoble appeared to have assumed a new *rôle* in the drama.

CHAPTER XVI

THE NEW STEAM-YACHT MAUD

JOHN SCOBLE, under the name of Wade Farrongate, claiming to be an honest and upright man, had married the widow of Paul Belgrave, Louis's father. Her son had proved that he was a thief, an embezzler, and a villain in general terms, and wrested from him an immense sum of money as he was on the point of sailing for England, which he had stolen from those who, like the widow Belgrave, believed him to be a man of integrity. For over two years Scoble had remained in England, serving out his term of enlistment in the regiment from which he had deserted and fled to the United States.

What was then the missing million, but which was now the fortune of Louis, had come to the knowledge of Scoble, and he had married the lady to obtain this wealth. It was believed by those who understood the matter best, that the villain intended to get the son out of the way, so that his mother could inherit the fortune as provided in her husband's will.

Scoble had used every means in his power to effect a reconciliation with his wife, as she had formerly been for two years; but the lady repudiated him with

loathing and disgust since she discovered who and
what he was. He had deceived her and married her
under an assumed name, and Squire Scarburn believed
that the union was invalid. The discarded husband
returned to the United States in a schooner he had
fitted up as a yacht, and contrived to entice Louis and
his mother on board of her, with Captain Ringgold
and Felix McGavonty. The vessel got under way as
soon as they were on board; but the villain succeeded
in getting rid of Louis and the shipmaster, and sailed
for the Bermudas.

The Guardian-Mother had been purchased mainly,
in the first instance, for the purpose of pursuing the
Maud, as Scoble had impudently named his schooner,
after the wife who had discarded him. The magnificent steamer had come in sight of the Maud as she
was approaching the islands. Though the villain had
been to sea in his younger days, he was not a skilful
navigator, and had run his vessel on the reef which
nearly surrounds the Bermudas, where she became a
total wreck. Her crew and passengers were saved by
the Guardian-Mother.

The lady and Felix were in this manner reclaimed
from the custody of Scoble, and he and his ship's company were landed on one of the islands. Louis was
supremely happy when he had redeemed his idolized
mother, but neither of them landed at that time, so
great was the dread and terror of the lady of meeting
again the man who had well-nigh wrecked her happiness in this world.

Scoble was informed on board of the steamer that the missing million had been found. This knowledge inflamed his wrath, and he threatened vengeance on Louis, whom he charged with being the cause of all his misfortunes, as he called them; and the charge was certainly a "true bill," for he had done his duty faithfully to his mother.

Two months had elapsed since Scoble and his associates had been landed at St. George's, and nothing had been directly heard from him, though Kimpton had followed the passengers in the steamer to New York, and had attempted to capture the object of his employer's bitter hatred. It did not occur to Captain Ringgold that Scoble might still be at the Bermudas. The villain had inherited the large fortune of his brother who had recently died at St. George's, and the captain estimated that he must be worth over half a million dollars, according to the information he had obtained of a custom-house officer stationed on board of the steamer while he was at the islands two months before.

The discarded husband was capable of achieving any villany in order to obtain even nothing more than his revenge, though he still hoped and believed that he could bring about a reconciliation with the lady if he could only get her son out of the way. The brother of Scoble, who was also a man with an unenviable reputation, had lived and died at St. George's. The custom-house officer who had given Captain Ringgold the facts in regard to him also communicated to him another piece of very important information.

From him he learned that Scoble had had a wife in England, and that he had deserted her. His informant's friend, also in the service of the customs, and living in St. George's, was an own cousin of the first Mrs. Scoble. She had gone out to Nassau as a nurse, but had left there six months before, and no one knew what had become of her. Captain Ringgold had treasured up this information, but he had been very careful not to reveal it to any person, lest Louis and his mother should be told of it. The commander did not regard the information as entirely reliable, so that he was not yet willing to make use of it; and he was not altogether certain that the genuine Mrs. Scoble could be found, even if the story proved to be true in all essential points.

Captain Ringgold was greatly astonished when he recognized Scoble as the latter took his seat at the table of the hotel with the most perfect assurance. With the large fortune that had fallen to him he thought he would probably hasten back to England to enter at once upon its enjoyment. It was likely that the villain knew his former wife's cousin was a resident of St. George, and the appearance of the Guardian-Mother's party in the Bermudas again must have suggested to him that his former marriage would come to their ears.

Whatever Scoble thought, feared, or believed, he conducted himself like a man of the world, and the acquisition of his fortune appeared to have improved his manners, however it might be with his morals. He did not seem to be at all abashed in the presence of the party, which included the wife who had cast him off like a loathsome reptile, and her son, on whom he had been concentrating his hatred and thirst for revenge for more than two years.

He glanced frequently at Mrs. Belgrave, but he did not yet venture to speak to her as he had to Louis, though her son did not doubt that he would do so if he could detach her attention from Dr. Hawkes and the commander, who were doing their best to amuse her and occupy her mind, for the surgeon saw that something affected her, though he could not tell what it was.

"Then you are the owner of the steam-yacht we saw in the harbor as we came into port this forenoon, Captain Scoble?" replied Louis, determined to be as courteous as his late step-father, heartily as he detested his character as a man, and in spite of all the injuries he had inflicted upon him.

"I am the owner of her," replied Scoble, with abundant assurance in his tone and of self-esteem in his manner and expression.

"She looks like a very fine vessel, and she is certainly a very handsome one," added Louis, uttering no more than he felt to be the truth.

"You will say so more emphatically when you have been on board of her. I have taken the governor and all the principal officers of the army stationed here on several excursions, though the Maud arrived less than a week ago," added the owner of the yacht in question.

"The what did you call her?" asked Louis, and something like a flush passed over his face.

"The Maud. I named her after a very dear friend of mine. She is a new vessel of about four hundred tons, and they say that she is good for twenty knots an hour, though I have not tried her at her best."

"I suppose you found some discontented yachts-man here who desired to dispose of her," suggested Louis indifferently, for he had no interest in the pretty steamer unless it was in the use to which she might be applied, for he could not even then forget that the implacable man on the other side of the table had threatened to pursue him all over the world to accomplish his vengeance upon him.

" Not at all, Mr. Belgrave," replied Scoble, shaking his head.

Louis could not help noticing that his opposite called him " mister," though he had ridiculed the application of this handle to his name when he first heard it on board the steamer at her former visit.

" You were fortunate to find so fine a craft ready for use."

" I did not come upon her by accident, I assure you, Mr. Belgrave ; " and he seemed to take a malicious delight in repeating the title of his late step-son, though he did so in rather a satirical tone. " As you are aware, Mr. Belgrave, I purchased a sort of yacht last spring which I called the Maud, for it is a name very dear to me, and I crossed the Atlantic in her; but she was unfortunately wrecked on the reefs of the Bermudas, as you are also aware, Mr. Belgrave."

"I remember the circumstance perfectly well, Corporal Scoble," replied Louis, mixing a proper quantity of the satirical in the dose, for this was the rank he had borne in the army.

The captain of the new Maud frowned, and his face flushed, for his warrant as a corporal had been taken from him after he deserted.

"I am no longer a corporal," said he, scowling in his former style.

"I understood that you lost your warrant after your absence in the United States," added Louis very quietly. "But you were speaking of your steam-yacht."

The owner of the new Maud evidently realized that he was losing ground by permitting his chagrin to get the better of him; but it took a minute or two for him to recover his self-possession, during which he studied the bill of fare and called the waiter.

"When I was looking for a suitable yacht last spring I came across the Maud, as she is now called. She was perfectly new; but her owner had lost all his property before she was fitted out for a voyage. But I could not afford to buy her at that time. Since I came to Bermuda I have inherited, by the death of my brother here, a million dollars, — more than that, but I wish to keep within bounds."

"Then you came into possession of *your* missing million," added Louis, as he noticed that the amount he named was double the sum reported by the custom-house official.

"I am as rich to-day as you are, Louis."

"Then we need not quarrel, even if we cannot agree."

"Precisely my idea; and I hope we shall be friends, and let bygones be bygones," said Scoble with apparent enthusiasm.

"You bought this yacht when you came into possession of your fortune ? " replied the young man, changing the topic a little.

"I did; and fortunately most of my brother's money was deposited in a bank in London, though he had a large sum in cash here, so that I had only to send my draft, and get the steamer at once. It was not by accident, you see, Mr. Belgrave."

"I see that it was not, Corporal Scoble."

The ex-corporal frowned; but he did not put a bad emphasis on Louis's title any more.

"Now, Louis, I hope you will allow me to take your party out on an excursion in the new steamer. I will treat them all like lords and ladies."

"We are all strong republicans; but as you are aware, Captain Scoble, I am the fortunate owner of a steam-yacht somewhat larger than yours, and we really do not stand in need of any such courtesies as you so kindly tender. Besides, we have just come in from a four days' voyage, and we should prefer to take in some of these beautiful shores before we go to sea any more," replied Louis.

Of course, this was only another scheme to enable the wretch to approach Mrs. Belgrave, and he could not encourage it. The fact that he had so promptly purchased a steamer after he went on board of the Guardian-Mother, and learned what use was to be made of her, looked suspicious, to say the least; and Louis had no intention of putting his head into the lion's mouth.

He did not take to the excursion in the Maud; but declared that he meant to go a-fishing while at the islands, for he knew they were noted for this sport. Scoble promptly offered to take him to the best grounds.

CHAPTER XVII

THE MISSION OF PENN SHARP

AFTER dinner the party from the Guardian-Mother went to the principal parlor of the hotel. Mrs. Belgrave took the arm of Dr. Hawkes, and looked over her shoulder as she walked through the hall, to see whether or not Scoble was following her. He did not venture to do so, for he saw that there would be no opportunity for him to speak to the lady while she was surrounded by such a large party.

The story of the Belgrave family had been told on board of the steamer during the voyage, and had been thoroughly discussed, so that every member of the company was familiar with it. While Scoble was conversing with Louis, Captain Ringgold wrote a couple of lines on a piece of paper, and passed it to the surgeon, informing him that the last comer to the table was the former husband of the lady at his side. Mrs. Blossom, who had seen Scoble on board of the ship after the wreck, conveyed the same information to Professor Giroud.

All the visitors from the steamer now knew who and what the owner of the new Maud was, and they all kept quite near Mrs. Belgrave on their way to the parlor. Some of them seemed to fear that he might even make an assault upon the lady, and she could not have had a more efficient body-guard if she had been supported by the ship's company of the Guardian-Mother. Louis kept near his mother; and Scoble, doubtless trusting to future opportunities, did not seek to continue his conversation with the principal object of his malice.

There were none of the few hotel guests in the spacious apartment when they entered, and the party grouped themselves together near one of the large windows. Mrs. Belgrave was certainly nervous, but she had behaved like a heroine during the trying situation at the table. She had hardly permitted herself to look a second time at Scoble, but she had been conscious all the time that she was under the fire of his eyes. The doctor, after he learned the cause of her embarrassment, had devoted himself to her with redoubled interest. One of his specialties, if he could be said to have any such, was nervous diseases, and he was an expert in the management of a situation like the present.

"Captain Ringgold, are you ready to leave these islands at once?" asked Mrs. Belgrave as soon as they were all seated, the doctor taking a chair at her side.

"Why, my dear madam, we have hardly begun to see the beauties and the wonders of this fairy-land," replied the commander, taking as much the manner of the doctor as he could, and laughing very pleasantly.

"We are in the enemy's camp, Captain," she persisted. "Did you hear what that man said?"

"I suppose I heard every word of it; and I was quite astonished at his gentlemanly manner. He must have taken lessons in etiquette since we landed him on St. George's Island two months ago," replied the commander.

"Oh, he always knew how to conduct himself like a gentleman when he was disposed to do so, and he did not need any lessons," added the lady. "But you do not expect me to be at peace near that man, do you?"

"I expect you to be in perfect peace, Mrs. Belgrave," interposed the doctor. "This is just such an experience as you need to enable you to overcome for all time these nervous yieldings to unpleasant circumstances."

"I think I can control myself, and I succeeded better at dinner in doing so than ever before in my life."

"That is excellent testimony that you are making progress," replied Dr. Hawkes. "You have only to persevere in order to win a complete victory over yourself."

Both Captain Ringgold and Louis had talked with the surgeon upon the subject of the lady's nervousness, which amounted to almost a malady, and he had actually begun the treatment of her case, though the patient had no suspicion of it.

"I am certainly less nervous than formerly, though

I cannot tell why," added Mrs. Belgrave. "But I wish you all to understand that I have no fears in regard to myself, and I should not have any if that man succeeded in making me a prisoner on board of his new steamer, as he did in the Maud. I am not afraid of him on my own account. I judge from what I heard him say that he intends to force himself into my presence."

"Then he will have to force himself into the presence of all the rest of us, and I am sure that we can protect you. Brother Avoirdupois and myself will constitute ourselves your especial champions; and then you will always have a heavy force at hand."

"Four hundred and fifty-three pounds of it, Brother Adipose Tissue," answered Uncle Moses.

"I don't need any body-guard, gentlemen; I only fear that man will entrap Louis into something that will deprive me of my son," persisted Mrs. Belgrave, as she glanced at the owner, who was talking French with the professor.

"Don't be alarmed about me, mother," interposed Louis. "You have seen for yourself that I have always been able to take care of myself, sometimes even under desperate circumstances, and there is not the least propriety in your worrying about me;" and he went to her and took both of her hands in his own.

"I don't believe that man will dare to kill you, my son."

"If he does, the wrong man may go down, like our friend McGinty."

"I won't let you out of my sight for the millionth part of a second, my darlint," interposed Felix.

"Brother Avoirdupois and myself will drop down on the fellow if he attempts to harm you, Mr. Belgrave," added the doctor. "And if he comes out of that at all, he will be as thin as a sheet of note-paper."

"That is too thin, doctor," laughed Louis. "If he does not shoot me from behind a tree or a corner — and even my mother does not believe he will dare to do that — I am very sure I can manage him. Since I had my first tussle with him, I have grown into a rather stout boy; and I do not believe that, with the experience of past events in his mind, he will care to pitch into me."

"You are too confident, Louis," added his mother, shaking her head. "Why has that man bought the steam-yacht we saw in the harbor?"

"Because he wanted it, and had money enough to buy it," replied Louis lightly.

"His very first move is to get you on board of her, my son."

"But he desired to get all the rest of you on board of her at the same time, so that I do not think I should be in any great peril if he attempted to indulge in any sort of foul play. I did not accept his very polite invitation, and practically declined it on the part of the entire company. I should like to see the interior of the new Maud, but I promise you, my dear mother, that I will not voluntarily go on board of her."

"That settles the matter, and I think we need not say anything more about it," interposed Dr. Hawkes, with a look which Louis understood, and he said nothing more on the subject.

The surgeon changed the topic of conversation by asking the commander several questions in regard to the islands; and he answered them, as none of the rest of them could, for not one of them had been ashore there. He said enough to enable the rest of them to get into a lively conversation in regard to the Bermudas, and the captain took the opportunity to leave the room. In the vestibule he found Penn Sharp walking back and forth, while Scoble was seated on the veranda smoking his cigar.

"I am keeping my eye on that man," said Sharp, as he nodded his head in the direction of the owner of the new Maud.

"You knew him, then, when he came to the table?" queried Captain Ringgold.

"Hardly, for I had never met him face to face; but I soon made out who he was from his conversation with Mr. Belgrave," replied Sharp.

"He appears to have changed his tactics," said the commander, as he led the quartermaster to the farther end of the vestibule, where the subject of their remarks could neither see nor hear them. "I do not apprehend any violence from him, and I think his first object is to obtain an opportunity to speak with Mrs. Belgrave. Our party will prevent him from giving her any annoyance, for it would greatly disturb her if she were addressed by him."

"I noticed that when he attempted to thorn the young gentleman by his scornful use of the title we all give him, Mr. Belgrave was able to thorn him quite as effectively in return," added Sharp, who had evidently enjoyed the conversation between them at the table.

"I believe we can take care of Mr. Belgrave and his mother, and I have other business for you, Sharp," said the captain.

"I supposed that my occupation was to consist mainly in looking out for the safety of the young gentleman," replied Sharp, "but I am very willing to do anything that may be required of me."

"I don't know but I ought to give you a better position than that of quartermaster, Sharp, for in your double functions you are likely to be more fully occupied than I at first anticipated."

"I am entirely satisfied with my position in the pilot-house, Captain Ringgold," returned Sharp, who had proved himself to be a competent seaman and an especially attentive wheelman.

"I may be able to put you in a position which will better enable you to do the work I have laid out for you, and which I at first intended to do myself," continued the captain, after looking about him to be sure there were no listeners to what he was about to say.

"You know something about the unfortunate marriage of Mrs. Belgrave?"

"You told me all about it from beginning to end at the time of our first conversation."

"I do not remember how much I told you; but if you know all about it, that is enough, and I need not go over it again."

"The lady has repudiated the man she supposed she married, and he is laboring to effect a reconciliation with her, and to be reinstated as her husband."

"That is the whole of it; and I am anxious to be able to prove that he could not legally marry any lady, and that the marriage with John Scoble was illegal under the laws of any country except those of the Mohammedan religion. In other words, I believe he has a legal wife living. It is to establish this point that I need your services."

"It looks as though you had the weather gage of him," said Sharp, rubbing his hands as though he enjoyed the prospect of handling a case like the one indicated.

"I am not quite sure of my facts. When I was here in the Guardian-Mother, two months ago, I made the acquaintance of a custom-house officer by the name of Stockling, and I inquired of him about John Scoble's brother Henry, who died here about three months ago. From him I learned that John had deserted his wife in England."

"Did you learn the maiden name of this woman?"

"I did: Ruth Hastings. This woman has an own

cousin here, whose name is also Hastings, a friend of Stockling, and likewise in the custom-house."

"We have something to begin upon, at least," added Sharp.

"We have that certainly; but the woman left England and went to Nassau as a nurse, probably in the family of some government official. Her cousin here learned that she had left Nassau, and he had been so far unable to ascertain where she had gone."

"Probably back to England," suggested the quartermaster.

"That is good for a guess. and that is all. If we can find this woman. or obtain evidence that she was living at the date of Scoble's marriage to Mrs. Belgrave, we shall be forever rid of the pestilent fellow who pursues her."

"I should say that we should either find her. or. if Scoble actually married Ruth Hastings, we can obtain the evidence of the fact."

The commander said he should send Sharp to St. George's the next day.

CHAPTER XVIII

A PROPOSED FISHING-EXCURSION

CAPTAIN RINGGOLD instructed the quartermaster not to divulge what had just been communicated to him, for no one on board but himself and Uncle Moses knew anything about the case in this new phase. The party from the steamer went on board in the evening, for the ladies preferred to sleep in their cosey rooms on board to occupying chambers in the hotel; and when they went to them, they found the attentive chief steward had placed a fresh bouquet in each of them.

In the course of the evening the captain invited Louis and Uncle Moses to a conference in his state-room. The presence of John Scoble at the Bermudas, and especially of the new Maud, were considered for a long time; but they had no knowledge of the intended movements of the commander of the handsome steam-yacht, and they could only indulge in conjectures in regard to his future conduct.

"So far as Scoble is concerned, the only real question is, whether or not he has abandoned his intention to capture Mr. Belgrave, and persecute his mother," said the captain, finding that they did not get ahead at all in their conjectures. "We cannot settle the matter, and I did not invite you here to discuss it. I find that I need a third officer, and the best man I know for the position is Penn Sharp, who took the place of a quartermaster because I had no other. I look upon him as a very valuable man, and the additional expense will be insignificant."

"Do just as you think proper. I have been looking over the books of Flix, and I find the expense of yachting is less than I anticipated," added Uncle Moses, who provided the money for all the disbursements. "I think we can afford to swell the amount within reasonable limits. I know nothing about the man, and I leave that matter entirely to you, captain."

"I like Sharp very well indeed, and I am sure he is better educated than the crew generally," said Louis. "I heartily approve the making of the position and the appointment of the quartermaster. He is a very inquisitive fellow, and he asks me rafts of questions about our family, and especially about John Scoble. I believe I have told him as many as three times about the robbery at the race course, and the manner in which I took possession of the robber's plunder."

The commander understood why Sharp had been so inquisitive, if neither of the others present did, and he was pleased that the employé with a double function was making a good use of his opportunities.

"Is that all, Captain Ringgold?" Louis inquired when the plan had been fully approved, with a long gape, for he was in the habit of retiring at nine o'clock in the evening, and of getting up at six or earlier in the morning.

"That's all, Mr. Belgrave; you can turn in now," replied the commander, with a laugh at the length of the yawn.

After he had gone the captain told Uncle Moses all about the use he intended to make of Sharp's services, and for another hour they discussed the subject till the squire began to yawn as heavily as Louis had done.

The next morning Captain Ringgold called Sharp to his room, and had another long talk with him before breakfast, and gave him some legal points he had obtained from Squire Scarburn.

"I have decided to appoint you third officer of the Guardian-Mother, Mr. Sharp," said the captain, giving him his new title for the first time.

"I am very much obliged to you, Captain Ringgold, though I was quite willing to do all you required of me as a quartermaster," replied the new third officer.

"The new position will enable you to do what I require of you to better advantage. We have a good room for you, and you can obtain such a uniform as you need at St. George's at very short notice. Mr. Boulong, will you call all hands?" continued the captain, going to the door of his room. "Fortunately, we have an extra seaman I shipped simply because I thought he was an extra-good hand."

Captain Ringgold explained to Mr. Boulong and Mr. Gaskette that he had appointed a third officer in the person of Penn Sharp, though he was unable to explain to them his precise object in doing so. They could not object, even if they had been disposed to do so; and the commander proceeded to introduce the new third officer to the crew, who "must be obeyed and respected as such." Then he called Nathan Bangs from the crew and appointed him quarter-master in the place of Sharp, promoted, and this action called forth a volley of cheers from the men. Bangs thanked the captain, and went into the pilot-house, the scene of his future duties.

After breakfast Mr. Sharp, as he must now be addressed, went on shore, and took a carriage for St. George's, in order to enter at once upon his special function. He did not return till after dark, and Mr. Gaskette suggested to Mr. Boulong that he had been appointed third officer for some other reason than because he was needed in that capacity. But they were wise men, and they did not exercise their sailor's prerogative to grumble at the action taken by the captain.

Mr. Sage had been in the Bermudas before as an assistant in one of the hotels, and he was a competent guide for the party. He suggested that the passengers should dine at least once at the Princess, in which he had been employed, and the captain assented to the plan for the second day. He was sent on shore early to engage the carriages needed.

All that day the party consumed in a ride to the south end of Long Island. as it is called, though it really has no name, frequently alighting to view in detail particular localities which the drivers pointed out to them. The ladies were in ecstasies, and Mrs. Belgrave even forgot that there was any such person in the world as John Scoble. Some of the gentlemen proved that they could "gush" moderately on an emergency, and they found the occasion during this trip.

The excursion was repeated every day for a week to different parts of the islands, though the barge and first cutter were sometimes used instead of carriages. Pleasant as it would be to report these agreeable trips in detail, it would require a volume to do justice to the subject, and it has been faithfully done by abler hands. During this busy week John Scoble was hardly seen or heard from. A boat came one day from the Maud, but the imperative order of Captain Ringgold was enforced, and no uninvited persons were permitted on board.

Louis received a letter from Scoble renewing his invitation to give the party an excursion in his steamer, which was respectfully declined. Another letter came in which the owner of the Maud made a sort of an apology for his conduct towards the young millionaire, and proposing that they should be friends in the future. To this Louis replied in formal terms, assuring Scoble that he had no ill-will towards him, and as long as he was not interfered with by his correspondent or his agents, he should not be guilty of any unfriendly act; and this was precisely the principle upon which the young millionaire had always acted.

If Louis did not accept the olive branch held out to him by the owner of the Maud, he did not reject it, though he was unwilling to establish intimate relations with one who had proved himself to be a most malignant enemy. He showed this letter to the captain, as he had the first one, and both of them had been approved. It was delivered on board of the Maud, and he heard nothing more from Scoble.

Louis had never been a sportsman in the proper sense of the word, and his taste as a hunter or a fisherman had never been cultivated. He had never had the opportunity to amuse himself as an angler, for there were no streams available within walking distance of Von Blonk Park. He had sometimes fished from the deck of the Blanche, or in one of her boats, and he was fond of the sport so far as he had been developed as a fisherman.

He had heard a great deal about the fishing of the semi-tropical islands, and read about it in the books relating to the regions of the earth the party expected to visit, which had been abundantly supplied by the forethought of the captain. Felix was more enthusiastic on the subject than the owner, and they had already planned a trip to the fishing-grounds. They had talked with a white man they found at their usual landing-place who was engaged in the business.

While they were engaged in a conversation with Lopez, as he was called, and he appeared to be a Portuguese, they noticed that a boat from the Maud landed Scoble near them. He paused a few moments by the side of the water, and looked at Louis; but he did not approach him. The fisherman was willing to take them to the best grounds for a consideration, and Louis engaged him for this purpose. The Guardian-Mother had been at her anchorage a week, and the excursion was arranged for Monday morning. On Sunday the entire party went on shore in the barge and attended Pembroke Church, and the captain announced his intention to sail at four o'clock on the afternoon of the next day.

"But, Captain Ringgold, Flix and I are going a-fishing to-morrow," interposed Louis. "We have been talking about such an excursion since we arrived here; but we have been so busy on shore with the rest of the company that we could not get a single day for it before."

"You can go a-fishing, certainly, if you desire to do so," said the commander, laughing at the earnestness of his owner.

"I don't wish to leave these islands without a day's sport of this kind," added Louis.

"Very well; I shall not be likely to sail without you, Mr. Belgrave, even if I have to wait a month for you," continued the captain. "This cruise is for your amusement as well as for your instruction, and I should be very unreasonable to curtail your enjoyment, especially after you have devoted yourself as closely as you have to your studies. Besides, you are the owner of the ship, and it is for you to give the order when we shall sail."

"I don't do it in just that sort of way, Captain Ringgold, as you are well aware," replied Louis, much amused at the humble position the commander assumed. "I leave all these matters to your judgment, and I do not intend to interfere with you in the discharge of your duties."

"But I should say, Mr. Belgrave, that you would have an abundance of time to do your fishing and get back before four o'clock in the afternoon, though I will put off our departure till Tuesday if you desire me to do so. Will you take the barge or the first cutter for your trip?"

"What good would one of our boats do us if we knew nothing at all about where to find the fishing-grounds? We shall use neither the barge nor one of the cutters; we have engaged Lopez, the fisherman you sometimes see at the landing."

"You have engaged him?" queried the captain thoughtfully.

The commander was on the lookout for any trap which the presence of Scoble at the islands suggested to him; but he could not see any danger in the proposed fishing-trip. The young men were to go with a resident of Hamilton, who was not in the employ of the owner of the Maud, so that he could hardly be one of his agents, like Ovid Kimpton. But he determined to consider the matter before the next morning, and cause some inquiries to be made in regard to Lopez.

The commander made no objection to the arrangement, and the subject was dropped. He had decided to have Mr. Sharp look into the character of the fisherman when he returned from St. George's. The new third officer had been back to the ship several times to report the progress he was making in his investigation to the captain; but he had gone over again on Saturday, and had not yet returned.

It was nearly dark when he came back, for he had said before that he had had great difficulty in finding Hastings, the cousin of the woman, and Sunday was the most favorable day for his operations. As soon as he came on board, Captain Ringgold sent for him to come to his room.

CHAPTER XIX

A COLICKY EXCURSIONIST

In order to keep up appearances on board of the steamer, Mr. Sharp had been back to the ship nearly every day during the week, passing a portion of the time there. Saturday night was the first that he had been absent. It was given out that he had friends at St. George's with whom he desired to pass as much time as possible ; and certainly he had done his best to make friends of Stockling and George Hastings. He had spent his money as freely as the occasion required, for he had been authorized to do so, in dinners and luxuries for his companions ; and he had succeeded in opening their mouths as wide as nature ever intended, for the custom-house officials really had nothing to conceal.

"We sail to-morrow afternoon, Mr. Sharp, and I hope you have brought your investigation to a satisfactory conclusion by this time," said Captain Ringgold, when they were alone and the doors were both closed.

"I have, Captain, for to-day I obtained three letters written by Mrs. Scoble to her cousin George Hastings at St. George's," replied the third officer as he produced them. " I should have finished the business three days ago if it had not been for these letters, which contain all the information in possession of Hastings in regard to his cousin."

" Stockling mentioned to me one or more letters Hastings had received," added the captain.

" The woman's cousin spoke to me about these letters the first time I met him. Of course I did not inform her of the nature of my business in relation to the woman, and he bothered himself a great deal to discover what I was driving at. He seemed to think I meant to injure his cousin, and I was finally under the necessity of leading him to believe that I was seeking to redress the wrongs she had suffered at the hands of her husband. I did this at a little dinner I gave to him and Stockling at the hotel."

" Of course a man must open his mouth at dinner," said the captain dryly.

" Hastings did so, at any rate. He had told me before that he supposed the letters had been destroyed, though he was not sure of it. I was satisfied that they had not been destroyed, and that he had some motive for holding on to them. He promised to find them if they were still in existence; but every day he reported that he had been unable to do so."

" I should have known what to do under such circumstances, for that class of Englishmen are not as reserved and sensitive as most Americans," added Captain Ringgold.

" To make a short story of what has been a long

one to me, I offered him yesterday ten pounds for the letters," said Mr. Sharp, reading the thought of the commander.

"That was the way to reach him, and I will cheerfully pay all such expenses as you may have occasion to incur."

"I took care to make this offer when Stockling was not present. Hastings seemed to have some scruples about making such a trade. I assured him the letters would be valuable to me, and it was a proper thing for me to pay for them. I invited him to dine with me alone at the hotel to-day. He accepted if we were to be alone, for he said he did not wish Stockling to know that he was making money out of his cousin's letters. He promised me before we separated yesterday that he would make a diligent search on Sunday morning, the only time he had, for the correspondence, and that I should have the letters if they could be found. I felt pretty sure he would find them, and he did. I paid him fifty dollars in our money after I had examined them, and was convinced that they were genuine."

"You have managed the case very judiciously, Mr. Sharp."

"I have done the best I could, though it has taken me a long time to get at this result. The envelopes of the letters have the Nassau postmark upon them; and the writer mentions persons and localities on the island of New Providence which satisfied me that the writer of the epistle was there."

"Have you been in Nassau, Mr. Sharp ? " asked the captain.

" I have ; I was the mate of a schooner that brought a cargo of sponges, pineapples, and such things from there the very last voyage I ever made to the West Indies. After I had the letters in my pocket, and Hastings had the fifty dollars in his, I questioned him for a full hour in relation to the past history of Ruth Scoble, born Hastings, and I wrote down all the important answers he gave me," continued Mr. Sharp, as he drew from his pocket a paper covered with writing in pencil.

"You have executed your mission very faithfully," added the captain, glancing at the paper.

"I will write these answers all out carefully while my memory of the conversation is still fresh. The first item of any importance is to the effect that the marriage took place in the parish church of Aldenham where the record of it can still be found," the third officer proceeded. "I procured half a dozen names of persons residing there, for this was the home of the Hastingses, though Mrs. Scoble was a bar-maid in London before her marriage."

"Then you had better write at once to one or two of these persons to ascertain if the record is still available," suggested the captain.

"I thought of doing that, and for that purpose obtained the names."

"Do so ; and enclose a small gold coin to pay postage and expenses, say half a sovereign," added the commander as he handed him a coin of this value.

"I will attend to this matter to-morrow. But where shall I tell my unknown correspondent to direct his reply?"

"To Havana, Cuba, Hotel Pasaje; but I will direct an envelope for you, and I happen to have a few English postage-stamps on hand. Now that matter is disposed of, I wish you to go on shore this evening, and ascertain what you can in regard to one Lopez, who is a fisherman, and lands his catch where our boats usually go in," continued the commander.

"I have seen him and talked with him about the fish he was selling."

"Mr. Belgrave and Felix are set upon going a-fishing before they leave the Bermudas, and I do not object if this Lopez, whom they have engaged for to-morrow, is the right sort of man. Strange as it may appear after what occurred in New York harbor, Mrs. Belgrave is perfectly willing her son should go."

"It does not look like very dangerous business to go out and catch a mess of groupers and other fish," added Mr. Sharp with a smile as though he considered it a perfectly safe excursion.

"Experience has taught me that we must be extraordinarily cautious in regard to our owner. I have not set you to watch John Scoble, for I had another occupation for you, though perhaps I ought to have done so. He seems to be perfectly harmless just now, and he has made overtures to Mr. Belgrave proposing to be on good terms with him in the future. But he is a malicious villain, and I will not trust him."

The third officer left the apartment of the commander, and the second cutter put him on shore at once. He found Lopez at work cleaning up his boat for the excursion the next morning, though it was Sunday. He talked with him for a while. He was rather small in stature, and Mr. Sharp was satisfied that Louis could handle him if he attempted any foul play; at least, he could use that handy revolver he still carried in his right hip pocket.

But the captain's agent was not satisfied with the examination of the fisherman alone. He found a number of strollers about Front Street near the landing, and they seemed to be at home there. He spoke to several of them, and they all said Lopez was a quiet and harmless man, and some thought he was a sort of simpleton. They believed as a rule that he was an honest and industrious man. The boat in which Louis was to make the excursion was good enough, substantial and strong, but far from handsome, and not to be compared with the trim sailboats belonging to the members of the yacht club.

When Louis left his stateroom the next day the first person he met was Mrs. Blossom coming out of the stateroom of Felix. It was only six o'clock in the morning, and he was rather surprised to see the lady about at so early an hour, and especially to see her coming out of the stateroom of his crony.

"You are up early, Mrs. Blossom," said he.

"I have been up about three hours, for Flix called me by rapping on the partition," she replied. "The poor fellow has been quite sick."

"Felix sick!" exclaimed Louis. "I never knew him to do such a thing before in my life."

"I have, for he has had occasional attacks of colic, resulting from indigestion the doctor says," added the lady.

"Has he had the doctor?" asked Louis, fearing that the case might be serious.

"Yes; Dr. Hawkes was with him over an hour, and entirely relieved him of the severe pain he was suffering. He is quite comfortable now."

"Is he awake?"

"He is, though he has been asleep, and he will do very well. There is no occasion for any anxiety on his account now."

"Can I see him?"

"Certainly, if you wish," replied Mrs. Blossom as she opened the door of the room.

"You are a pretty fellow, Flix!" exclaimed Louis as he took the hand of the patient. "I suppose you forget that you were to go a-fishing with me to-day, and have made up this fiasco as an excuse for getting rid of it."

"Faix, me b'y, if ye's had the gripes as I got it this morning, you w'ul'n't be a bit loikly to call it a fiasco, though upon me sowl I don't know at all at all what the wurrud manes," replied the patient in a rather feeble tone for him, though he struggled to be as jolly as usual.

"It means a failure after high hopes, a failure to go a-fishing in this instance," replied Louis.

"Sure Oi'm goin' a-fishin' all the same," protested Felix.

"No, you are not, Flix!" protested Mrs. Blossom. "The doctor said you must not get out of your bed to-day."

"No, Flix; I wouldn't have you do any such thing. I will give up the trip since you are not able to go with me," added the owner in the kindly tones of sympathy.

"I suppose I must do as the doctor and Mrs. Blossom say," replied the patient, suddenly dropping his Milesian brogue when he began to feel a little more serious. "They mean well by me in spite of the stuff they made me take internally, externally, and eternally, and I must obey my orders. But you need not give up the trip at all, my darling. You have no need to make a shotecary pop of your interior as I have. Promise me that you will go; and take the captain with you if you need company."

There was nothing dangerous or even serious in the condition of Felix, and after some persuasion Louis promised to attend to the fishing that day. When he went out into the cabin, he found his breakfast all ready and he disposed of it without interruption from any one, for the party were not in the habit of coming out of their staterooms till after seven o'clock, and it was now only half-past six.

When he went on deck he discovered that the firemen and engineers were getting up steam at this early hour. He asked the captain about it, and was told that he intended to give those who remained on board a little excursion during the day. The Maud was doing the same thing, and a black volume was rolling out of her smoke stack. There was no concert between the two steamers, and it appeared to be a simple coincidence.

Lopez's boat was at the platform of the gangway, and, descending the steps, Louis took his place in the stern.

CHAPTER XX

A DISAGREEABLE SKIPPER

IT was seven o'clock in the morning when Louis embarked in the fisherman's boat. While the millionaire at sixteen had never cultivated a taste for hunting and fishing, he thought it probable that he might desire to amuse himself with one and the other, and Captain Ringgold had advised him to provide himself with a good double-barrelled fowling-piece and a sufficient supply of fishing and angling gear. From his store of the latter he had taken a couple of lines with heavy sinkers, such as he had used when fishing from the deck of the Blanche.

Lopez shoved off and set his three-cornered sail. A gentle breeze was blowing from the south, which was fair in getting out of Hamilton Harbor, and the boat made about three miles an hour. The fisherman appeared to be a man of about forty, and he was not especially agreeable in his manners or gentle in his speech. Louis tried to get up a conversation with him, but the Portuguese answered him so crustily that he abandoned the attempt, and gave himself up to a study of the islands which made a miniature archipelago of Great Sound, an enclosed sheet of water like the bend of a fish-hook, which is about the shape of the Bermudas as they appear on the map.

As the boat was approaching Timlin's Narrows, the passenger observed that Lopez was headed for the shore of the main island. He did not understand this movement, but he concluded that the skipper was going to some place to obtain bait, or for some similar purpose. Not far from the Narrows was a small house, from which he saw two men walking towards the water.

"Whose house is that, Lopez?" asked Louis.

"I live there," replied the skipper curtly.

"Who are those men?"

"My men."

"Do you keep men?"

"Two."

"What do they do?"

"Fish."

"Are you going to take them in the boat, Lopez?"

"Yes."

"But I hired your boat, and she belongs to me for the day," protested Louis, for he did not like the idea of having any company in the boat with him.

"No!" replied Lopez gruffly. "You hired me to take you out fishing, and I am going to do it."

It seemed to be useless to argue the question, even if it were of importance enough to need consideration, but Louis did not understand the matter as the fisherman did. He supposed when he engaged the boat he did so for his own exclusive use, though he certainly had not so stipulated in the agreement, and on second thought he concluded that he "had no case," as Uncle Moses would have put it if he had been present.

There was nothing in the situation to excite the suspicion of the passenger, though he kept his eyes wide open to discover anything that looked like treachery, for though he had seen little or nothing of John Scoble, and he had professed to be friendly, he was still within working distance of him. Captain Ringgold had charged him to be on the watch for every moment of the time when he was not on board of the Guardian-Mother. He had done and was still doing so; but he could not conceive in what manner the two additional men could do him any harm.

When the boat came up to the shore, he took the precaution to place himself in the bow, where he should have his three companions in front instead of on both sides of him. He even put his hand on the handle of his revolver to assure himself that it was ready for use in any possible emergency. He adopted these means of safety simply because the captain had so solemnly warned him to be on the lookout for treachery at all times, and not because he detected any signs of danger in the present situation.

"Sit here!" said Lopez, pointing to the place in the stern he had just abandoned.

"No!" replied Louis stoutly, and in a tone as commanding and as crusty as the boatman used.

"You must sit here!" added Lopez.

"No, I will not!"

"I say you must sit here!" said the skipper, rising from his seat.

"I say I will not!" protested Louis in the most determined tone.

The passenger acted as he did, and spoke as he did, simply to keep even with the boatman, whose imperious manner was not at all to his taste, and the fellow seemed to be inclined to bully him. He could not realize that Lopez acted from any other motive than the desire to have his own way.

"I run this boat, and those on board of it must obey my orders!" persisted the skipper as he began to move forward.

"Must they? Then I am no longer on board of her," replied Louis, as he picked up his fishing-tackle, and leaped upon the shore, where the boat had grounded.

The two men had not yet reached the landing-place, and were walking very leisurely towards it. Lopez appeared to be nonplussed by the unexpected movement of his passenger. He had not condescended to explain why he wished his companion to sit in the stern, and his imperative order had raised a doubt rather than a suspicion in Louis's mind. The two men reached the shore while things were in this position, and Louis wondered if the fisherman would attempt to enforce his order.

The two men in the employ of Lopez looked as though they might be Portuguese like himself; but they were younger men, and of rather small stature.

They were very meanly clad, like the fisherman himself, and there was something repulsive about their
expression which Louis did not stop to analyze. He
placed himself with his back against a ledge of coral
rock, and he had a sublime assurance of his ability to
take care of himself. His father had been a soldier
in the war of the Rebellion, and he was reported to
be the most brave and daring man in his regiment;
and Louis appeared to have inherited his courage and
assurance from him.

The two men looked peaceable enough in spite of
their ill-favored expression, and Louis could not see
even a "speck of war," for the fisherman had ceased
to be imperative; in fact, he was sporting a smile on
his bronzed face, and the skirmish seemed to have
resulted in a complete victory for the passenger.

"What you about?" asked Lopez, putting on his
sweetest expression, albeit not very sweet one at that.

"I am about to go back to Hamilton," replied Louis
as mildly as the other had spoken. "I think I had
rather take a two-mile walk back to the steamer than
go a-fishing with such an uncomfortable fellow as you
are."

"You must excuse me, Mr. Belgrave; I forgot that
you were a passenger, and not one of the crew. I did
not mean any harm, and I am very sorry that I was so
saucy. I won't do it again, and if you will come on
board again, you may sit where you please, and I will
not say a word to you about it," said the fisherman
in a very mild and even humble tone.

Louis had agreed to give him ten shillings for the use of his boat, and he was to put all the fish caught by the passenger on board of the steamer. This was a considerable sum of money for a man of his class in the Bermudas, and Louis could readily perceive that the anticipated loss of it had a very salutary effect upon the skipper, and had quickly brought him back to his senses.

"Do you suppose the owner of a steam-yacht like the larger one on Hamilton harbor will submit to be addressed as you spoke to me, Lopez?" demanded Louis, putting on more importance than he had ever been known to assume before in his life, for he wished to make a strong impression on the mind of the fisherman.

"The Guardian-Mother, as they call her? Be you the owner of that fine steamer?" asked the fisherman in a very fawning manner, his head bowed as he spoke.

"I am the owner of her; and I am not to be domineered over by the skipper of a little tub like this one," replied Louis, very smartly for him. "But it makes no difference who or what I am. I agreed to give you ten shillings to take me out a-fishing, and I supposed I was to have the boat to myself. I did not expect to be treated like your servant, and I will not stand anything of the sort."

"I ask your pardon, Mr. Belgrave, and I am very sorry that I was rough to the owner of such a fine ship," pleaded Lopez. "If you will come in the boat again, I will treat you like a lord, and let you do any-thing you please."

"All right; I will try it again. If you try to lord it over me again, I shall compel you to return to Hamilton at once, whether you have caught any fish or not," added Louis, as he drew his revolver from his pocket to assure the skipper that he could enforce his commands; and he displayed the weapon quite as much for the benefit of the two men, who had now seated themselves in the middle of the boat.

"I will agree to go back when you say the word, sir," answered Lopez, evidently thrown aback by the sight of the pistol.

One of the men shoved off the boat with an oar, and Louis took the seat he had chosen before in the fore-sheets. The fisherman said no more, and Louis prepared one of his lines for use. The prospect of some good fishing was very pleasant, but he did not enjoy the company he had in the boat. He had been looking up, in the books on board of the steamer, the fish he expected to catch, and he anticipated a day of exciting sport.

There was one other amusement he was not inclined entirely to neglect, though no other person in the com-pany was disposed to participate in it, and this was bathing. The transparent waters that surrounded the island were very enticing to him, and he was deter-mined to have a swim, if possible, before his depart-ure. Perhaps five shillings more would induce Lopez to take him to a suitable place near the shore, for he was not willing to dive off the boat at a distance of eight or ten miles from the main island, where the festive shark might gormandize upon his dainty body.

"Do you know of any good place to bathe, Lopez?" he asked, when the skipper furled his sail at the fishing-ground, which was near Chubb Cut in the outer reef.

"Plenty of them, Mr. Belgrave," replied the fisherman, who had become very respectable to his passenger. "But not out here, for there are too many sharks."

"Sharks are not agreeable companions in the water," added Louis.

"There is an island about four miles from here which is one of the best places I know of," answered Lopez; and the passenger thought there was some meaning in the smile with which he glanced at his Portuguese companions in the boat.

"Are there no sharks there?"

"Only little ones that won't hurt anybody."

"I will give you five shillings more if you will take me over there, and wait till I take a swim, for I think I may need a wash after we get through fishing."

"All right, sir;" and Louis thought he looked exceedingly glad to make this small sum.

A dish of bait was passed forward to Louis, and he soon had a line in the water, with the sinker near the bottom. A minute later he felt a heavy tug at his line, and he hauled away with all his might, and brought

up an angel fish that the skipper said would weigh
fifteen pounds. He was an ugly-looking beast, and
there was nothing angelic about him. He was not eat-
able ; one of the men killed him and threw him overboard.   Louis's next fish was a grouper, and he
caught half a dozen of them.

CHAPTER XXI

THE PRISONER ON AN ISLAND

THE grouper is a very gamy fish, and after Louis had been instructed by the fisherman, he heaved out a long line, and then trolled it back to the boat. This fish bit ravenously, and the young millionaire had his hands full to haul them in. Most of them would weigh from fifteen to thirty pounds, though they are sometimes seventy-five. Louis pulled in several "margate," a name not found in the books, but Lopez said it was the nicest fish he had caught.

The sea was rather "lumpy," and catching such large fish as the grouper was hard work, and by noon he was so tired that he had had enough of the sport. He ate the luncheon he had brought from the ship with a decided relish. He was ready to refresh and restore himself with his bath, and he intimated his desire to the skipper. He and the two men had taken all the fish they could stow in the boat, and Lopez had no occasion to remain any longer.

"There comes your steamer, Mr. Belgrave," said the fisherman, pointing to the entrance to the harbor.

"The captain said he should make a little excursion to-day," replied Louis as he glanced at the steamer.

She was coming out from behind Ireland Island, where the dockyard is located, and the party had already visited it. She was all of six miles distant, and he could not make her out very distinctly; but he wondered if the captain had taken into his bunkers a supply of soft coal while at Hamilton, for the smoke from her funnel was very black. She was not headed in the direction of the fishing-craft, but stood off to the north-west.

Lopez set his sail, and headed his boat a little south of east. The breeze had freshened since morning, and in about an hour he touched at an island west of Somerset, and not far from it. Louis looked into the water, which was as clear as crystal, and not very deep, to see if there were any sharks in sight, for he had a mortal aversion to being chewed up by one of them.

"The sharks will not trouble you here, Mr. Belgrave," said the boatman after Louis had spoken of them again.

"But I saw a shark larger than I should care to meet in the water," suggested Louis. "What is to prevent them from coming here? There is no fence to keep them at a respectable distance."

"I will look out for that," replied Lopez. "While you are in the water I will keep my eye to seaward of you, and will tell you if I see a big back fin coming this way."

Louis went on shore, where the two men had gone before him, one of them carrying a piece of canvas to protect his clothing on the rocks, for the spray dashed upon the island, and the surface was quite wet. The bather divested himself of his clothing, and hastened to plunge into the clear water. The Portuguese on shore carefully covered his garments with the canvas ; and the swimmer thought they were taking excellent care of his suit, which was an old one he wore when working in the garden, which he had brought with him for occasions like the present.

The two assistants of the skipper got into the boat, which immediately shoved off from the shore, the two hands taking to the oars. As he swam away from the shore, Louis wondered if this movement was entirely regular. The boat passed quite near him, and he hailed the fisherman.

"Where are you going now, Lopez ? " he inquired.

"I am going out here a little distance to look out for the sharks," replied he. "If I see a back fin, I will call to you, and you must swim for the shore. You can keep out of his way easy enough."

The swimmer concluded that he did not care to try a race with a shark, and he would not go any farther from the island. He swam, dived down, swam under water, and turned somersets, as he had learned to do in the swimming bath at the natatory. He enjoyed himself so thoroughly that he gave no attention to the boat, and even forgot that sharks existed in these waters. When he had had enough of it, he swam to the shore, leaving the boat behind him.

He had no towels, and he was compelled to shake

himself like a spaniel, and then dry himself in the sun. As soon as he had seated himself on a rock for this purpose, he looked for the boat. He discovered to his astonishment that Lopez had set his sail, and was standing to the north-west. He shouted the name of the skipper several times; but he could obtain no reply, and the boat continued on its course.

"These fellows are playing some trick upon me; but I am in fifteen shillings on the game," said he out loud, though there was no one to hear him.

A look beyond the fisherman's boat revealed to him the approach from the north-west of the steamer he had taken for the Guardian-Mother, or, rather, Lopez said it was she. She was not two miles distant now, and a second look assured him beyond a doubt that the vessel was not the one he ownĕd, but the new Maud. He did not wait for the sun to do its full work upon him, but dressed himself very hastily.

The fisherman's craft was still within hailing distance of the island; but he had hailed in vain when it was nearer, and he decided to do so again with his revolver, though it was too far off for an effective shot. But the weapon might intimidate the trio in the boat. When he felt for the pistol he found it was no longer in his pocket. Perhaps it had dropped out when he undressed himself, and he made a diligent search near the canvas. It was not to be found, and he could come to only one conclusion — that one of the Portuguese had taken it from his trousers when he covered the clothing with the sail-cloth.

By this time it was patent to Louis that he was the victim of a trick such as that which had been worked against him in New York. It was part of a plan to entrap and capture him, engineered by John Scoble. The Maud approaching him at full speed was abundant confirmation of the suspicion that he was the victim of another treacherous scheme. The situation was worse than before, for he had been deprived of his revolver, and he had no means of defence, — nothing with which he could intimidate and keep at bay any force sent to capture him.

When the Maud came up with the fisherman's boat, Louis saw her stop and take on board the two Portuguese who had been the companions of Lopez during the day, and he had no doubt they were a couple of seamen from Scoble's steamer, who had been detailed for the duty they had accomplished, though they had not been called upon to do anything. His plan to bathe before he returned had been taken advantage of by the wily skipper, and he had permitted the victim to set his own trap, and then fall into it without any assistance.

The Maud was approaching the island with the evident intention of taking him on board; and Louis was not at all willing to fall in with the programme of his great enemy, though he might be compelled to yield to a superior force. He looked about him to find some means of resistance. He walked around the island, and found it was separated from the connected portions of land which form the chain of islands by a channel not more than half a mile wide, as its width seemed to him.

He was confident that he could swim this distance even with his clothes on, though he could throw away most of his garments, and have enough to cover him partially while he walked back to Hamilton. This seemed to be the only practical way to escape, though it would require a walk of about a dozen miles. Anything was preferable to falling into the hands of the enemy. Across the island he could see that the Maud was not more than half a mile distant, and he felt that he had no time to lose, and the chances were that the foe would be upon him before he could succeed in reaching the main island.

He threw off his coat after taking from it his wallet, which contained but little money, and removed his shoes. As he did so he examined the channel he was to traverse in order to find the narrowest place, and to find a landmark which should be his guide in directing his course in swimming. As he looked out on the water he saw what he took to be the back fin of a shark projecting from the surface. He had seen them before, and he knew what it was. He might be mistaken, but he had no means of settling the question.

He could see no reason why the big sharks should not make an occasional excursion to this lonely part of the islands, though Lopez protested that they did not; but it would not have greatly disturbed the Portuguese skipper, and certainly not his employer, if he had perished in the voracious maw of a man-eater. Louis realized that he might be destroyed; but he had a very decided choice in the present instance in the means of his destruction, and the very least to his liking was being crunched by the teeth of a shark.

The projecting fin moved along in the water, and Louis waited a little while to ascertain what course the piratical fish would take. He seemed to be on a foraging expedition. Suddenly the shark dived and disappeared; but in a minute or two it came up, headed in the opposite direction. He had no longer a hope that the fish would leave the channel, and permit him to swim across it. He seated himself on a rock, and gave himself up to the further consideration of his disagreeable situation.

He could see no boat except that of the fisherman, and there appeared to be no hope of assistance in any quarter. The appearance of the Maud just as the boat had suspended the sport of fishing indicated that the plot had been definitely arranged beforehand. The two men from the steam-yacht were to make a prisoner of him, and convey him to this island, which Lopez had chosen as his bathing-place, and the Maud was now coming to take him off.

Doubtless Lopez felt that he was to raise his hand against his passenger, and perhaps for this reason he had got up some feeling against him. His servility when Louis left the boat and proposed to walk back to Hamilton was fully explained. Of course the fisherman was to be paid a considerable sum for his treachery to his passenger, and he was not willing to lose it. The fifteen shillings Louis was to pay him was only a bagatelle compared with the amount to be received for his treason.

The Maud stopped her screw while she was still in the deep water about an eighth of a mile from the island. A boat towing astern of her was brought to the gangway and at least half a dozen men embarked in it, and dropped four oars into the water. They gave way with a will, as though they were in a hurry to accomplish the villanous task assigned to them. Louis was not at all surprised to see that the boat was headed directly for the island, which had become his prison. There was a man who appeared to be an officer in the stern sheets. As the boat came nearer to the island Louis was satisfied that this officer was Scoble himself, in the uniform of a yachtsman.

The prisoner was not yet quite prepared to give up all hope of relief from some quarter. He remained on the shore of the channel over which he had not dared to swim, and he could see across what little land intervened between him and Great Sound, from which is the entrance to Hamilton harbor. He noticed a volume of smoke rising in that direction, not so black as that cast out from the smoke stack of the Maud ; and a moment later he made out a steamer coming through the Narrows.

She was over four miles distance from him, and more than double that by the circuitous ship-channel she would be compelled to follow before she could do anything to relieve him.   He could not identify her at such a distance, but he concluded that she was the Guardian-Mother, though the only evidence he had was the color of the smoke.   Captain Ringgold had announced his intention to make an excursion in her that day, and this confirmed him in his belief.

Would the commander discover, or even suspect, that his owner had again become the victim of a treacherous scheme?   The boat from the Maud touched the shore of the island, and Scoble and his five men landed.

CHAPTER XXII

THE BATTLE ON THE ISLAND

THE party landing from the Maud's boat could not help seeing the prisoner on the island as soon as they landed. They drew the boat up and made the painter fast to a bush. Scoble led the way, and among his followers Louis recognized one of the men who had served with Lopez in his boat. From the uniform he wore it was evident that the owner of the Maud did not employ a sailing-master, but intended to command the steamer himself.

As he advanced upon his prey Louis saw that he had made a great improvement in his personal appearance since he came into possession of his brother's fortune. He had at different times made changes in the style of his beard, and now he wore "Dundreary" whiskers, and seemed to have taken a great deal of care of them.

"I am glad to see you, Mr. Belgrave," said Scoble when he came within speaking distance of his intended victim.

"I can't say that I am particularly glad to see you, Corporal Scoble," replied Louis, noting the emphasis he put upon the title he applied to him in a derisive tone.

"Let me remind you in the first place that I am commander of the steam-yacht Maud; and if you call me 'corporal' again, I shall take it as an insult," replied Scoble, while a flush of anger covered his face.

"But I shall take the liberty of calling you so as many times as you address me derisively as 'mister.'"

"But that is the title by which you are addressed by the captain of your steamer."

"He does not use the word to ridicule me as you do."

"I desire to be on friendly terms with you, Louis, as I have told you before; and learning that you had been abandoned on this island, I have come to take you back to Hamilton," continued the commander of the Maud in quite a gentlemanly tone for him.

"Is that what you came for, Captain Scoble?" asked the prisoner, looking him earnestly in the face.

"That is precisely what I came for; and if you will take a seat in the boat I will put you on board of the Maud at once, and get under way for Hamilton immediately," replied the captain, glancing across the land to Great Sound, where he could not help seeing the Guardian-Mother steaming just south of Spanish Point.

Might it not be possible that Scoble was carrying out a scheme to propitiate his mother by returning her son to her? It was possible; but it was hardly probable. So far as he had seen the captain at all, his whole purpose seemed to be to obtain an interview with Mrs. Belgrave. Captain Ringgold might fail to discover that he had been made the victim of a treacherous scheme, for Lopez would be very likely to keep out of the way of the steamer, though he had just seen his boat go through an opening south of Ireland Island into Great Sound.

It was impossible for Louis to have the least confidence in Scoble, or to place the slightest reliance on anything he had said. After a moment or two of consideration he decided that he would not voluntarily do anything which the enemy suggested. It looked a little like hauling down his flag and surrendering at discretion to go on board of the Maud.

"The boat is all ready for you, Louis," continued Scoble, rather uneasily, as he glanced again at the steamer in the Sound.

"If it is all the same to you, Captain Scoble, I will remain where I am," he replied as gently as possible, for he did not care to rouse the anger of the implacable enemy unnecessarily, though he was braced up to fight his battle if the occasion required.

"It is not all the same to me," replied the captain of the Maud very briskly. "I learned from Lopez that he had played you a trick, and I came over here to take you from the island. I think the fisherman means to make some money out of you, for all the people here know that you are a young millionaire."

"He will make more money out of you than he will out of me," added the prisoner quietly.

"What do you mean by that, Louis?" demanded Scoble.

"I am not so blind and stupid that I can fail to see that all this is one of your schemes to get me into trouble. You saw me talking to Lopez, and you bought him over at a bigger price than I paid him. Here is one of your men, sent to help the fisherman carry out the plan," replied Louis, as he pointed to the fellow who had been with him in the boat all the forenoon.

"I will deny all that at another time. I came to this island to save you from spending the night here, and I am going to put you on board of the Maud, whether you are willing to go or not," said Scoble, as he advanced upon him, closely followed by all his men.

The enemy had evidently prepared for just the occasion which had now developed itself in the refusal of the prisoner to go on board of the steamer. He had been robbed of his revolver in anticipation of this event. He had looked about the island when he realized the meaning of the situation, and found a piece of drift wood, which he had placed on a rock within his reach.

"Do you mean to put me on board of your steamer whether I will or not?" demanded Louis, grasping the stick, and placing himself in the attitude of defence. "How long do you think it will take you to conciliate my mother in this manner?"

"I have no time to argue the point, and I am no

lawyer, as you are, Mr. Belgrave. Two of you, rush upon him ! " said Scoble in a loud tone.

The two men, who had evidently been selected beforehand for this part of the enterprise, sprang forward and attempted to grasp him by the collar of his coat, which he had put on again when he abandoned the idea of swimming across the channel. But the prisoner on the island did not wait for them to do so; he retreated a pace, and then his stick fell in a blow which carried one of the two down upon the rocks. The other would have retreated if Scoble had not driven him on. He was a little shy after the fall of his companion; but he came near enough to receive a blow on the head, though it had not been well directed, and he was not injured.

Scoble directed two more of his men to support the attack, and he spoke in a low tone to the fellow who had been in the fishing-boat. The leading assailant dodged the club, but one of the others received a blow on the shoulder, for Louis had no time to use his weapon with anything like deliberation, and he rained his blows rather at random, so that most of them were avoided. The fellow to whom the captain had spoken succeeded in getting to the rear of the prisoner, who was too busy to notice his movements, and before he was aware of the peril in that direction, his arms were pinioned behind him in the embrace of the coward detailed for this purpose.

The club dropped on the rocks, and the rest of the men, no longer fearing the weapon, threw themselves upon the struggling prisoner, and he was powerless to make any further resistance. Cords were at hand, for everything seemed to be prepared beforehand for such an event as had just transpired, and his arms were bound behind him.

"That will do, my men," said Scoble, plainly pleased at the victory of his force. "Now, Manuel and Leon, walk him to the boat as lively as you can!"

Louis was not disposed to be "walked," lively or otherwise; he refused to take a step, and dropped on the rocks. He was not disposed to make any vain and foolish resistance, for he wished to gain all the time he could, hoping that the Guardian-Mother would get out in season to redeem him from the hands of the enemy. The last he had seen of her, she was approaching the anchorage off Long Point.

"Don't fool with him!" shouted Scoble, "Pick him up, and carry him to the boat!"

Louis had delayed the movement as much as he could, and when they picked him up, he submitted quietly to his fate, whatever it might be. He was placed at the side of the captain in the stern sheets, while all the men took their original places in the boat. The bowman shoved off, and the rowers were urged to "bend their oars," for Scoble was clearly in a desperate hurry.

As soon as he was seated Louis had an opportunity to make another observation of the position of the Guardian-Mother. He had studied the chart of the islands with Captain Ringgold, who had pointed out

to him the direction of the various ship channels.
A large vessel coming out of the harbor first made
the anchorage off Long Point on the West and Spanish Point on the East. From this locality the channel turned at right angles to the north-east.

The steamer had reached this point, and here
stopped her screw. She hastily dropped the first
cutter into the water, which the prisoner knew from
the fact that the davits of this boat were on the starboard side of the ship. Then Louis discovered Lopez's
boat coming into view from the inlet through which
it had passed. The treacherous rascal instantly came
about, and stood towards the opening between the
islands which he had just come through. But the
stout oarsmen in the cutter soon overhauled him.

The Maud's boat was now in position to see clearly
all that took place on board of the fishing-boat the
other side of Boaz Island. Louis rose from his place
in his interest to see what transpired to better advantage. Mr. Boulong usually went in the first cutter
when she left the ship on any service, and the prisoner had no doubt he was the officer he saw leap into
Lopez's craft. It looked as though a stormy interview
followed this movement.

Then a couple of seamen leaped into the fisherman's
boat, and dragged the skipper into the cutter, after
one of them had thrown the anchor overboard.

"Rather high-handed that!" exclaimed Scoble, who
had observed the scene with quite as much interest
as his prisoner, though he had not ceased to hurry

the rowers in his own boat. "If Captain Ringgold ordered his officers and men to commit that outrage on Lopez, he will have to answer for it in the courts of Bermuda."

"And who will answer in the courts of Bermuda for the outrage committed upon me?" asked Louis in his quiet way.

"Oh, well, my dear boy, I think that will be easy enough to manage, for you are my refractory step-son, and I simply picked you up when I found you on that island. But I don't think the matter will ever come before a Bermuda court, for I am going to sea at once, and I don't believe they will send a man-of-war out after me on account of such an insignificant vagabond as Lopez," replied Scoble with all his usual assurance.

The boat came alongside the gangway of the Maud, and Louis was hurried up the steps to the deck. The boat was hastily hoisted up to the davits, the gangway hauled up, and the screw began to turn. There was a Bermuda pilot at the wheel, and the Maud was headed for the main ship channel, and she came into it at a point about three miles to the north-east of where the Guardian-Mother lay.

The crew were hoisting in the first cutter. Louis had lost sight of her after the Maud got under way, for the buildings at the dockyard on Ireland Island concealed her from his view. He concluded that Captain Ringgold had spent all this time in an examination of Lopez in order to ascertain what had become of his late passenger. It was evident enough that he and his officers had recognized the fisherman's boat, and discovered that their owner was not in it.

But the commander had evidently reached a conclusion, for the Guardian-Mother started her screw, and she was headed to the north-east, the course of the channel, while vast clouds of smoke poured out of her smoke stack.

CHAPTER XXIII

THE PROSPECT OF A LIVELY RACE

As nearly as Louis Belgrave could comprehend the situation, the Maud had about three miles the advantage of the Guardian-Mother, and both steamers were going at their best speed. Both vessels had pilots on board, for it was not practicable to make even an excursion inside of the surrounding reef, which was about ten miles distant from the main island, without one.

Captain Scoble had come out of Hamilton harbor with his eyes open, for he had no doubt planned his enterprise beforehand, so that he knew just what was going to happen. Louis concluded that he had made his arrangements to go to sea, and must have prepared his vessel for the purpose. On the other hand, though Captain Ringgold could have no suspicion that his owner would be captured, he had made everything ready to proceed to the next port in the programme of his voyage.

Both of the steamers were therefore in condition to go to sea, and a lively race between them was impending; the stakes seemed to be the safety, and perhaps the life and liberty, of Louis. The speed of the two steamers was a vital question with the prisoner on board of the Maud. He knew that the rate of the Guardian-Mother was sixteen knots an hour, and probably one or two knots more could be got out of her if the engine was driven to its utmost capacity.

On the other side of the question, Scoble had claimed a speed of twenty knots an hour for the new Maud; but he had also declared that the fortune he inherited from his brother amounted to a million, and according to the general report this was double the amount. It was not unlikely that he had increased the speed .of his steamer in the same ratio, and Louis felt sure that he had exaggerated the truth.

The Guardian-Mother was two hundred tons larger than the Maud; and it was possible that her owner had added something to the size as well as to the speed of his vessel, for she did not appear to the prisoner on the deck of the Maud to be more than half as large as the other, though he was not an expert. He was hopeful, therefore, that his own steamer would overhaul that of his enemy.

But even if she overtook her any time during the voyage to Nassau, what could come of such a meeting on the ocean? Neither ship was a man-of-war, and neither was capable of attacking the other. If Captain Ringgold succeeded in coming up with the Maud, Louis could not see that he could do anything to liberate him. If his steamer came near enough he might jump overboard, and be picked up by her people; but this would be a hazardous experiment.

Captain Scoble had been busy so far observing the movements of the Maud, and he had given no attention to his prisoner. Louis had been walked up the gangway with his arms still bound behind him, and left in the waist. The cord had been passed around his arms near the elbows, and drawn very tight, so that it gave him a great deal of pain. In the course of an hour the Maud passed through the narrow and circuitous channel among the reefs at the north of the islands, and in doing so the pilot had slowed down, so that the pursuer would gain something upon her by this necessity, though she would lose the advantage in passing through herself.

The Maud threaded her way through all these perils in safety, and discharged her pilot about a mile distant from the nearest land. The Guardian-Mother could be seen at this time, but she seemed to be at the same relative distance astern as at first, as Louis supposed she would be. She came out of the entrance of the channel, and both vessels were on the open ocean where nothing was likely to interfere with the exciting race in prospect.

The pursuer was evidently making all the steam her boilers would permit, as indicated by the color and density of the smoke that was pouring out of her smoke stack. The Maud was doing the same thing, and the inky cloud that trailed astern of her was more dense than that of the other vessel. Louis was not sufficiently versed in the working of steamships, though he had already acquired a fund of ideas on the subject, to make any calculations on the result of the race. He walked about, suffering from the pain in his arms, but observing everything that transpired very carefully. He had hardly seen Scoble since he had been put on board; but as soon as the course of the Maud had been laid to the south-west, the latter appeared in the waist, and approached his prisoner.

"Well, Louis, I hope you are comfortable," said he with a smile on his sinister face.

"No, sir; I am not comfortable at all," replied the young man in painful bonds.

"In spite of the manner in which you have treated me, in spite of the cruel wrongs you have done me, I am still disposed to be your friend, though I must admit that I am so for your mother's sake rather than your own," said Scoble, in a mild tone for him, and one that was intended to be impressive. "If you are uncomfortable, I desire to make you comfortable."

"Then take the rope off my arms, for it is cutting me to the bone," replied the prisoner.

Not a little to his astonishment, the captain proceeded to untie the cord, and in a moment had released him from his confinement, without speaking a word.

"Thank you, Captain Scoble; I am very much obliged to you for this relief from pain," said Louis promptly, as his kidnapper cast the rope into the scupper.

"I am sorry you have suffered any pain or discomfort, and I should have removed the cord before if I had thought it gave you any serious annoyance. I shall do my best to make you comfortable and happy on board of the Maud," added the captain.

"I am not likely to be very happy in my present situation," replied Louis with a rather sickly smile. "The circumstances are not exactly favorable to the enjoyment of life for me at present, though I hope they will change for the better."

"They will not change till I change them, Louis," answered Scoble with all his old assurance, though he was evidently in a pliable condition, believing that he had successfully carried out his vicious scheme, in which he was certainly right, and, as the gamblers would say, he held all the winning-cards in his own hand.

"Perhaps not," added Louis dubiously, as he glanced at the Guardian-Mother, still at least three miles astern.

"You look at the steamer of which you are the sole owner; and she is assuredly a magnificent vessel, though I have not been on board of her; but she can be of no service to you in the present emergency," said the captain.

"I don't know that she can be, though she appears to be in hot pursuit of the Maud," answered the prisoner with a sigh.

"This steamer is somewhat smaller than the Guardian-Mother, as you call her, though that is a very odd name for her; but the Maud is good for twenty knots an hour, day in and day out, as was assured by her former owner, though I have never had the opportunity to get that speed out of her," Scoble explained. "Perhaps you will not object to telling me the steaming capacity of your steamer, Louis."

"I do not think she has ever been driven to her utmost speed; but she can make sixteen knots when she is put to her best ordinary running," replied the prisoner, who had no motive for concealment.

"Then we can do her four knots better," added the captain with a triumphant expression on his vicious face. "It must be plain enough to you, my boy, that your steamer can never overhaul the Maud if she should chase her all over the world."

"I should say she could not if your estimate of the speed of your vessel is correct, of which, of course, I know nothing," said Louis; but he hoped and even believed that Captain Scoble had exaggerated the sailing ability of the Maud.

"Then I trust you will accept the situation as you find it without attempting to do any foolish and unreasonable thing, as you have been in the habit of doing."

"I am not disposed to jump out of the frying-pan into the fire," replied the victim of the plot, somewhat cast down by the circumstances that surrounded him.

"You have always misjudged me, Louis."

"And you have often abused me."

"As I have considered the matter since my arrival

in Bermuda, I am forced to admit that I have sometimes been rather rough on you, my boy," continued
Scoble, bringing out a couple of stools from a mess-
room, and seating himself and Louis. "I was
brought up in England, and I have never been able
to get used to the pert and priggish ways of American
boys. I have had the opinion that you were much
more given to those ways than the generality of boys."

"I was not aware that I ever was pert, and I don't
know what you mean by 'priggish,'" replied Louis,
looking curiously into the face of the captain, who
had certainly improved his manners, whether or not
he had his morals, which made the prisoner the more
willing to converse with his captor.

"I mean by pert what you Yankees call 'smart,'
forward; and a priggish fellow is one that is stuck
up," Scoble explained. "You think ever so much
more of yourself than any English boy I ever saw."

"I have been told that American boys are more
forward than those on the other side of the ocean."

"Because they are encouraged to be so by their
parents and friends, and I was afraid that your
mother, as you were an only son, had spoiled you
by indulgence. In England we keep a boy in subjec-
tion; and if he is getting ahead too fast, we snub
him and subdue him; and that is what I tried to do
with you. If your mother had not taken your part, I
should have made a decent fellow of you before this
time," added the captain in a tone of raillery, soft-
ened by a pleasant laugh.

"Not many boys in our country are used to this sort of thing," added Louis. "I tried to do my duty all round, and I was obedient to my mother and respectful to you when you became my step-father. I did my best to conciliate you."

"I dare say you did; but you went about it in the wrong way. You talked up to me as though you were my equal, and boys had always treated me with deference at home. You talked as smartly as though you were as old as I was, and it was impossible for me to endure that sort of thing."

Louis made no reply, for he saw that it was useless to argue a question like this one; and whatever boys may have been in England, he knew that his late step-father was exceedingly self-sufficient and tyrannical by nature. The explanation he gave fitted his own case only.

"It is best for us to have an understanding of the situation, Louis," continued the captain, as his prisoner was silent. "You have charged me with wicked intentions toward you; you have even led your mother to believe that I desired to deprive you of your liberty, and even take your life."

"My present situation seems to show that I was not far out of the way."

"I utterly deny it!" protested Scoble.

"Why then did you send Ovid Kimpton to New York by the next mail-steamer that left the Bermudas after the arrival of the Guardian-Mother, two months ago," demanded Louis, very quietly, "to entrap and make me a prisoner?"

"Kimpton?" repeated the captain, as though he knew nothing of him; and probably he did not know what he had done.

"He is in the State prison for five years for the outrage upon me."

This was news to Scoble, and he seemed to be greatly moved by it.

CHAPTER XXIV

A WILFUL COLLISION

AT this season of the year American papers were not abundant in the Bermudas, and Louis was satisfied that Scoble knew nothing of the adventure of Ovid Kimpton in New York, and he was ready to enlighten him. He related the details of the affair in full to him. The captain was moved by the narrative, and then he became as glum as an owl at midday.

"That matter does not concern me, Louis, and you might have spared your breath," said he after a long pause; but it was apparent that his assumed amiability had suffered a severe shock, for his manner had essentially changed.

"I have a collection of letters taken from Kimpton which were written by you, Captain Scoble; but I suppose they are of no consequence," added Louis in a very indifferent tone.

"I neither know nor care anything about them. I think we had better proceed to business," continued the captain, taking what appeared to be a letter from his pocket. "As I have said before to you, there is no occasion for us to quarrel. According to your own statement and that of Captain Ringgold, you are in full possession of what was the missing million, which you insisted was the cause of what you were pleased to call my hatred of you, and to furnish my motive for desiring to get rid of you, as you romantically put it. Of course that motive no longer exists."

"Of course I know nothing of the secrets that are locked up in your bosom, Captain Scoble," replied Louis in a careless manner.

"Locked up in my bosom is very telling! You mean, I suppose, that you cannot read my motives," added the captain with a sneer.

"That is just what I mean. Thank you for your clever interpretation of my meaning."

"You are in the full enjoyment of your grandfather's million now."

"About a million and a half, Captain."

"Of course that fortune can no longer influence me, if it ever did, as you insist."

"You discovered the hiding-place of the missing million."

"Not till after I became one of the occupants of your mother's house. I desired to be of service to her; for though the fortune nominally belonged to you, I knew she would have the full benefit of it."

"As she has at the present time."

"Whatever you may have foolishly fancied in regard to my intentions towards you, I can have no motive now to harm you," continued Scoble, his former suavity restored.

"Why have you been so desirous to meet my

mother since you found her in the Bermudas, then ? " demanded Louis. " Why were you so anxious to have our party make an excursion in this steamer ? "

" I do not deny that I desire to meet your mother ; and if anything can excuse me for the means I have used to secure your presence, Louis, on board of the Maud, it was my intense, earnest, and sincere desire to have an interview with your mother. You know that I am wholly devoted to her ; and I look upon her as my wife by all the laws of marriage, human and divine, whatever may be lacking in the forms. I am a millionaire, and you ought to be able to understand that I am actuated only by pure, sincere motives."

Louis did not care to make any reply to this eloquent speech, and he gazed in silence at the planks in the deck.

" Why don't you speak, Louis ? " asked Scoble.

"I have nothing particular to say."

" If you object to what I have stated, speak out."

" I don't object to it if it pleases you to indulge in such talk ; but I can assure you that it will amount to nothing, whatever may become of me," replied Louis, thus pushed for a reply.

" My motives are good."

" I have no means of knowing as to them."

" Financially I have nothing to gain by a reconciliation with your mother," Scoble insisted.

" I am not so sure of that," answered the young millionaire, who began to feel that the wrath of the captain was rather to be preferred to his cajoling.

"Not sure of it! Can you point out any motive?" demanded the pleader, beginning to be excited.

"I do not care to discuss this matter, Captain Scoble; it is not my affair, and I must refer you to Squire Scarburn for the legal bearings of the matter," said Louis very gently.

"It has no legal bearings, and I will have nothing to do with that old lobster! You are in my power, you young reprobate!" stormed the captain, rising from his stool.

"I am well aware of it; but I do not intend to sell my soul in order to get out of this scrape. You seem to be getting excited, Captain Scoble, and I think we had not better talk any more on excitable topics."

"It is enough to make an angel mad to have his highest and truest motives questioned and condemned. You are quite as much of a lawyer as that old jelly-tub, and I ask you again if you can point out any motive of mine of a mean and sordid character for desiring a reconciliation with your mother."

"You have probably read the will of my father," added Louis.

"What has the will to do with it?"

"My mother is my sole heir; and if I should disappear or die by some unforeseen accident, she would succeed to the million and a half," replied the prisoner.

Captain Scoble took in this suggestion with a vengeance, and perhaps, as the Belgrave family and their friends fully believed, it was just precisely the motive

that actuated the villain in his efforts to effect an
arrangement with the lady who had repudiated him.
He dashed across the deck with a fury which looked
dangerous to the captive, and walked back and forth
in a sort of desperation. He could hardly help realizing that he was playing a useless as well as a
dangerous game. He marched back and forth on
the deck till his wrath appeared to have abated in a
degree.

"I am glad to get the truth out of you, Louis, at
last, stupid and unreasonable as your conclusion is in
respect to my motives."

"I ought to have said before, Captain Scoble, that
I am absolutely sure an interview with my mother
would be utterly useless, and that she would refuse
to the last day of her life to be reconciled to you,"
said Louis, the captain still retaining the place he had
taken in front of him.

"Why should she be so implacable ? "

"Because she despises you."

"Why should she despise me ? "

"You seem to forget the record you have made in
and about New York."

"I have before explained to you that I had no intention of keeping the money used at the race-
grounds."

"Which was the particular reason why you carried
it on board of a steamer bound to England. Could
my mother ever forget that you are a robber, an embezzler, and even a highwayman ? "

Captain Scoble tried to get up a hearty laugh as an answer, but it was not a brilliant success. Then he marched across the deck half a dozen times more, and his passion became controllable.

"I do not believe that your mother is such a pronounced heathen as you are, Louis, and I am determined to have an interview with her, and one with no witnesses present either; and she will be glad to grant it to me when I have made my next move on the board," said the captain, as he again drew the letter Louis had seen before from his pocket.

"What is your next move, Captain Scoble?" asked Louis very innocently.

"Excuse me, if you please. Here is a letter I have written to your mother, asking her for the interview to which I have alluded. You may read it yourself, and then, if you are reasonable, I may make you the bearer of it to her."

The captain handed him the letter; but several of the ship's company, including an officer, were moving aft, one of them bearing a log-line, and Louis had nothing to say. Captain Scoble followed them, for they were about to heave the log in the old-fashioned way, and he had a tremendous interest in the speed of the steamer at that particular time. Louis was even more interested than the commander, and he went after them. By the exercise of some skill, he contrived to keep out of sight of the captain, who might object to his knowing the result obtained from the log, and secured a position behind the mainmast.

"Fourteen knots," said the officer, in whom Louis recognized Wilson Frinks, who had been the mate of the original Maud.

"Fourteen!" exclaimed Captain Scoble, with a blood-curdling oath, which probably indicated his disappointment at the result from the log-line. "You have made a mistake, Frinks."

"I don't think so, Captain," replied the mate, or whatever he was, though he wore the uniform of a superior officer. "I will heave the chip again."

"You are a blunderer, Frinks!" raved the commander. "Do you mean to tell me the ship is making only fourteen knots?"

"I give you what the log-line measures," pleaded the mate, who was not as saucy as he had been on some former occasions.

"Go forward, and ask Mr. Scarbury to come aft."

Frinks obeyed the order, though with a very ill grace. The person sent for soon appeared, and Louis concluded that he was the first officer. He was directed to superintend the heaving of the log. He proceeded to discharge this duty in a very careful manner.

"Thirteen knots and a half," reported Mr. Scarbury, when the operation was completed.

"Thirteen and a half!" exclaimed Captain Scoble, with a string of heavy oaths, which Louis knew would alone have set his mother against him forever. "That is half a knot worse than Frinks made it. Is the log-line all right, Mr. Scarbury?"

"I overhauled it very carefully, and I think it was all right," replied the officer, not pleased with his superior's manner.

"Try it again, Mr. Scarbury," said the commander.

The result of the second trial gave fourteen knots; and Mr. Frinks was fully justified. The captain stormed, and then rushed forward, where he mounted the bridge, giving no further attention to Louis. The prisoner obtained a position where he could get a view of the Guardian-Mother. He was not trained to measuring distances with his eye at sea; but he felt convinced that the pursuer had gained something on the chase since he last saw his own steamer. His very heart had been thrilled with joy when he heard the first report of the log, and Mr. Scarbury had fully confirmed it.

At dinner-time Louis was called to the cabin to partake of the meal. The captain did not appear, and he dined alone. The steward showed him to the stateroom assigned to him; but instead of occupying it, he went on deck to watch the progress of the Guardian-Mother. He was sure now that she was gaining on the Maud, for she appeared to be not more than a mile distant. She seemed to have only just obtained her best speed, and in half an hour she was abreast of the chase.

"Come to, and stop your screw!" shouted Captain Ringgold in stentorian tones.

The answer that went back from Captain Scoble

was mingled with a string of oaths, and was too bad
to be repeated ; and Mrs. Belgrave heard it.

A minute later the bow of the Guardian-Mother
crashed into the Maud abreast of her foremast.
Captain Ringgold was in earnest.

CHAPTER XXV

NOT TWENTY KNOTS AN HOUR

THE Guardian-Mother had run perhaps half a mile in the position she had taken abreast of the Maud; and it was during this time that Captain Ringgold had hailed, and had received the scornful and contemptuous answer of Captain Scoble. Mr. Scarbury, the first officer, was at the port end of the bridge, and the captain had come over to that side of the steamer to reply to the hail.

"I wash my hands of all this business, Captain Scoble," said the chief mate, shaking his head very dubiously.

"Do you mean to be a traitor to your employer?" demanded Scoble furiously.

"Better to my employer than to God and my own conscience," replied Mr. Scarbury with dignity.

Louis Belgrave had gone forward when the Guardian-Mother ranged alongside the Maud the better to observe what passed, for it looked like a very critical moment to him. He heard his captain's hail and the beastly reply of the commander of the Maud, who had plainly been worked up to the highest pitch of wrath by his disappointment at the failure of his vessel to attain the speed he expected of her.

The prisoner saw his mother and Mrs. Blossom standing with Dr. Hawkes and Squire Scarburn on the deck-house abaft the bridge, where a small promenade had been railed in for the use of the officers. Captain Ringgold was on the starboard end of the bridge with his hand on the bell-pull of the gong, where he could overlook the deck and bridge of the Maud. The expression on his face was that of terrible earnestness.

The Guardian-Mother was still going at her highest speed, and was forging ahead of the struggling Maud, which was not half a ship's length from her; but it was not the intention of the commander of the larger vessel to run away from the other. When she was half a length ahead of the Maud, Captain Ringgold rang his bell, and the screw of the steamer stopped.

"Hard a port the helm!" he shouted to Bangs who was at the wheel.

"Hard a port, sir!" repeated the wheelman, who evidently shared the earnestness of the commander.

The Guardian-Mother promptly responded to her helm, and turned her head in such a manner as to strike the Maud abreast of the foremast, and just forward of her bridge.

The headway of the larger steamer had been checked, but she still had momentum enough to cut through the iron sides of the smaller with her sharp bow; but at the instant before she struck the commander gave two strokes on the gong, and her screw was working backwards at the instant of the collision, or she would

"THE BOW WENT THROUGH THE SIDE OF THE 'MAUD' AS FAR AS THE DECK-HOUSE."   Page 219.

have cut her into two pieces. Captain Ringgold had timed his manœuvre in such a manner as to accomplish just the effect he had produced.

As it was, the bow went through the side of the Maud as far as the deck house. At this moment Mr. Scarbury, either because he believed his ship was going to the bottom, or because he desired no longer to sail with such a reprobate as Scoble, dexterously vaulted from the bridge to the top-gallant foercastle of the other steamer. Louis saw him make this movement, and, leaping on the rail, climbing the stanchions that supported the bridge, he made his escape in the same way, caught in the arms of the late chief officer of the Maud.

Captain Scoble on the bridge saw that he had lost both his principal officer and his prisoner, and his curses were loud and deep. The commander of the Guardian-Mother made a careful observation of the effects of the collision he had wilfully brought about, and sent Mr. Boulong and the boatswain to make an examination of the bow of his own ship to ascertain if it had received any serious injury.

The iron plates of which the sides of the Maud were composed were cut through and driven inboard; but on account of the structure of the bow which had done the mischief and the greater size of the Guardian-Mother, most of the rupture and the damage was above the water line, though the sea was pouring in at the lower part of the opening. Captain Ringgold rang his gong several times till he had brought his vessel into a position within talking distance of the injured steamer; and the sea was not rough, though the long billows surged in a gentle swell as usual in mild weather.

"Do you need any assistance?" demanded the commander of the aggressor.

"Assistance, you infernal pirate!" responded Captain Scoble. "You have cut a hole through the side of my ship, and she is going to the bottom!"

"If she goes down, my boats are all ready to pick up your ship's company," replied Captain Ringgold, apparently as unmoved as though he had not been the author of the calamity which had overtaken the Maud.

The screw of the damaged vessel had been stopped at the moment of the collision, and both steamers were at rest on the long rollers. Louis Belgrave had made his way to the promenade where the passengers were standing, and in two minutes after he boarded the vessel he was folded in his mother's arms. She was in a state of violent agitation, for she had not recovered from the shock of the collision. The commander had not spoken to any one on board in regard to what he intended to do, and no one knew what was coming till it came.

"Pass a line under the bottom of your ship, and draw a sail down over the hole in your side! She will not go down if you look out for her!" shouted Captain Ringgold from the bridge.

Up to this time Captain Scoble seemed to be in a

dazed condition, as much because he was crazed with wrath as on account of the shock of the collision. But the words of the commander of the Guardian-Mother seemed to produce a partial restoration of his senses. Frinks had come upon the bridge, and he appeared to have given him the order to carry out the suggestion of Captain Ringgold.

"If you need any assistance, I will send a force to help you!" shouted the captain of Louis's steamer. "You are not badly damaged, and you can easily save your ship!"

Captain Scoble made no reply to this kindly offer; but Captain Ringgold ordered Mr. Boulong to board the Maud in the first cutter with ten men, and do what was necessary to keep the vessel above water, for she would certainly go down if nothing was done, and he could see that Frinks went to work in a very bungling manner. With the old salts from the Guardian-Mother, Mr. Boulong soon checked the leak so that no danger was to be apprehended from it.

"I will stand by you till you get to the entrance of the Burmuda channel!" called Captain Ringgold for the last time.

Scoble responded with a volley of abuse and profanity, and threatened vengeance upon his triumphant adversary in the race and its sequel; but as his ship was safe, no further notice was taken of him. As a last word, he demanded that Scarbury, his mate, should be sent back to the Maud. This officer was informed that if he desired to return, he should be sent back in the first cutter, which was still at the gangway.

"No, sir; I do not wish to be sent back," replied Mr. Scarbury. "I have had enough of that brute of a captain. When I saw what he was about and that the young gentleman had been purposely left on the island, I remonstrated with the captain, and begged him not to take him on board as a prisoner, for it was kidnapping, and he would get us all into trouble; but he only cursed me as a traitor to him."

"You were vastly less wicked, and a good deal more sensible, than your captain," added Captain Ringgold. "How happened a man of your good character to be in Captain Scoble's employ?"

"I brought the Maud out to the Bermudas from Southampton with the expectation of getting the command of her; but the new owner chose to be captain himself, and I took the place of mate, for I was out of employment," replied Mr. Scarbury.

The passengers on the promenade had retired to the boudoir, the preparations on board of the Maud had been completed, and the latter started her screw, laying her course back to Bermuda. By this time it was dark, and the Guardian-Mother followed the crippled steamer to insure the safety of her ship's company in case of any further danger.

Dr. Hawkes had succeeded in restoring Mrs. Belgrave from her nervous agitation, and considering the peril of her son, she had behaved much better than usual on trying occasions. The commander joined the party in the boudoir, and Louis related all that occurred during the day, and the conversation he had had with Scoble. He was still as confident as ever of his ability to take care of himself.

"If they had not stolen my revolver, I should not have been made a prisoner on the island, or have been put on board of the Maud," he added.

"But that is a thing that might happen to you in any of these affrays," suggested his mother. "I wonder that Kimpton did not think to disarm you. But, thank Heaven, you are safe once more. I should like to know whether we are ever to be free from this life of storm and turmoil."

"I should say Scoble saw that I meant business this time, and I doubt if he troubles us any more," added the captain.

"What a terrible man he is!" exclaimed Mrs. Belgrave, with something like a shudder, as she thought of her former relations with him. "I cannot think what he expects to accomplish by getting you into his possession, Louis."

"I think his only object is to effect a reconciliation with you, mother," replied Louis, as he thought for the first time of the letter Scoble had given him to read, and which the catastrophe had prevented him from reclaiming.

But he promptly decided not to produce the letter in the presence of his mother, for he had had no opportunity to read it, and she was too much agitated still to consider such an exciting subject. The commander had brought Mr. Scarbury into the boudoir and introduced him to his passengers. He questioned him in regard to the Maud and her captain.

"Do you know for what purpose Captain Scoble purchased that steamer?" asked the commander, after he had drawn from him the particulars of the purchase.

"He never told me what he intended to do with her; only that he should use her as a yacht, and thought he might make a voyage around the world in her," replied the late first officer of the Maud. "He changed her name without authority to do so, for she was called the 'Viking' when I brought her out. But he only put the new name on a tin outside of the old one, and he can take it off if he ever goes back to England with her."

"Did you know her former owner?" asked the captain.

"I did, for I sailed a schooner for him last season; but he failed and then died just as he had completed the Viking."

"Did this Viking have a reputation as a fast steamer?" inquired Louis, recalling the heaving of the log on board of the Maud.

"Mr. Beachford, her owner, intended that she should make twenty knots an hour, and I think he died in the belief that she would do it. She was never fairly tried, and fourteen knots were the most I could ever get out of her," replied Mr. Scarbury.

"Captain Scoble believed she would make twenty

knots, for he told me so himself," added Louis.   "He depended upon her to do so in order to enable him to carry out his plan with respect to me."

"I have no doubt Mr. Beachford's brother, who had the selling of the Viking, understood from what he had heard her owner say that she was good for twenty knots, and said so to Captain Scoble, who believed it.   I knew she couldn't do anything of the kind, and I did not think I was in a position to say anything about it."

"His scheme failed because his steamer was not fast enough to make a success of it," added Louis; and the conversation closed.

About midnight the Maud anchored off Bermuda; the Guardian-Mother came about, and steamed off to the south-west.

CHAPTER XXVI

A WEEK IN NASSAU

No pilot would take the Maud through the intricate channels among the reefs to the harbor of Hamilton in the darkness, and she had been obliged to anchor. Captain Ringgold was in the pilot-house of the Guardian-Mother when the disabled steamer swung round as she came up to her cable. He went near enough to her to ascertain that she was still all right, and no signal for assistance was made. He waited for a boat when one was reported to have put off from the Maud.

The screw had been stopped and the steamer was at rest. The commander went to the gangway himself to ascertain the object of the boat's visit. It soon came alongside; but the gangway had been hoisted up, and was not available for any messenger from the other vessel.

"Guardian-Mother, ahoy!"

It was the voice of Captain Scoble in which the hail came, and the commander was satisfied that he did not come for assistance, for in that case he would have sent an officer.

"In the boat!" replied Captain Ringgold.

"I wish to go on board of your steamer," added the captain of the Maud.

"I decline to admit you on board."

"What kind of an idea is that?" demanded Scoble angrily. "You have stove my vessel!"

"It is my idea. I have nothing to say to you."

"I shall bring a suit against you for felony and for damages!"

"All right."

"I want you to appear and answer to the charge."

"Bring your suit in a United States court! Good-night;" and the commander walked forward, rang his gong, and the Guardian-Mother started on her voyage to the south-west.

The next morning, when the passengers came on deck, Louis found Captain Ringgold in his stateroom, studying a chart of the West Indies spread out before him. The commander was the hero of the event of the evening before, and Louis had to step into the shade; but the latter was as profuse in his praise as the rest of the company. Mr. Boulong went so far as to say that he did not believe there was another captain in the world who would have taken such decided and perilous action to right a wrong.

Louis was exceedingly grateful to his friend for taking such a bold step to release him from his imprisonment. There was no knowing where Scoble would have taken him, or what would have been the result of the adventure. When he went to his stateroom the night before, Louis had opened and read the letter which the captain of the Maud had confided to his care. It was addressed to Mrs. Belgrave, and the first part of it set forth that his feelings remained the same as when he had "led her to the holy altar."

Then he pleaded for a reconciliation, and enlarged upon the purity and sincerity of his motives. He was a millionaire himself, and nothing mercenary influenced him. He had captured her son; but he should be treated with the utmost kindness and respect. His only object in doing so was to obtain an interview with her. If she would give him her written consent to meet him, Louis should be returned to her immediately. Otherwise, the young gentleman might make a voyage around the world in the Maud instead of the Guardian-Mother.

It was just about what Louis supposed it would be. The last line was a threat to keep him a prisoner on board of the Maud until Mrs. Belgrave consented to see him. He handed it to the captain, and while he was reading the epistle, Uncle Moses came into the room.

"You have sent for me and I have come," said the trustee as he entered.

"Thank you, Squire Scarburn. Take a seat, and I will see you in a minute or two," replied the commander, who was deeply interested in the letter he was reading.

"Well, Sir Louis, anything stirring going on just now ?" asked Uncle Moses.

"Nothing at all, sir; it looks like a dry time," answered Louis.

"Read that, squire," said the captain as he turned the letter over to the lawyer, which he read through, his companions in the room remaining silent while he did so.

"What do you think of it?" asked Captain Ringgold, when he had finished the reading of it.

"I think I could have written the letter myself so far as it conveys any information in regard to the rascal's intentions," replied the squire, wiping the perspiration from his brow, for the weather in this latitude was beginning to be very warm for December.

"But we learn from it that he intended to keep Sir Louis a prisoner on board of the Maud until his mother consented to an interview with him," added the commander. "However, I understood that before, and so did you, squire."

"Perfectly."

"It appears from what Mr. Scarbury said, that Scoble honestly believed the Maud could steam twenty miles an hour, for her former owner was satisfied in that respect," continued Captain Ringgold. "You may call it an exceedingly lucky stroke, or a special interposition of Providence, in Sir Louis's favor that Scoble was deceived in regard to the speed of his steamer."

"But suppose he had not been deceived, and the Maud had been able to steam twenty knots an hour, what would or what might have happened?" asked Uncle Moses.

"He might have been able to make good the threat contained at the end of his letter, though I fancy we could have got the bulge on him in some manner. Beating us by four knots an hour, he could have found time to coal his ship and keep out of our way. I might have procured the intervention of our government to have him arrested, or obtained it by a requisition for his extradition on the part of the State of New York on the charge of robbery and embezzlement; but that would have been a tedious process, and the villain might have resorted to some desperate measure if he discovered what we were doing. I think we managed it in the safest and surest way."

"I think you did, Captain Ringgold, and I for one am greatly obliged to you for your summary action," added Uncle Moses.

The commander then related to him the incident of the boat from the Maud the night before. The legal gentleman laughed, and declared that he should like to have that case in court; for when a man went before a judicial authority he must go with clean hands, and Scoble was engaged in an illegal proceeding when his steamer was damaged.

They discussed the matter for a time, and Louis, tired of the subject, interested himself over the chart on the table.

"Do you understand it, Sir Louis?" asked the

captain, when they had finished the discussion, in which they cordially agreed.

"I see the Bahama Islands on the chart; but I don't know which way you are sailing," replied the owner.

"Look over your head," added the commander, pointing to a tell-tale adjusted in the skylight; and this is a compass set upside down so that the occupant of the room could see at a glance the course of the ship.

"I can hardly read that, for I have given no attention to navigation, I have had so much else to study."

"You must learn to box the compass, Sir Louis. Our course is south-west by west a quarter west, as Bangs would tell you if you went into the pilot-house," the captain explained. "We are running for the southern point of the island of Great Abaco, which is called Hole in the Wall, as you see on the chart. The distance from the Bermudas to that point is seven hundred and forty-eight miles, and we have made eighty-four of the distance since eight bells last night; we shall get there in two days and seven hours, if nothing interferes with our voyage."

"Thank you, Captain. I am going to study these things up now," added Louis, as he left the room to meet his mother whom he saw on deck.

The captain and Uncle Moses agreed that Scoble's letter should not be shown to Mrs. Belgrave, for it would only make her uncomfortable to know the intentions of their persecutor, even in the past and

when the danger was over. Everything went on
pleasantly on board, and all the occupants of the
cabin were happy. Louis studied six hours a day,
which Professor Giroud and the surgeon declared was
quite enough for him.

The captain gave him lessons in seamanship and
navigation, assisted by Mr. Sharp, who had become
quite interested in the young millionaire. Amuse-
ments of all practicable kinds were in order. Felix
had entirely recovered from his colic, and he insisted
that Louis would not have been captured if he had
been with him. On Thursday at two o'clock in the
afternoon, the Guardian-Mother was off Abaco light,
and at six she let go her anchor in the harbor of
Nassau.

During the voyage from Bermuda the party had
studied the books relating to the Bahamas and especially Nassau, and when they arrived at their destination they were well informed in regard to the pirates
who preyed upon the commerce of the Spaniards, the
capture of Nassau by the Americans during the Revo-
lution, and had obtained a general idea of the island
they were to visit. As they had remained on board of
the steamer at Hamilton, making excursions from her
among the islands, the commander thought they had
better board for a week at the Royal Victoria Hotel
for a change, especially as they were not likely to
have such an opportunity again for several weeks.

Before dark, therefore, the boats conveyed them all
to the shore, and they took carriages for the hotel.

The next day they took the first of a series of drives through the town and outside of it. They found the region a semi-tropical paradise, even more interesting than Bermuda, and more novel. The cocoanut palms were the especial admiration of all, to say nothing of the orange-trees, and an immense variety of plants and trees which were strangers to all of them.

It was a summer air, but not hot, and the stout gentlemen did not suffer after they were dressed for the climate. After riding for four days they took the boats for excursions on the water, the clearness of which was a constant marvel to all of them. They visited the sea gardens, and saw the wonders of vegetation on the bottom of the sea. They saw all there was to be seen of the sponge fisheries without going out with the boats employed in that business.

They employed guides to conduct them on the water as well as the land; and though they remained there but a couple of weeks, they carried away with them a very good knowledge of the town and the Island of New Providence. On the last day they made an excursion in the Guardian-Mother to Eleuthera Island, which they explored, and visited the "Glass Window," as it is called, which is a natural arch in the coral rock, through which people entering a cave look out on the ocean.

As at the Bermudas, it would take a whole book to describe all the sights the company saw and expatiate upon them; and as this is a story, those who wish to know more are referred to the books which were to be found in the ship's library.

All hands on board of the steamer were given all the liberty they wanted to go on shore, and Mr. Sharp was taken to the hotel to enable him the better to prosecute his investigation in regard to the wife of John Scoble, of whom no one but the captain and Uncle Moses had any knowledge. The letters of this woman from Nassau, of which he had obtained possession at St. George's, enabled him to make a beginning.

He found the family in which she had been employed as a nurse; but Mrs. Scoble had left her place of her own accord, and they did not know where she had gone, as the letter from the head of the house had informed her cousin. But Mr. Sharp discovered that the woman had a very intimate friend employed in the same family, who had left some time before Mrs. Scoble did. Her name was Mary Bordling, and she had gone to Crooked Island.

CHAPTER XXVII

RUTH SCOBLE AND OTHERS

THE gentleman in whose family Mrs. Scoble had lived as a nurse was a government official who had grown up on the island from small beginnings to be a person of considerable importance, and he lived in good style. He was largely interested in the culture of *sisal*, a fibre plant valuable for rope-making, which promised to redeem the fortunes of the island. Mr. Sharp knew all about this plant, and at one time had thought of regaining his shattered health by settling in Nassau, and engaging in its culture.

The name of this gentleman, Mr. Crandall, was given in one of the letters in possession of the third officer. When he inquired for him, he learned that he was engaged in sisal-planting. He went to his house the first evening after the cabin party landed, and made inquiries about the wonderful plant. Mr. Crandall was an enthusiast on the subject, and his visitor was hardly less so. In the course of the week Mr. Sharp became a subscriber for fifty shares in a company of which the Nassau gentleman was the president.

This operation on the part of the third officer lubricated the machinery of his mission, and opened the way for him to obtain all the information he desired, though he did not begin his real work at the place till he had given a draft for his shares on his cousin in New York, who took charge of his affairs in his absence.

"I think it probable that my cousin will take some shares in your company, Mr. Crandall, when I have written to him about it, for both of us have studied up the subject," said Mr. Sharp, after he had given the draft.

"If he has any spare capital, he can't do better with it," replied the president.

"Now, sir, I have attended to one matter I had in view when I came here, and I am interested in another. I learned from a letter I obtained from George Hastings in the Bermudas, that a woman by the name of Ruth Scoble lived in your family," the third officer continued.

"But she does not live in my family now, Mr. Sharp," replied the official. "In fact, she left me more than six months ago. I don't remember just when it was; and I wrote to Mr. Hastings, in answer to his inquiries, that I did not know where she was."

"What kind of a woman was Ruth Scoble?"

"A very good woman indeed. I went home to England on a visit, and found her as the attendant in a bar at a hotel in London. She was a very good-looking woman, with a very agreeable expression. I got acquainted with her. I asked the landlady about her character, and learned that it was excellent."

"I am very glad to hear this of her," added Mr. Sharp.

"I was told that she had had several offers of marriage, but declined them all. She was so pleasant that I became interested in her, and gossiped a great deal with her. She told me, as she had not told the landlady, that she had been married, though her husband had deserted her. She still clung to him, and hoped for a reconciliation with him."

"She would not if she knew what her husband had become since he left her," said Mr. Sharp.

"Then you know him, sir?"

"Hardly; but I know that he is a bad man, though at the present time he is rich."

"Ruth was in rather poor health at the time I saw her, and when I offered her a situation in my family as a sort of governess, she accepted it, for she knew that Nassau is the paradise of invalids; and so it proved to her, for she entirely regained her health. She and Mary Bordling, my housekeeper, became very intimate friends. Mary left me to go to Crooked Island. After her departure Ruth became discontented, and left me to take a position as housekeeper in a small hotel."

"You never had any trouble with her?"

"Not the slightest. I had a high regard for her, and saw her at the hotel. But after a few weeks, when I called, I was astonished to learn that she had left the house and the island. She had taken the mail-steamer going south ; and that was all that was known about her departure."

"Her movements were very singular. Do you suppose she went to Crooked Island to join Mary Bordling ? "

"Decidedly not, for the mail-steamer makes no landing there."

"How do you account for her singular conduct ? "

"I can't account for it at all," replied Mr. Crandall. "I had a suspicion that her husband might be at some point in the West Indies, and that she was in communication with him, though she never admitted to me that she ever had a word from him."

"It looks as though it would be a very difficult matter to find her," added Mr. Sharp.

"Then you wish to find her ? "

"I am very much obliged to you, sir, for the information you have given me, Mr. Crandall; but I can only give you an idea of my object in making these inquiries. Ruth's husband, John Scoble, deserted from the army, and went to New York. He was a thorough jockey and expert in horses, and did exceedingly well in his new home. He married an excellent lady in New Jersey.

"But Scoble was a scoundrel. He had assumed the name of Wade Farrongate. Sporting gentlemen of wealth had confidence in him, and he robbed them of a vast sum of money in his keeping, and escaped to England. He was arrested as a deserter,

and compelled to serve out the term of his enlistment.
His wife repudiated him when he attempted to return
to her. This lady is the mother of the owner of the
Guardian-Mother, now in your harbor."

"Bless me!" exclaimed the operator in sisal. "I
hope you will find Ruth, for her husband's marriage
to this lady was sheer bigamy."

"Nothing less."

Mr. Crandall offered to do anything in his power
to assist his visitor, but he had callers in the next
room who had been announced to him, and Mr. Sharp
hastened his departure. If he had looked into the
reception room as he passed its closed door, he would
have seen the two heavy men of the steamer, Dr.
Hawkes and Squire Scarburn. The former had heard
all about sisal from one of his patients, and both of
the gentlemen were looking up an investment in the
new fibre.

The third officer was hardly outside of the door before he remembered that he had not requested Mr.
Crandall not to mention the fact that he had made inquiries about Ruth Scoble. If he had known who the
visitors in the reception room were, he would have
returned and corrected what he regarded as his error.
The doctor and the trustee made their inquiries in
regard to sisal, and the president of the company set
forth its merits in glowing terms. Each of them put
his name down for fifty shares, and the trio became
quite familiar.

" A gentleman belonging to your steamer subscribed

for fifty shares just as you came in," said Mr. Crandall. "Mr. Sharp is his name."

"He is the third officer of the steamer," replied
Uncle Moses. "The captain told me that he was
worth quite a little fortune."

"He was interested in a woman who was formerly
a sort of governess in my family, and was very anxious to ascertain where she is at the present time."

"I hope you were able to inform him," added the
trustee.

"Unfortunately I was not, for she left Nassau without informing any one of her destination," replied the
president of the sisal corporation; and he repeated
enough of the conversation between his late visitor to
enable Uncle Moses to understand the matter.

The two passengers of the Guardian-Mother parted
with the president, feeling somewhat richer on pro-
spective dividends on sisal stock. Squire Scarburn
realized that Mr. Crandall had "let the cat out of the
bag," as he expressed it, on the Scoble affair; but he
thought it would be easy to induce the surgeon to be
silent.

Mr. Sharp realized after he had left the house that
he had not used proper precautions for the concealment of the Scoble matter, and he went back a few
hours later to correct his error, but Mr. Crandall was
not at home. The servant said the bishop had called
upon him, and he had gone out with him. At his
next visit he found him at home; but the president
informed him that he had already told the adipose
twins all about the Scoble affair.

"But I have just met the Bishop of Nassau, and I made some inquiries in regard to Mary Bordling. The reverend gentleman keeps as fine a yacht as you would ever wish to look upon, and in the discharge of the duties of his see, he visits the various islands of the Bahamas, and holds services in a chapel he has on board of the vessel. He has recently been to Crooked Island, and informed me that Mary Bordling was married to a prosperous planter there," said Mr. Crandall. "If you take the trouble to go there, perhaps she can inform you as to the present residence of Ruth Scoble."

"The island lies directly in our course to the south; but whether I can go there or not depends upon the captain of the steamer," replied Mr. Sharp.

"I hope I have not seriously compromised you by what I said to your passengers," said the president, as the visitor was taking his leave.

"I think not, for the information in our possession at the present is ample enough to render further secrecy unnecessary.

When he went on board of the steamer he spoke to the captain about the feline which had escaped from the sack, as the doctor put it, and regretted the slip that had been made.

"I don't think it makes the least difference in the world, for you have facts enough now to satisfy anybody that Mrs. Scoble is not a myth," replied Captain Ringgold. "On the contrary, I think Mrs. Belgrave should be told all about the matter; for it will give her another assurance that she has nothing to fear from her repudiated husband, who could be prosecuted for bigamy as well as embezzlement if we had him in the United States."

The Guardian-Mother had been a week in Nassau; but the party, including Louis, were in no hurry to leave. The owner found the fishing very agreeable sport, and the bathing was exceedingly refreshing as well as delightful to the senses. There was nothing to call the company away, and the steamer remained in the port another week. Through Mr. Crandall they became acquainted with some of the prominent families in the town, and came into social relations with them. They were entertained at dinner several times, and Louis suggested an excursion in the Guardian-Mother for the benefit of those who had extended their hospitality to them.

The commander assented, and M. Odervie was instructed to "spread himself" on an elaborate dinner for the occasion. No reporters were present; but it was a most delightful affair. When the guests had been landed in the barge, Louis and the captain felt that they had properly reciprocated the attentions bestowed upon them in the town. On the following Monday morning the steamer was ready to pursue her voyage to the south, and the public wharf was well covered with the ship's late guests and the inhabitants of Nassau generally to witness her departure.

The seamen manned the yards on the foremast, and

cheered lustily, aided by those on deck, as she moved off. It was high tide, and she went over the bar without accident. Louis was in the pilot-house with the captain and the pilot.

"You are headed the wrong way, Captain Ringgold," said he with a laugh. "You are going to the north-east."

"If you go into my room and look at the chart, Sir Louis, you will see that we have to make a course in this general direction before we can point her to the south."

Louis adopted the suggestion, and found that the steamer had to go to the northward of Eleuthera before she could lay her course to the south.

CHAPTER XXVIII

THE LANDFALL OF COLUMBUS

CAPTAIN RINGGOLD had studied his chart as well as the owner, and for a reason of his own which he did not explain, he instructed the chief engineer to keep the speed of the steamer down to eight knots an hour. In the afternoon the Guardian-Mother was on the broad Atlantic to the eastward of the Island of Eleuthera. The sea was very calm, and the ship was hardly affected by the long rollers. All the rest of the day she was in sight of this island, and the cabin party enjoyed every moment of the time.

Louis had attended to his studies in the forenoon, and was at liberty in the afternoon, though he was so earnest in his pursuit of Spanish as the ship was approaching Cuba, where it might be of use to him, that he used a great deal of his leisure in practising it with the professor and Mr. Gaskette. He liked to know just where he was, as all voyagers do, and he spent some of his time in the examination of the chart which was spread out on a table in the captain's room. The commander kept the steamer nearer to the shore of the island than vessels usually go, and pointed out to him the various capes on the coast.

In the evening there were no lights in sight, and there was nothing to be seen. As the darkness came on the ship stood out from the shore. In the morning Louis was up very early. The weather was delightful, and he and Felix walked the deck till breakfast time. At this meal Captain Ringgold invited the entire party to assemble on the little promenade abaft the bridge, though he did not explain his object in doing so. The occupants of the cabin had abundant space for "planking the deck," as naval officers call it, on the quarter-deck abaft the boudoir; but the officers' promenade, as it had come to be called, suited them better, for it enabled them to see the coast or other vessels more distinctly from its elevated position.

The commander went with them. The steamer was approaching an island, and was headed as near to it as the depth of water would permit, for most of them in the Bahamas are surrounded with shoals and sandbars, some of them with coral reefs, which render them very difficult of access. The captain said the other side of the island in sight was bordered by a shoal extending out eight or ten miles, which could be navigated only by small vessels.

"But what island is this, Captain Ringgold, for I have not looked at the chart this morning?" inquired Louis.

"This island is better off than some of them, for it has two names, and it has had three," replied the commander. "However, it is not uncommon for the islands in this region to have two names, one given by the Spanish discoverers, and the other by the English or French into whose possession they have afterwards come. The first name of this particular one in sight was Guanahani, given to it by the natives before any Europeans had been this way."

"Then this was the first land that Columbus discovered on this side of the Atlantic!" exclaimed Louis, rather thrilled to have the lesson of the discovery of America he had learned from his school books made so real by the presence of the very land on which he had first set his foot. " Guanahani, or Cat Island. That was just what I learned when I was a smaller boy than I am now; and I suppose all the rest of the boys in the United States learned the same thing, and did not think they should ever see the very land he trod on that memorable occasion, as I do at this moment."

The party all laughed heartily at the enthusiasm of the owner of the steamer, though a few of them had some of the same feeling. When in Granada, in Spain, the writer descended into the tomb or vault under the royal chapel, in the cathedral, and saw the coffins in which rested the remains of Ferdinand and Isabella. They seemed to give a reality to the facts of history which they had never possessed before.

" It is hardly worth while to gush over this island, Sir Louis ; but you shall have the opportunity to do so later in the day," said Captain Ringgold.

" I thought you said this was the island on which

Columbus first landed," added the owner, rather taken aback by the words of the commander.

"I only said it was the original island of Guanahani, and you jumped at all the rest, Mr. Belgrave. That was the Indian name of it; our friend Captain Columbus changed its name and called it St. Salvador," the captain proceeded. "The English called it Cat Island; and that makes up the three names."

"But didn't Columbus land here?" asked Louis, who appeared not to be as well posted as he generally was on miscellaneous topics.

"If you had examined the chart which covers the course we are to follow the rest of the day, and until we reach the coast of Cuba, you would have seen it stated that this was formerly San Salvador. This is not where Columbus first landed. An officer of the English navy has proved conclusively that his landfall was at another island south of this one."

"How could he prove that this was not the right one?"

"By comparing the description which Columbus gave of the island with the facts as he found them in a visit to this one. The great discoverer of the New World located a lagoon, or lake, in the middle of it; and there is no such sheet of water on Cat Island. Again, Columbus rowed around the island in one day; but Cat Island is fifty miles long, and he could not possibly have done it. The island which is now called San Salvador on the chart contains the lake, and it is not more than fifteen miles long. It is now generally agreed that the more southerly island is the right one, though some other inquirers have located his landfall on other islands."

"Can we see the true San Salvador?" asked Louis.

"You can, for it is visible from the deck of every vessel bound down this channel; but I propose, as the weather is so pleasant and the sea so smooth, to do better by you than simply give you a view from the deck of this historic island. It is about sixty miles from here."

It was time for Louis to attend to his studies, and he thought no more of Columbus and his landfall. After lunch he went to the captain's room and devoted himself for a considerable time to the study of the chart; but there was not a word about Columbus upon it. Then he went into the pilot-house, from the window of which he saw two islands on the starboard and one on the port side of the ship.

"We have three islands in sight, Captain Ringgold," said the young millionaire, who was very much interested in the geography of the region for one with so much money in his coffers.

"The smaller one on the starboard is Conception Island, and the larger is Rum Cay, which looks as though there were hills upon it. That on the port hand is Watling's Island; and that is the one you are looking for, and over which you may gush moderately without the danger of wasting any of your enthusiasm, for it is the real Columbus island," replied the commander.

"But you have nearly gone by it."

"Not at all; we shall make the landing at the southerly end of the island, for the approach from the north is dangerous on account of the reefs."

"There are a couple of tall rocks near it."

"Those are the Hinchinbroke Rocks, sometimes called the Pigeons."

"This island is inhabited, for I see several houses on a hill."

Half an hour later the Guardian-Mother was near the lofty rocks Louis had mentioned, and ran to a point quite near the shore. The screw was stopped, and the anchor let go. The gangway was rigged out, and the barge and first cutter were lowered and brought to the platform. The party embarked at once, and were landed in a few minutes. The only white man on the island gave them a hospitable greeting, and proved himself to be a gentleman in every sense of the word.

"But it was not at this part of the island that Columbus landed," said Captain Nairn, when the object of the visit was explained to him; and he indicated where the precise spot could be found. "I shall be happy to be your guide, if you will accept my services."

"We shall be very grateful to you for such assistance," replied the captain. "I hope it is not far from here."

"A considerable distance, Captain."

"Shall we go on foot, or in the boats? Some of

our party are heavy men, and perhaps they do not care to walk any great distance, especially as the weather is rather warm on shore."

"Then, you had better go in the boats," added the inhabitant of the island.

The party embarked again, Captain Nairn taking a place in the stern-sheets of the barge with the ladies. They questioned him in regard to his life in this solitary region; and he gave them a great deal of information about the Bahamas, to which Louis was an attentive listener. The boat came to a large bay, which the boats entered under the pilotage of the resident. As they approached the shore, the guide pointed out the monument, about six hundred feet from the beach.

"I didn't know there was any monument to commemorate the landing of Columbus," said Louis, who thought it very strange he had never heard of it.

"There are a great many things in this world, Sir Louis, which you are yet to hear about. Probably there are thousands, if not millions, of people in the United States who have never heard of this monument. I acknowledge that I did not till very recently," added the commander.

"This monument was erected by the *Chicago Herald* to mark the spot on which Columbus first set foot in America," said Captain Nairn. "I supposed every reader of that paper knew all about it."

"Yes; and most of the readers of all other papers, though a great many people, myself among the number, contrive to miss a great many things that are printed for their information," said Captain Ringgold, laughing.

The party landed and took a survey of the surroundings, and they could see the coast to the north and to the south for miles. They walked directly to the monument, which had been erected under the supervision of a couple of the employees of the *Chicago Herald*. It was built of the stone found on the spot, and consisted of a solid square foundation, with buttressed corners, with a shaft rising to a considerable height containing many stones from public and private buildings in Chicago, contributed by friends of the enterprise. A tablet of marble had been set in the masonry, on which was the following inscription: —

ON THIS SPOT
CHRISTOPHER COLUMBUS
FIRST SET FOOT ON THE SOIL OF
THE NEW WORLD.
ERECTED BY THE
CHICAGO HERALD,
June 15, 1891.

After the company had inspected the monument, they were conducted to a hill from which they could obtain a view of the greater part of the island, including the lagoon, or lake, which has gone into history. The landscape was well covered with semitropical trees, and the resident pointed out the fields he cultivated. The only collection of houses that could pass for a village was that on the hill which they had seen from the sea.

About sunset the boats reached the steamer, and Captain Nairn was invited to dine on board and spend the evening, for the commander had decided to lie at his anchorage till morning, so that he need not have to make his landing at Crooked Island in the darkness. The dinner was an excellent one. The guest seemed to enjoy it prodigiously; and he did a great deal to entertain the party.

CHAPTER XXIX

A RICH WEST INDIAN UNCLE

WHEN Louis went on deck the next morning the Guardian-Mother was under way, having sailed at daylight. The weather was still delightful, and the owner of the steamer enjoyed every moment he spent on deck. When he went into the captain's room to look at the chart and ascertain what islands were to be seen during the forenoon, he remarked that he should like to live in such a climate all the time.

"You would not find it so charming all the time," replied Captain Ringgold. "There are ups and downs in the weather here as well as in New Jersey."

"We have not had a drop of rain since we left New York," added Louis.

"There is not much rain in this region at this season of the year; but the summer is the time for rain, and if you were here at that time you would see rain enough."

"Of course I know that the two seasons in the tropics are the wet and the dry; and I have not seen both of them."

"I have no doubt you will get into some pretty hot weather before you are a month older. If you take

the summer at home, you find that it has its discom-
forts and its annoyances, and you are likely to experience them down here, with some additions which do
not affect you at the North. You will not want many
blankets on your bed when you get to the south side
of Cuba, where you will be within the tropics. Then
I suppose you are not especially partial to mosquitoes,
Sir Louis."

"I can't sleep a wink when there is a single one
buzzing about me."

"There are plenty of them in this region; but the
berths are provided with mosquito bars, which I must
have Mr. Sage put in place very soon."

"The flies were very numerous at Nassau, and they
bothered Uncle Moses so badly by lighting on his
bald head that he had to put on his silk cap. He
will not allow one in his house at home," added Louis.
"Are there any snakes down there?"

"I think not on these islands; but in Cuba there
are some, though they are not numerous. The *maja*
is a large fellow, sometimes a dozen feet long, but he
is not poisonous; yet he will fight when disturbed.
He climbs trees, and drops down on his prey. The
tarantula and the scorpion are about the worst nui-
sance in the island."

"I don't like them."

"No one does. Speaking of the climate, if you
were to see a few hurricanes, and witness the destruction they bring about, I imagine you would prefer
New Jersey to the tropics as a steady dwelling-place."

"I don't think I should care to be here in the summer, for I have read about the effects of hurricanes."

" We certainly shall not stay here during the summer; but we have the means in our floating home of going to any climate that suits us."

" How far is it to Crooked Island, Captain ?" asked Louis, as he looked out the window at Rum Cay, which lay on the starboard side.

"From our anchorage at Watling's Island to Bird Rock, a small island, with a light on it, off the northern end of the island the distance is sixty-seven miles," replied the captain, taking from the table a pamphlet with a blue cover. " This is the second part of the West India Directory which comes with this large chart. Perhaps you would like to read it, for it contains some meagre descriptions of all these islands."

"I should like to refer to it as occasion may require; but I think it must be rather dry reading."

In the middle of the forenoon the steamer was in sight of Bird Rock, and Louis consulted the blue book; but he found nothing but a description of the lighthouse. Although the captain spoke of Crooked Island as a single one, he found that there was a group of four called by that general name. At Pittstown, where the steamer was to make a harbor, he found there was a post-office, and he improved the opportunity to write a letter to Morris Woolridge, though he would have preferred to write one to his sister, which he had not the courage to do.

About noon the Guardian-Mother let go her anchor at Crooked Island, the most northern of the group The barge dropped into the water, and the whole party were landed, the third officer being in charge o: the boat. Lunch had been served at an early hour in the cabin, and the passengers were to remain on shore all the afternoon.

By this time the especial mission of Mr. Sharp was well understood. Uncle Moses had told Mrs. Belgrave all about the Ruth Scoble affair. She was greatly astonished; but as it removed all doubt in regard to the illegality of her marriage to Scoble, she was all the happier for the information. In fact, she had been less nervous and even more cheerful than before since the steamer left Nassau.

The town on the island was not a very extensive one Mr. Sharp looked up the post-office at once, for that was where he was most likely to obtain information in regard to Mary Bordling, if she was still on the island. As her friend Ruth had gone in another direction, he feared that she would not be able to give him any clew to her present residence. He found the post-office in a store.

"Mr. Bondleigh?" said the third officer, as he ap proached the only person he found in the store.

"That is my name, sir."

"You are the postmaster, I am informed."

"Well, yes, sir; I hold about all the offices on this island," laughed the official.

"Then you are more fortunate than most of the office-seekers in my country."

"That is because we have more offices than men, and it is just the other way in the States."

"I have called upon you, sir, because I believed you would be the most likely to give me the information I am seeking, as you handle all the letters that come here."

"That is very true; but in a place like this the postmaster is not over-worked," replied the official. "I have not the pleasure of knowing your name, sir."

"My name is Penn Sharp; but I am not looking for a letter. On the contrary, I am looking for a lady."

"Not an unusual occupation for a good-looking person like yourself."

"Thank you, Mr. Bondleigh; and I dare say you have done the same thing yourself; and I hope you found the one for whom you were looking. You are certainly prepossessing enough to be successful in such a search."

"That makes an even thing of it between us. Yes, sir; and I married the lady. Now, if you will give me the name of the lady you are seeking, I will give you all the information I have in regard to her."

"The lady came here from Nassau, and her name is Mary Bordling."

"That name is no longer in existence," replied the postmaster with a smile.

"Is she dead?"

"Not at all, Mr. Sharp; the lady is my wife, and she is now Mrs. Mary Bondleigh."

"I see; and I congratulate you, for she had a most excellent reputation at Nassau."

"I knew her in England twenty years ago when she was a young girl; and when I heard of her at Nassau, I invited her to come over here; and I have told you the result."

Mr. Sharp explained his object in desiring to see the lady, and her husband conducted him to the finest house on the island, which was surrounded by his plantation. Mrs. Bondleigh was apparently about thirty-five years old, and she was still handsome enough to explain why the postmaster had sent for her. The visitor was duly presented to her, and he stated the object of his visit.

"Ruth Scoble was my most intimate friend in Nassau, and I was very sorry to leave her," said Mrs. Bondleigh.

"But you have heard from her since your departure?" suggested the third officer, fearful that the separation had been final.

"Oh, yes! Nearly every mail brought me a letter. She was perfectly contented in the family of Mr. Crandall, and I did not suppose she would ever leave Nassau. But her last letter from Nassau informed me that she had heard from her uncle, who went to the West Indies when she was a child. He had sent for her to come to him, and make her home with him. He had dropped out of the knowledge of the family, though Ruth had heard of him."

"Is he still living in the West Indies?" asked the visitor.

"He is, or was three months ago, when I last heard from Ruth. She had a great many doubts about going to her uncle's. She has never ceased to be attached to her husband, and she seemed to be confident that they would be reunited some time."

"So I learned in Nassau."

"She would never mention her uncle to Mr. Crandall, and for some reason which I do not understand, she distrusted her West Indian relative. She wrote me that she intended to leave Nassau without permitting her destination to be known, and return by the same steamer if she found she had been deceived. I think she believed it was a trick on the part of her husband to get her out of British territory, perhaps to obtain a divorce from her for desertion."

"Captain Scoble is capable of such a trick," added Mr. Sharp.

"Do you know him, sir?" asked the lady, manifesting a great deal of astonishment.

"I have seen him, and I know all about him," replied the visitor. "He is a thief, a robber, and an embezzler; and if Ruth Scoble knew him as I do, she would think no more of him."

Before the lady would proceed any farther with her story, the third officer was obliged to tell in as few words as possible what he knew about her friend's husband. She was astounded at the revelation, for she had derived all her information in regard to Scoble from the wife.

"There is a steamer coming down the passage, and

if she comes into the harbor, I must leave you, though I am much interested in this narrative," interposed Mr. Bondleigh.

The third officer looked out of the window to see the craft, and when he saw her he manifested the most intense surprise.

"Your friend Ruth's husband is the owner and commander of that steamer!" he exclaimed, as he identified the Maud in the vessel, which was hardly half a mile distant from the island.

She continued on her way without putting in at the port. The Guardian-Mother was behind a sort of bluff so that she could not be seen from the Maud. Scoble had evidently hastened the repairs of his vessel, and started in pursuit of the steamer which had thrust her bow into the side of his yacht, no doubt bent upon revenge and retaliation.

"She has gone on her voyage, and I am glad she did not come in at this island," said the visitor, resuming his seat. "You have not yet informed me where your friend's uncle resides."

"At Cienfuegos, on the south side of the island of Cuba."

"I have been there, and I know the place."

"Ruth wrote me that she had found her uncle David; that he was a very wealthy planter, though he had an elegant residence in the city. He was very kind to her, and she had decided to remain with him. He was seventy years old, and had married a Spanish lady who had died a year ago; but he had no children, and the poor old gentleman, rich as he was, was all alone in the world."

"Then she is likely to be an heiress."

"Probably; but Ruth says nothing about that. I have not had a letter from her for three months; and then her uncle was quite sick, and it required all her time to take care of him."

The subject was considered for another hour, and Mr. Sharp took his leave, hastening to find Captain Ringgold.

CHAPTER XXX

AN APPREHENDED DANGER

CAPTAIN RINGGOLD had employed a very intelligent negro, who smiled all over his face when he spoke, revealing a wealth of pure ivory in contrast with his black countenance, to guide the party about the island. It was very hot in the sun, and they were not disposed to prolong the promenade. The guide had taken them to a shady grove, where they had seated themselves to enjoy the cooling breeze from the ocean.

With some difficulty and the assistance of the postmaster's black clerk in the store, Mr. Sharp found the commander. As soon as he discovered their cool retreat, he saw at a glance that Captain Ringgold had not seen the Maud when she passed the island. From the high ground he had gone over the third officer had observed her in the distance, off Fortune Island, one of the Crooked Islands group.

"Take a seat, Mr. Sharp," said the commander, as the officer came into the bower, fragrant with flowers, which seemed to be a miracle to the ladies in December. "I hope you have found Mary Bordling."

"I have found her; but she no longer goes under

that name, for she is the wife of the postmaster, who is also a magistrate, a planter, and a storekeeper. He holds all the offices in the place. But I have another piece of news which I must mention first," replied the third officer.

"Is it possible there is news in such a place as this?" asked Dr. Hawkes.

"I picked it up myself. The Maud just went down the passage about two hours ago, bound to the southward."

"The Maud!" exclaimed the commander, rising to his feet, with the spy-glass he had brought with him in his hand.

"The Maud!" groaned Mrs. Belgrave.

"Don't be alarmed, madam," interposed Dr. Hawkes. "Captain Ringgold has proved that he is able to take care of his ship and all his passengers; and perhaps this fellow will give us a little more needed excitement."

"Are you sure it was the Maud, Mr. Sharp?" inquired the captain.

"I have no doubt of it; I have seen enough of her to know her very well," answered the officer confidently. "She is still in sight, though twenty miles off or more, and you can make her out with your glass from the hill over here."

The commander went to the hill indicated with Mr. Sharp, and directed his glass at the distant steamer. What he could see of her confirmed the announcement that it was the Maud.

"Where is she going now?" mused the captain.

"I am confident she is going in search of the Guardian-Mother. What else could she be doing in these waters?"

"I suppose you are right. That Scoble is the most diabolically malicious and revengeful fellow I ever knew or heard of," added the commander. "He must have gone in at Nassau, and ascertained that we were bound to the south side of Cuba. We hardly need be surprised at the appearance of the Maud in these waters. He had time enough to repair his damages, and he knew that we were bound to Nassau. I have no doubt he will retaliate to the utmost extent of his malice and his ability."

"What do you expect him to do, Captain?" asked Mr. Sharp.

"I expect him to run into the Guardian-Mother, and sink her in the deepest water in which he can find her!" said Captain Ringgold earnestly. "I don't believe he would scruple to drown every person on board of her."

"Even the lady whom he claims as his wife?"

"I don't know; perhaps that is the only thing that would deter him from such a savage act of retaliation. But I think I shall be ready for him," said the commander with a smile; but he did not indicate in what manner it would be possible to checkmate the desperate villain.

"I think he could be claimed and extradited from any part of the Spanish dominions," added the third officer. "Tweed, who was a mild criminal compared to this one, did not find it safe to remain in Cuba, and he escaped to Spain, where he was arrested and sent to New York. I think you had better put a stop to the villain's career by having a warrant for his arrest, and a requisition for his extradition from the governor sent to Cienfuegos."

"I will telegraph to Mr. Woolridge to have this done as soon as we get to Santiago de Cuba, which will be in a couple of days or less, if the desperado does not sink us before we arrive there," replied Captain Ringgold as they started on the return to the shady bower.

There could be no doubt that the commander of the Guardian-Mother was very anxious, and even alarmed, at the situation; but before he reached the little grove he had banished every appearance of disquiet from his face, for he feared that Mrs. Belgrave would be seriously disturbed if she understood the danger before them as well as he did. But he looked as cheerful as usual when he went to join the party.

"Have you ascertained anything in regard to this villain's wife, Mr. Sharp?" he inquired.

"Everything that is worth knowing, Captain; and it is quite a history," replied the third officer.

"It is four o'clock now, and I think we had better go on board of the ship, where we can hear your report to better advantage," added the commander, consulting his watch. "We should be late to dinner if we heard it here."

The company proceeded to the shore, where the boats were waiting for them. On the white, sandy beach they found the postmaster and his wife. They evidently expected to meet some of the excursionists, for they were both attired in their Sunday garments, so that Mr. Bondleigh looked more magisterial than when he was in the store. Mr. Sharp presented them to all the members of the party, and the captain invited them to visit the steamer and dine with them.

The officers were all occasionally invited to dine in the cabin, and the commander took this occasion to request the presence of the third officer at the table and in the boudoir. Some time was consumed in showing the guests from the shore over the ship; but before dinner Mr. Sharp, assisted by Mrs. Bondleigh, had imparted all the information obtained in regard to Mrs. Scoble. No one doubted that they would find the lady on the arrival of the ship at Cienfuegos; and the captain hoped he should be able to put an end to the career of John Scoble at the same time.

The dinner was heartily enjoyed by the islanders, and hardly less by the passengers, for the tramp on shore had given them excellent appetites. In the evening Mrs. Belgrave and Professor Giroud, who was a musician in addition to his other accomplishments, played the piano in the boudoir, and the company sang songs and hymns, the postmaster and his wife joining in the exercise. At a rather late hour the guests were landed in the barge, attended by the third officer. The ship remained at her anchorage over night.

But she was under way at daylight in the morning, for the commander desired that the occupants of the cabin should see all the islands on the course. Before he turned in the night before Captain Ringgold called all his officers into his room, for they had remained out of their berths to hear the music, and it was an unwonted treat to them. None of them except Mr. Gaskette and Mr. Sharp had seen the Maud when she passed. The second officer had been out fishing in the dingy, and had gone out far enough to see and recognize her. He was as positive as the third officer that the steamer was the Maud, and the captain could no longer doubt the fact.

The commander explained to his officers the peril he apprehended, and urged them to be on the watch all the time for the piratical craft, as he called Scoble's yacht. To them he explained in what manner he intended to defeat the undoubted purpose of the captain of the Maud to run into the Guardian-Mother, even at the risk of sinking her. They all of them noticed a repeating rifle they had not seen there before.

The course of the steamer during the early morning had been along the coast of the islands and outside of the extensive bay formed by the group which surrounded it. In the four hours which had elapsed before breakfast the ship had nearly reached the southern extremity of the cluster of islands. The captain sent an invitation to the cabin for the party to meet on the officers' promenade, and they promptly answered the summons.

"Why, there is a castle!" exclaimed Mrs. Belgrave, as the commander pointed to the shore.

"Is it a fort?" asked Louis.

"Neither a castle nor a fort," replied Captain Ringgold.

"It certainly looks like a white fort," added Dr. Hawkes.

"I look upon it as quite a remarkable formation," continued the captain. "I thought you ought to see it. It looks like a castle; and that is the reason why the little island on which the lighthouse is located is called Castle Island. We shall go out of sight of land for a short time in a couple of hours, and the next island we make will be Cuba. When you see the lighthouse on the point, that is Cape M-a-y-s-i; how do you pronounce that word, Sir Louis, for it is Spanish, and ordinary mortals cannot pronounce it?"

"Mah-ee-see, I should say," replied Louis, glancing at the professor.

"Quite right, Mr. Belgrave," added the learned gentleman with a smile.

"Very well; then the next land you see will be Cape Maysi," added the captain, pronouncing it correctly. "But it will be eight or nine hours before you see it."

The breakfast bell summoned the party back to the cabin. Everything went on as usual during the day, and the professor's ambitious pupil had nothing to disturb him till four o'clock in the afternoon, when the promised lighthouse was seen. An hour later the ship was approaching the great island, and later was abreast of it. The water was very deep, and the steamer went quite near the shore. The cabin party were on the officers' promenade again, observing whatever was to be seen of the country. It was no longer low and sandy, with coral reefs and bluffs, as when they entered the Bahamas, and which had been the outlook during the passage through them.

"That is a very desolate-looking region, and I would not live there if anybody would pay my board," said Louis, as he looked upon the sugar-loaf hills which extended as far as could be seen. "Nobody appears to live there, and a sheep or a goat would have a hard scramble to get his breakfast there."

"This is the least desirable part of the island as a residence or for cultivation," added the commander. "All this part is hilly and mountainous, and you will soon see some lofty mountains in the interior. They will continue to form the background of the picture for three or four hundred miles."

"So far? But how long is the whole island?" asked Louis.

"One English authority gives it as 620 miles, and another as 750, and American books generally put it at the latter figures. Its breadth varies greatly from thirty to ninety miles. The range of high mountains is mostly in the eastern part of the island, while

the western is more nearly level. It has no large
rivers, for there is no room for them. This hilly
region contains many valuable mines. The country is
generally well watered by small streams and rivulets,
and the soil in the parts cultivated is remarkably
fertile and productive. Now, don't forget anything I
have told you, for I have had to study it up in the
books," said the captain as he finished his remarks.

"You have not told us yet, Captain, that we are
now in the Caribbean Sea," suggested Louis.

" It appears that there was no need for me to do
so."

When the young millionaire went on deck the next
morning, he found the steamer had stopped her screw
off an opening in the coast.

CHAPTER XXXI

Louis looked about him like an old sailor when he
went on deck. The Caribbean Sea seemed to be an
improvement on the ocean, for it was almost as smooth
as a millpond. The air was delightfully soft and
pleasant, with a gentle breeze from the southward.
When he turned in the night before the ship was
still following the trend of the coast, which was due
west in this part of the island.

The opening before him was very narrow, and the
shores of it were rugged, with bluffs on the east side.
The young voyager did not know where he was, and
he went to the captain's room and there he found the
chart spread out on the table as usual. As he studied
the shore he concluded that the inlet must be Guantanamo, or Cumberland Harbor as the English call
it. Captain Ringgold presently appeared, only half
dressed, as though he had just turned out of his berth.

"Good-morning, Sir Louis. You are out before
me; but I have been up a good portion of the night,"
said he, as he proceeded to complete his toilet.

"I have been on deck, sir, taking a survey of the
sea and the land," replied the young man. "I see

there is an opening just ahead of the ship, and I suppose that is Guantanamo."

"You suppose wrong, Sir Knight. We passed the entrance of Guantanamo port four hours ago, as you could have seen if you had looked at the log-slate in the pilot-house. I thought of going in; but there is nothing of interest to be seen there, and the only object I had for going in was to ascertain if the Maud had made a harbor there. But I concluded not to go in."

"Then, this must be the entrance to the harbor of St. Jago de Cuba," added Louis, consulting the chart again.

"Precisely so; and I suppose you would write it out as the Spaniards do; but we generally write it and print it Santiago de Cuba. We are waiting for a pilot," said the captain. "If it had not been in the night, I should have called the attention of the party to the hiding-place of Tweed, the New York embezzler. It is only a short distance from Santiago, in a very desolate region, and there is really nothing more to be seen than you have observed all along the coast."

"I have heard of that man, and seen pictures of him in an old illustrated paper," added Louis.

"Those pictures of him which were caricatures, though the resemblance was perfect, brought him to grief; for they enabled the officers in Spain to identify him, so that he was arrested and sent back to New York. He lived in his Cuban retreat in a hut with a negro, which was a tremendous contrast with the

luxury he had purchased with his ill-gotten gains.
He succeeded in obtaining a passage in a sailing-vessel
to Spain, and he passed his last days as a prison con-
vict."

"There comes a boat out of the inlet, Captain."

"That is the pilot; and probably he does not speak
English. You can air your Spanish now," added the
captain with a smile.

"I haven't much to air; but I can say 'Good-morning' to him."

"Perhaps you had better walk Spanish a little
before you talk it, Sir Louis, for you will soon see
something that will remind you of the country of
that other celebrated knight, Don Quixote," laughed
the captain.

"You don't pronounce it right, sir."

"I think I do, my young friend, for I think it is
ridiculous for us to call it Don Kee-ho-tay. Do you
remember what the capital of France is?"

"Of course I do: it is Paris."

"But you don't pronounce it right, though you
speak French."

"I don't think I ever heard any person speaking
English who called it Par-ee," replied Louis.

"You might as well pronounce it so as to follow
the Spanish pronunciation when you talk English."

"Give it up!" exclaimed Louis.

"Still, it is the fashion to pronounce foreign proper
names as the natives do. Now, Sir Louis, if you
will walk Spanish as far as the cabin and invite the

party to the promenade, they will soon see something interesting," said the captain, as he went out on the deck.

By the time Louis returned from the cabin, the pilot had reached the deck, and his boy was rowing his boat back to the inlet. The man's complexion was dark. and he looked as though he was part Indian. Louis spoke to him in Spanish, and the pilot seemed to be delighted to hear his own language on board of a steamer flying the American flag. But the student's vocabulary gave out very soon, and Mr. Gaskette took his place.

Antonio, as he gave his name, went to the pilot-house, with Twist at the wheel. His English vocabulary seemed to be confined to three words, "starboard." "port," and "steady;" and he pronounced these well enough to be understood. The party from the cabin gathered on the "lookout," as Dr. Hawkes had christened the officers' promenade, and the commander rang the gong to go ahead.

The Guardian-Mother entered the narrow opening, and went ahead at about half speed. In a few minutes more the old Morro castle came into view, and some of the company began to indulge in exclamations. It was an ancient fort, most of which had been cut out of the solid rock. It was two or three stories high. and under it was a sort of arch which had been dug out of the rock by the waves which had been beating against it for centuries. It was an exceedingly picturesque ruin.

"You will be able to obtain photographs of it in Santiago," suggested Captain Ringgold, who had joined them on the lookout. "Santiago was the ancient capital of Cuba, and still has a population of fifty thousand; some place it at a higher figure."

"There are lots of holes and passages in that hillside where the fort is," said Louis, who was still gazing at the wonderful Morro.

"It is honeycombed with subterranean alleys. It was strong in its day; but a few shots from the big gun in the turret of a monitor would knock it all to pieces in a very short time. That is said to be the oldest fort in America; and I do not doubt the truth of the statement, for it must be over three hundred years old."

The scenery on both sides of the harbor was very beautiful, the slopes covered with fresh green foliage, with plenty of palms, laurels, cocoanut-trees, orange, lemon, tamarind, almond, and banana groves. The party were very enthusiastic over the prospect presented to them.

The distance of Santiago from the sea is about six miles, considerably increased by turns in the crooked channel in making the passage. Not a dozen miles to the northward of the city could be seen the lofty heights of the Copper Mountains, taking their name from the metal that abounds among them. They are said to be very nearly seven thousand feet in height; but figures in Cuba are very uncertain.

The city is built on rather hilly ground, and its

harbor is one of the finest in the world. The party found that the American flag could be seen on several two and three masted schooners, and lying at a wharf was a side-wheel steamer precisely like the in-shore boats about New York, and they concluded that she was built there. The pilot informed Mr. Gaskette that the steamer was the José Garcias, that she was American built, and plied between the cities of the southern coast of the island.

The steamer came to anchor a short distance from the principal landing-place of the city, near a rather small Spanish cruiser, which looked as though she might have been one of the " white fleet " of the United States, if her colors had not told a different story. The party landed in the barge and first cutter, much to the disgust of the numerous boatmen who surrounded the steamer as soon as her anchor went to the bottom. In most of the ports of Cuba but few wharves are available for loading vessels, as is the case at the ports of the Mediterranean Sea, and lighters have to be used for putting in the cargoes of large crafts.

Santiago seemed to be a hundred years behind the times, though it was progressive in some things, for a sign with letters a foot high informed visitors that the fancy tipples of the Americans could be obtained there. The party climbed a hill to the fish-market, after a guide had been procured, who gave them the names of the highly colored denizens of the deep. They were very pretty.

Before a block of stores near by the attention of the strangers was attracted by a string of a dozen mules, small in size, each having a pair of panniers filled with various merchandise. From the bridle of each animal was a rein passing to the one next ahead of him, and made fast to the saddle. On the top of the goods of the leader was seated the driver. There are no railroads of any length in this part of the islands, or any common roads outside of the city available for vehicles, and all the commerce with the interior has to be carried on with mules, as in many parts of old Spain.

The company visited the cathedral, where they found much to interest them, and a priest conducted them through the structure, pointing out and explaining everything to them in his own language, which the guide and Mr. Gaskette interpreted to them. Louis found that he could understand very little of what the padre said.

By this time it was one o'clock, and the party visited a restaurant for lunch. No one there could speak a word of English. The place was fitted up precisely like any eating establishment in New York, though it did not compare with those of the higher class. The guide had provided carriages for the party, and they were ready when they came out. Just then they heard military music, and a regiment of soldiers marched through the plaza in front of them. This was an exceedingly interesting sight to Louis and Felix. The soldiers were all sent over from Spain, though sometimes recruited to fill up the ranks,

"That is what I never saw before," said Louis. "Soldiers wearing straw hats!"

"I should say they would be vastly more comfortable than the woollen one worn at home," replied Felix. "The uniform is made of blue cotton drilling, with light stripes, or something of that sort."

"They have a bit of red on the hat, and the same color on their uniform. Just twig!" exclaimed Louis, as among the young people who had come out to see the soldiers, he discovered a boy and a girl of ten to twelve years old, each bearing a baby in the exact condition in which it came into the world.

The little ones did not seem to like the looks or the music of the military, and they were making a desperate resistance to the show in the arms of their nurses. It was with the greatest difficulty that the boy and girl could retain their hold upon their charges, for the naked bodies of the struggling little ones afforded no sufficient grasp upon them. Wherever the party went in the city these naked babies were to be seen; and it would be an interesting bit of statistics if any one could figure up the amount saved by not clothing the infants till they are two years old or more.

The strangers rode to barracks, hospitals, the city hall, and through the best streets of the town to see how the wealthy people lived. The ship remained a week in the harbor, and many excursions were made by land and water. Louis and Felix hired a couple of mules and took a ride over the hills of the interior;

and the former found more occasion to talk Spanish than before, for when he was obliged to do so, he got along much better than with the pilot.

On the first day of the stay in Santiago, Captain Ringgold had telegraphed to Mr. Woolridge to procure a requisition for the arrest and extradition of John Scoble, and to send a couple of officers to Havana to convey the prisoner to New York. Before the steamer sailed he received a reply to his message to the effect that the request had already been complied with. It was only three or four days that the voyager from New York required to reach Havana, and something less to make the trip by Tampa. He might expect these officers in Cienfuegos in a week.

CHAPTER XXXII

A SKIRMISH IN THE CARIBBEAN SEA

On the day appointed for the sailing of the Guardian-Mother, the voyagers were not sorry to depart from Santiago, for aside from the sight-seeing and the excursions to the Morro and elsewhere, they had not greatly enjoyed the ancient capital of Cuba. All of them had mailed letters to friends at home, and Louis had made a practical use of the little Spanish he had been able to learn in two months.

"I shall be glad to get out to sea again," said Mrs. Belgrave at breakfast. "It has been very hot in Santiago, and it is not much better in the harbor; and, besides, the mosquitoes invaded the cabin last night."

"But we have screens for the doors and the ports; and some one must have left them open, so that the lights drew them inside," replied the captain. "I noticed that the thermometer in the pilot-house has indicated ninety-four several times during the last week; and I think it must have gone up to a hundred in the city. We shall soon be out of it; and I shall expect to find it cooler in Cienfuegos, and certainly in Havana."

The party remained on board of the ship all day,

for the commander had fixed the hour for sailing at six o'clock in the evening, which would give daylight enough to enable the pilot to take the ship to the sea. Louis asked why he had chosen so late an hour, for he wanted to study the coast.

"We shall be out of sight of land for the next twenty-eight hours; so that there will be nothing to be seen till we make the light on Point Colorados, at the entrance to the harbor of Cienfuegos," the commander explained.

"As we are in no hurry, why not follow the coast?" Louis inquired.

"Because the bottom is too near the top of the water between Cape Cruz and Trinidad; and this city you shall see in the distance, for I will strike in shore in the morning, and you shall see the coast for about forty miles. That is the best I can do for you, Sir Knight."

"What is the name of that place we visit next, Captain Ringgold? I can never remember it," said Mrs. Belgrave.

"Cienfuegos; and it means a hundred fires. If you don't like the name, it has another which may suit you better. It is Xagua," replied the captain, giving it the Spanish pronunciation as nearly as he could.

"Gracious!" exclaimed the lady. "That is worse than the other. I think we had better learn to pronounce the first one."

"That is the one most commonly used; but if you

learned to pronounce it in pure Castilian Spanish, I am afraid you would find many who would not understand it.   I leave the pronunciation to you, Professor Giroud."

" Thi-ain-foo-ā-gos," added the professor.

" American officers of vessels call it Seen-fer-gus. But Cuban Spanish is largely *patois*," said the captain.

Louis and his mother both practised on the word with the assistance of the professor.   The son got it very well; but his mother conquered it only after many struggles; and when she had succeeded in pronouncing the name, she declared that she had enough of the language to last her the rest of her lifetime.

The steamer went to sea at the time fixed, and Louis did better with the pilot than before.   The company retired early, for it was cooler at sea in the evening, and some of them had been robbed of their sleep by the heat and the mosquitoes.   When they went on deck in the morning, the Guardian-Mother was still out of sight of land.   But it was very pleasant on the smooth waters of the Caribbean Sea; and as the commander had predicted, the wind, what there was of it, came from another quarter, and it was decidedly cooler.

" Sail, ho ! " shouted the lookout man on the topgallant forecastle.

The captain was smoking his cigar in the pilothouse, and he had already discovered it.   The stranger, which could hardly be made out in the distance, was a steamer, as indicated by the long streak of black high in the air beyond her. Spy-glasses were in immediate demand; but the steamer was too far off to be made out distinctly.

Half an hour later she proved to be a vessel of between three and four hundred tons, schooner rigged, and had the appearance of being a very jaunty craft.

Captain Ringgold said nothing, and he was very glad that his owner was studying his lessons or reciting in the after cabin. He went into his room from the pilot-house, and took in his hands the repeating rifle he had removed from its case the week before. He filled the magazine with cartridges, and then carried the weapon back into the pilot-house. Mr. Sharp had come in during his absence, but the commander said nothing to him; and he did not venture to address him after he had observed his resolute expression.

Captain Ringgold remained only a few minutes in the pilot-house; but taking his rifle in his hand, he passed out to the deck, beckoning the third officer to follow him. He proceeded directly to the top-gallant forecastle, where he deposited the arm in a convenient place.

"I suppose you have made out that steamer, Mr. Sharp?" the commander began, as he fixed his gaze upon the vessel, now not more than a mile distant, and sailing a course that would take her by the Guardian-Mother, perhaps half a mile from her, on the starboard hand.

"I hope the captain of that pirate craft will live

long enough to be arrested and sent to New York," he added, after he had watched the other steamer for some minutes.

"There seems to be some danger that he may not," replied the third officer.

"Of course I shall not use my rifle as long as I can avoid the fellow; and my chance of doing so is pretty good, for we can outsail him by two or three knots an hour. I have already spoken through the tube to Mr. Shafter, asking him to get up all the steam he can."

"I hope you will not be obliged to fire at Scoble," said Mr. Sharp.

"I hope not myself; and I shall do so only at the last extremity. But when you are attacked by a pirate, self-preservation is the first law of nature."

"The Maud does not act as though the captain of her had made out the Guardian-Mother," suggested the third officer.

"I do not see how he could have failed to do so before this time."

"There she goes! She has put her helm to port!" exclaimed Mr. Sharp, who was beginning to be somewhat excited.

"That is what I expected her to do," added the commander, who did not appear to be at all moved, though he could hardly fail to feel some anxiety, as the captain of the Maud indicated by changing his course that he had some object in view, and it was not difficult to decide what it was.

The commander returned to the pilot-house, still attended by the third officer. The belligerent steamer had evidently made a good calculation of her course in order to intercept the Guardian-Mother; and Captain Ringgold realized that the Maud would be very soon directly ahead of him, or in a position to make a dart into his vessel.

The Maud stopped her screw when she had attained the position which was satisfactory to her captain. Then she backed, and worked around till her bow was pointed to the west south-west, the course of the Guardian-Mother being to the west north-west. It looked as though Scoble expected the larger steamer to keep his course till it was convenient for the Maud to thrust her bow into her side.

"The idiot!" exclaimed the commander. "Is he stupid enough to suppose I cannot make out what he is driving at? Does he expect me to put my ship into position for him to sink her?"

"That seems to be what he is expecting," replied Mr. Boulong, who had come into the pilot-house a few minutes before.

"If I were disposed to do so, I could easily sink the Maud, for Scoble has arranged everything so that I could do it without the least difficulty," added the captain.

"She is starting her screw again," said the first officer. "He means to get headway enough to strike the blow when we are directly ahead of him."

"I see his plan. Hard a starboard the helm, Bangs!"

said the captain earnestly, to the astonishment of the other officers, who thought he was too proud even to have the appearance of running away from the miscreant's steamer.

The Guardian-Mother promptly swung her head round till it pointed to the west south-west, as did that of the Maud. The captain had not made this movement till his ship was within a cable's length of the Maud, so that her commander should not know what he intended to do; but as soon as she started her screw, it was quite time to do something.

It soon appeared that the chief engineer had fully obeyed the instructions of the captain as indicated by her increased speed. The ship shook under the pressure put upon her. The Maud had obtained headway enough to have driven in the steel plates of the Guardian-Mother, and in five minutes more she would have done it if her course had not been changed. It looked as though the skirmish had practically ended, for the safety of the larger steamer was insured by her superior speed.

"I knew that fellow was a villain and a pirate; but I did not suppose he was an idiot," said the commander, when he had given out the new course.

"Do you think this will be the end of this thing, captain?" asked Mr. Sharp, who was still observing the movements of the Maud.

"I am sure it will not," replied Captain Ringgold. "Scoble has evidently been looking for the Guardian-Mother ever since the repairs on his steamer were completed. Probably he learned in Nassau that we were bound to the south side of Cuba, for I made no secret of it, and he had to follow us to this part of the world. No doubt he looked in at Guantanamo, Santiago, and has been to Cienfuegos. Perhaps he obtained the shipping news at this port, and ascertained that we were at Santiago, and has come out in search of us."

"That looks clear enough," added Mr. Boulong. "I wonder how long she will chase us after her experience off the Bermudas."

"I have no doubt we can outsail him. Mr. Scarbury, whom we left at Nassau, said she never made over fourteen knots an hour, and could not always do even that. She ought to be satisfied in a few hours that we can run away from her," replied the captain.

"What's the matter?" demanded Louis, rushing into the pilot-house at this time.

"Nothing the matter, Sir Louis," replied the captain with a smiling face.

"What's the trouble, Captain Ringgold?" demanded Uncle Moses, appearing at the door of the pilot-house a moment later.

"No trouble, Squire Scarburn; we are still on the top of the water. If you will take the trouble to look out over the stern of the steamer, you will see the Maud chasing us with all the speed she can get up. We have had a skirmish on the Caribbean Sea, for she is trying to make a hole in our side, as we did in hers in a good cause; but we have got the weather gage of her, and we are all right for the present, though we are likely to try it over again at no distant time."

"But the steamer is shaking like a man with the palsy," said Louis.

"Because we are driving her just now, in order to leave the Maud out in the cold, if there is any cold in this region," the captain explained.

The Guardian-Mother proved herself to be the faster steamer for the second time, and in four hours the Maud abandoned the chase, laying her course for the west north-west, very much to the satisfaction of the ladies, who had learned about the skirmish.

"That means that she will try it over again off the entrance to the bay of Cienfuegos," said the captain, as he ordered the course to be changed to the north-west.

At noon the lighthouse at the entrance of the harbor was made out.

CHAPTER XXXIII

A FRIENDLY SPANISH CRUISER

THE Guardian-Mother had gone about eight miles farther to the west south-west than the Maud, so the latter had the "inside track" in the run to the light-house on Colorados Point, and those in the pilot-house of the former discovered the "pirate," as all of them called her, several miles from the shore. Coming up by the course the steamer had followed from Santiago was a white cruiser, hardly larger than the Guardian-Mother, and about five or six miles distant. Perhaps she was the one the party had seen at the ancient capital.

Mr. Gaskette had made the acquaintance of some of the officers of the cruiser at Santiago, and at the suggestion of the captain had given them a dinner on board of the steamer, at which the commander presided; and he found that two or three of them could speak English, including the captain of the man-of-war.

The Maud had stopped her screw, and appeared to be lying in wait for the Guardian-Mother. From what he had seen of Scoble, Captain Ringgold concluded that he was still intent upon retaliation for the hole made in the side of his vessel, and he insisted upon giving it in kind with the injury done to his craft. For the time being he seemed to forget that Mrs. Belgrave was on board of the object of his vengeance, or he had abandoned his attempt to effect a reconciliation.

The black smoke was pouring out of the smoke stack of his steamer, and he was evidently prepared to carry out his desperate purpose. When the Guardian-Mother was within a mile of her, the Maud started her screw and steamed at her best speed towards her. All the passengers of the doomed vessel, as the pirate evidently regarded her, were on deck, wishing to see the coast as the ship approached it. They had been present at one collision, and did not consider it a very serious affair as the commander managed it. They had been assured that the steamer would come out of it all right. They were considerably excited, but not very much alarmed.

"It goes against my grain to run away from the pirate, and if I had not so many precious lives in my care, I would fight it out with him," said Captain Ringgold, who was in the pilot-house. "During the war I saw some of this sort of play, and I think I could put the Maud a thousand fathoms under water, for I should hit her less tenderly than off the coast of the Bermudas."

"I can hardly conceive of a more reckless fellow than that Scoble," added Mr. Boulong. "He entirely ignores the fact that he was the aggressor in the affair

at the Bermudas, and that he had kidnapped and was
actually carrying off the owner of this steamer. He
acts as though he had not been guilty of an illegal
and outrageous act."

"He is a pirate at heart, if he has any heart or
soul, and I am determined not to be molested again
by him, even if I have to send him and his piratical
craft to the bottom," continued the commander.
"When we met him this morning, I was determined
to do his vessel no injury; but I am inclined to
believe now that is not the best policy."

"She is headed so as to strike the ship directly in
her stem," said Mr. Sharp.

"If he would hit us there, I think I should be willing to let him try it on, for I think the Maud was
very cheaply built from what I saw when we cut into
her; and our steel bow could resist a pretty smart
blow."

"He is putting his helm to port," added Mr.
Boulong.

"He sees that he is more likely to hurt himself
than us if he strikes the ship in the bow," replied the
captain.

Louis and Felix were on the lookout with the rest
of the denizens of the cabin, and they were greatly
excited; but the commander requested the owner not
to come into the pilot-house, and not to speak to him,
for he must give his entire attention to the affair in
hand. All the ship's company were on deck where
they had been called for any duty that might be
required of them.

"Port the helm, Twist!" said the captain sharply, as soon as he had made out the purpose of the enemy.

"Port, sir," repeated the quartermaster; and the steamer answered her helm as promptly as usual.

The result of this change was that the two steamers were pointed directly towards each other, and if they came together each would strike the stem of the other. This did not suit the captain of the Maud, and he changed his course again. Captain Ringgold followed his example, and the two vessels were again pointed towards the bow of the other. Then the Maud stopped her screw in order to prevent an undesirable collision under the conditions to which her commander was utterly opposed. It was his purpose to strike the Guardian-Mother on her broadside.

Captain Ringgold again followed the example of the pirate; but a little later he rang to back her, and she was soon going astern at the rate of six knots an hour. Scoble started his propellor again, going ahead. The engine of the larger was reversed, and the two were again approaching each other. For half an hour they faced each other.

The Spanish cruiser had come within half a mile of the steamers, and had stopped her screw to observe the manœuvres. Evidently her officers did not know what to make of the menacing attitude in which they faced each other, and they could hardly know which was the aggressor. Captain Ringgold decided that they should know, and he backed the steamer till she was a mile from her enemy. Then, with full steam

on, he suddenly came about, and stood off to the southward.   The Maud attempted to follow her.

"The officers of that cruiser will soon know which
is the one that means mischief, and which is the one
that desires to avoid it," said the commander.

"It is a plain case to them now," replied Mr.
Boulong.

Captain Ringgold was tired and disgusted with this
idle skirmishing, and he saw that he was likely to
be kept there all day.   At the end of an hour the
superior sailing of his ship had put a couple of miles
between the two vessels, and he again laid his course
for the lighthouse.   But the Maud immediately
headed her bow to the west; and as she was two
miles farther in shore, she was sure to intercept the
Guardian-Mother, with the probability that the same
manœuvres would be repeated.

The Spanish cruiser manifested a great deal of
interest in the affair and had started her propellor as
soon as the larger steamer headed to the south.   She
was now following the Maud, and gaining rapidly upon
her.   As Captain Ringgold anticipated, the two vessels were soon confronting each other, bow to bow,
for he would not expose his broadside to the blow of
the enemy.

Scoble undertook a new manœuvre, for he came
about so that his broadside was fairly exposed to his
enemy, evidently for the purpose of tempting the
Guardian-Mother to move towards her, and afford him
the opportunity to strike the blow where he desired

to give it. Captain Ringgold declined to avail himself of this opportunity, and began to back away from the Maud again. When he was not more than a quarter of a mile from the enemy, he rounded to, and presented the chance to the pirate for which he had been seeking all the morning.

This change in the tactics of the commander was made for the benefit of the cruiser, to enable her officers to understand the intentions of the Maud. Scoble evidently believed, when he saw this inviting position of the Guardian-Mother, that his moment for action had come, and he started his screw, driving her at his utmost speed. Captain Ringgold had time enough to come about, and he was about to do so, when a cloud of smoke rose from the bow of the Spanish man-of-war, and the report of one of her guns broke the stillness of the hour. It was followed by another report, and a shot was seen to drop into the water ahead of the Maud.

The cannon shot, which must have whizzed near enough to the bow of the Maud to be heard by Scoble in the pilot-house, evidently produced an impression on his mind, if the smoke and noise did not, for he immediately rang his bell to stop her.

"The cruiser has decided to take a hand in this game," said Captain Ringgold.

"That is the cruiser we saw at Santiago, and with whose officers we dined in the cabin," added Mr. Boulong.

"I am very much obliged to my friend her captain

for interfering, though I think I could have managed the affair myself," added the commander, as he passed out to the lookout to assure the party that there would be no further trouble.

The cruiser ran up within hailing distance of the Maud, and one of the officers who spoke English announced that she would fire into her as a pirate if she made any further attempt to collide with the Guardian-Mother, which had come out again, and was heading for the port of her destination. As she passed the man-of-war, the colors were dipped, and the ship's company responded with three rousing cheers, when the salute was returned. The cruiser followed her, and the Maud brought up the rear, which seemed to prove that Scoble intended to seek another opportunity to wreak his vengeance.

Pilots were obtained off the light, and the cruiser followed the Guardian-Mother to her anchorage, and secured a position within half a cable's length of her. The Maud did not appear till an hour later. The anchor had hardly touched the bottom before a tug boat was observed approaching the steamer. The gangway was promptly rigged out, and all the party were absolutely astonished when they saw Mr. Woolridge himself step down from the rail.

Very earnestly, and with a very smiling face, he grasped the hand of Captain Ringgold, and then of Louis who was at his side. He was conducted to the boudoir, where he was very cordially received by Mrs. Belgrave and Uncle Moses, and where he was introduced to those whom he had not met before.

"This is a very unexpected pleasure, Mr. Woolridge," said the commander, as they seated themselves in the boudoir.

"I received your telegraphic despatch from Santiago, Captain Ringgold, and I was greatly surprised to learn that this miserable Scoble was pursuing you in these waters," replied Mr. Woolridge.

"I could not tell you the whole story in a telegram; but this very morning he has done his utmost to drive the bow of his steamer into the side of the Guardian-Mother;" and he proceeded to relate the particulars of the kidnapping of Louis, the manner in which he had recovered him, and the two skirmishes he had had with the Maud in the Caribbean Sea. "I hope you have been able to obtain a requisition for the arrest of this pirate, Mr. Woolridge."

"I have, and two officers from New York came off with me in the tug, as well as three Cuban officials," replied the magnate from the North. "The warrant for his arrest was already out, and I knew just where to put my hand upon it. The Governor of the State, who is a friend of mine, happened to be in the city, and I produced all the necessary evidence before him, for Scoble's robbery of the pools and stakes was so notorious that there was no difficulty in my way. The police department of the city promptly detailed the officers for this duty. Then I took it into my head to come down here and see that the business was properly done; and I am very extensively acquainted in the island, for I have some heavy investments here."

"I am very glad you came; and you have certainly done your part very expeditiously," added the commander.

"By the aid of my influential Spanish friends in Havana, to which we came by the way of Tampa, I obtained an interview with the Captain-General, who is all-powerful here, and my business was hurried through without any delay; but we arrived here by the train from Havana only last evening. Now, where is Scoble?"

"The Maud is just coming into the harbor," said Louis.

The commander was happier than he had been for a month.

CHAPTER XXXIV

THE END OF JOHN SCOBLE'S CAREER

AT this stage of the proceedings on board of the Guardian-Mother a boat from the Spanish corvette came alongside, in charge of one of her English-speaking officers. He was received on board at the gangway by the commander and treated with the "most distinguished consideration." The captain of the cruiser desired an explanation of the extraordinary scene he had witnessed in Spanish waters, and he extended a very polite invitation to him to visit the commander on board his ship.

Captain Ringgold promptly accepted the invitation, and proceeded at once in the barge, fully manned, taking Louis with him. The captain of the man-of-war, having met him before, received him with the greatest courtesy, which was also extended to the youthful owner. They were invited to the cabin, where the commander of the cruiser, Captain La Cadeña, desired an explanation of what he had seen from the deck of his ship.

Captain Ringgold related as much as was necessary of the history of the Belgrave family, of the kidnapping of the owner, and the previous skirmish at sea.

He gave a full account of Scoble, and finished by informing him that officers had arrived the night before from Havana to arrest the commander of the Maud, and convey him to New York to answer for his crimes.

"I congratulate you, Captain Ringgold, on the skill with which you have managed your affair; and I tender you the services of my ship's company in making the arrest," said Captain La Cadeña. "I will see that the Maud does not leave the harbor."

"I thank you, Captain. The Cuban officials are on board of the Guardian-Mother; and if they need assistance doubtless they will call upon you, for the Captain-General has already acted on this case," replied Captain Ringgold, as he took his leave after the captain had invited him to dine on board of his ship.

The Maud had anchored not very near the Guardian-Mother, for Scoble evidently did not like the neighborhood of the man-of-war. During the absence of the commander and Louis, Mrs. Belgrave had explained to Mr. Woolridge all the details of the voyage. It was decided that the arrest of the pirate should be made at once, and the Spanish and American officers went on board of the tug.

The Cuban officer who had charge of the business said that he must have at least two persons who could identify their prisoner, and Mr. Woolridge, the captain, and Louis were to join the party for this purpose. The tug started for the Maud, which had anchored by this time, and was soon alongside of her. The application of the officer in command to be admitted on board was denied by Scoble in person. The official replied in English that he came in the name of the law, and that he should go on board whether the captain was willing or not.

"What do you want on board of my vessel ?" demanded Scoble.

"I will inform you when I reach the deck of your ship," replied the official.

"Then you will never reach the deck !" exclaimed Scoble with a volley of oaths.

"She is weighing her anchor," said Captain Ring-gold. "He has a suspicion as to the meaning of this visit. But there comes the corvette; and she has got up her anchor in short metre."

The man-of-war was moving to the scene of action, and long before the captain of the Maud could get his anchor out of the mud, she was alongside. The officer of the law made a formal demand upon Captain La Cadeña for assistance, and in three minutes more a dozen sailors and a file of marines dropped down upon her, and were in possession of the disputed deck. The crew of the Maud were heaving away at the cap-stan, while Scoble remained at the gangway.

The officers from the tug came on board when the Spanish sailors had rigged out the gangway. The captain of the pirate had been crowded to one side, for the officers of the law did not know their intended prisoner.

"What do you want on board of my vessel?" demanded Scoble, when all the officials had gained a footing on the deck.

"Who are you?" demanded Captain Ortiz, the chief official.

"I am Captain John Scoble, the commander of this steamer! I demand the reason of this outrage!" replied the embezzler.

"John Scoble!" exclaimed Captain Ortiz, as he consulted a document he took from his pocket. "Then, you are the man I want, and you are my prisoner."

"Your prisoner!" exclaimed Scoble, and he looked a shade paler than usual, though he tried to laugh a moment later. "I suppose I am to be arrested for fooling with that steamer yonder."

"What does he mean by fooling?" asked the officer of one of the Americans at his side.

"He means joking, playing," replied the New Yorker.

"The captain of that steamer over there did the same thing with me, for he actually run into my ship, and stove a hole in her side," continued Scoble, as the trio from the Guardian-Mother came upon the deck. "I will show you just where the new plates were put in at Bermuda after he had made a hole in my vessel."

"I know nothing about that matter," replied Captain Ortiz. "I arrest you on a requisition from the American government on the charge of robbery, stealing, embezzling the sum of sixty or seventy thousand dollars at a race course."

Scoble's head sank so that his eyes were fixed on the planks of the deck. He was plainly overcome by the charge; but in a few minutes he rallied and fixed his gaze upon Captain Ringgold.

"I suppose that I owe all this to you!" he exclaimed bitterly.

"I am happy to inform you that you do. When I realized that the Guardian-Mother and her owner were to be pursued by you, and annoyed to the extent of your capacity, I decided to put an end to your infamous career."

"You fight the battle of that whelp of iniquity for him, or I should have made a decent young man of him before this time," added the pirate captain, as he glanced at Louis, who would say nothing to irritate him.

"You will have ten years of solitude and seclusion to make a decent man of yourself before you attend to Mr. Belgrave's case," said the commander of the Guardian-Mother.

"But where is my wife? Why did you not bring her with you to witness my humiliation?" asked Scoble, who seemed to be rapidly breaking down before the accumulation of miseries that beset him.

"I think your wife is in Cienfuegos, where her uncle has an elegant residence," replied the captain.

"Maud? An uncle?"

"I do not mean Maud, but Ruth, your veritable

"TWO OF THE CUBAN OFFICERS SEIZED HIM."   Page 303.

wife, who was Ruth Hastings, of Aldenham, England."

"What do you mean by that ? " demanded Scoble, so far overcome that he had to seat himself on a step at the door.   "I thought Ruth was dead."

"But you deserted her, as you did the army, and you never took the trouble to find out whether she was dead or living. Your marriage to Maud Belgrave was a fraud, doubly illegal as we find now."

Captain Ortiz did not appear to be interested in all this talk, and he approached his prisoner with a pair of handcuffs. The wretch sprang to his feet, and recoiled at the sight of the manacles. Two of the Cuban officers seized him each by an arm, and the irons were applied in another moment in spite of his struggles. Scoble was in the hands of the law, as he ought to have been more than two years before; but justice had overtaken him at last because he had neglected his opportunity to become a decent man, if not an honest one.

"This is an outrage !" groaned he, reviving from his dejection. "I am not a criminal ! I am a wealthy man, worth a million, and I am voyaging over the world in my own steam-yacht."

"That is all very well, but I shall have to commit you to a prison in the city till the American officers are ready to convey you to New York. Take him on board of the tug !" said the chief official.

He was permitted to take his trunk with him. He desired to know what was to become of the Maud ;

but the officials knew nothing about that, and declined to answer the question. As soon as he was on board with his baggage, the tug left for the shore. The commander of the cruiser sent Captain Ringgold and his companions to the ship in her boat.

Mr. Sharp had landed in a shore boat as soon as the steamer had let go her anchor, and knew nothing of the disaster which had overwhelmed the captain of the Maud. He went to the American consul in the city, and soon obtained information in regard to Mr. Hastings, the uncle of Mrs. Scoble.

"But he died about a month ago," said the consul. "It is understood in the city that he left his immense fortune mainly to his niece, who came out to him about three months ago."

Mr. Sharp took a carriage and proceeded to the late residence of the English Don Philip, as he was called. It was an elegant mansion in Spanish style, and he was seated in a richly furnished apartment to wait for the signora. In a short time she appeared, dressed in deep mourning. She was still handsome, and her expression was kindly and very pleasing.

"I have taken the liberty to call upon you, Mrs. Scoble, on the part of a lady who was known by the assumed name of your husband," the visitor began, thinking it best to proceed to business at once.

"I never knew that he had an assumed name," replied the lady, much embarrassed when she found that the call related to her husband.

"He called himself Wade Farrongate in America,

and under that name he married a most estimable lady, who is now on board of a steamer in the harbor of this city."

"Married a lady!" gasped Mrs. Scoble.

"I am sorry to say, Mrs. Scoble, that your husband was a villain, a swindler, and an embezzler. He inherited the fortune of his brother in Bermuda, calls himself a millionaire, and has a steam-yacht."

"He must be a villain if he married another woman," added the lady, wiping the tears from her eyes.

Mr. Sharp proceeded to relate the history of her husband from the time of his desertion from the army; and no one knew it better. She listened with the most intense interest, weeping and sobbing at times. He told her about the missing million, and his persecution of his wife's son, bringing the narrative down to that very day, so far as he knew it.

"I have neglected to mention the most important fact of the whole, which is that John Scoble is now on board of his steam-yacht the Maud, named after the lady he married last," added Mr. Sharp.

"I will not see him if he married another woman!" exclaimed the lady, springing to her feet, and weeping bitterly.

Possibly she might have forgiven his crimes, but she could not his infidelity. She expressed a desire to see the lady who had been known as Mrs. Farrongate, and the third officer promised to consult her about it, and call again with her answer in the afternoon. On board of the steamer he learned that Scoble was committed to the prison, and that the American officers would leave with him on the train the next morning for Havana.

Mrs. Belgrave was happy now, exceedingly happy, for she realized that the persecutor of her son had been deprived of the ability to do him any further harm. She was willing to see Mrs. Scoble, and would receive her on board of the steamer. Mr. Sharp conveyed the reply to that lady, and informed her that her husband would probably spend the next ten years of his life in the State prison, and that he was in prison and in irons then. He conducted the lady to the ship, and presented her to the owner's mother. They retired to her stateroom, and what passed between them was not revealed. Both had been deceived, and they became good friends on the moment. She was presented to all the party, and invited them to her residence.

CHAPTER XXXV

THE COMMANDER OF THE VIKING

WHILE Mrs. Scoble was on board of the Guardian-Mother she asked for and obtained an interview with Captain Ringgold. For several months she had been in a strange land where she could not even speak the language ; but she had been so busy in the care of her uncle that she had had no time to notice the absence of friends. The planter's business man was a lawyer, and had proved to be a very honest person. He had managed all her affairs, and she had already informed him that she did not intend to remain in Cuba.

While the lady was on board, one of the American officers came off to the ship with the request that Louis Belgrave should visit Scoble in his prison. The messenger also said that he had promised to find Mrs. Scoble, of whose presence in Cienfuegos the prisoner had been informed, and to request her to go and see him.

"Rather strange requests, both of them," said the commander. "Is there any danger to Mr. Belgrave if he should go into the presence of this man ? "

"Not the least in the world," replied the officer. " He is kept in irons, and he could not harm any one if he desired to do so, which I don't think he does, for he seems to have entirely broken down."

"I don't wonder at that, for it is a tremendous contrast between his condition to-day and what it has been for the last three months," added Captain Ringgold. "But he is an unmitigated villain, and lately he has been at work to obtain his revenge for the mishaps he has brought upon himself. What do you say, Mr. Belgrave?"

"I don't object to seeing him, and I am not afraid of him," replied Louis.

"It is possible that he has some important communication to make to you, and it will do no harm to see him. As to Mrs. Scoble, she must consult her own feelings."

The lady decided to comply with the request of her husband, and the party, including the commander, went on shore in the barge. Louis was the first to see the prisoner, and he was impressed by the change which had come over him in a few hours.

"You see to what you have reduced me, Louis," Scoble began, in a broken tone, as he sat on his bench with his wrists manacled behind him.

"I do not wish to say anything harsh to you, Captain Scoble; but it seems to me you have reduced yourself to this condition," replied the visitor in gentle tones.

"Where is your mother?" demanded the prisoner, suddenly changing the subject of the conversation.

"She is on board of the Guardian-Mother."

"Is she coming to see me?"

"She did not say that she was."

"Has she no pity at all for me? Louis, you can do anything with her; and I implore you to induce her to come and see me. In my present distress you cannot refuse to grant me this favor. I feel that I am already convicted, and sentenced for ten years. With health and an abundant fortune, I shall be the occupant of a prison cell. You will never see me again, and I want you to look upon me as a dying man, and I hope you will grant my last request."

"Why do you wish to see my mother?" asked Louis, who could not but pity the fallen man.

"How can you ask such a question?" demanded Scoble, with some of the dramatic energy he had used on occasions. "She was my wife!"

"Excuse me, Captain Scoble, but she was never your wife, only your victim. Your only legal wife is waiting to see you in the guard-room of the prison," replied Louis rather warmly.

"Your mother can save me from the fate to which you have doomed me," groaned the prisoner, when he saw that he had made no impression on his visitor.

"She could not save you if she would. You have doomed yourself, and no one else has had any hand in it. You have relentlessly pursued me and my mother for months. Because my mother would not be reconciled to you, a step against which her whole soul revolted, you have let loose the vials of your wrath upon me. If I had submitted to your will and pleasure, at the sacrifice of my mother's peace and happiness, I have no doubt you would have ceased to persecute me, at least till you found an opportunity to get rid of me," replied Louis, somewhat aroused by the words of Scoble.

"A few words from your mother would release me," pleaded he.

"They shall never be spoken," said Louis firmly.

"As to Ringgold, I shall hate him to my dying day."

"Simply because he has been the protector of myself and my mother."

"But be a Christian, Louis!"

"A strange appeal from you; but this interview has been long enough," added Louis; and as soon as he said the words, the door of the cell opened, for the officers had been looking through the grated window at him all the time.

Mrs. Scoble was next admitted to his presence. He appealed to her as he had to his last visitor, but she only replied by reproaching him for his desertion and infidelity. She was evidently as disgusted with him as she who had borne the name of Farrongate. She retired leaving the prisoner in utter despondency in regard to his immediate fate. The next morning the officers conveyed him to Havana by train, and to New York by steamer, where he was convicted and sentenced to ten years.

Mrs. Scoble had become quite interested in the party on board of the steamer, and the next day they all visited her in her elegant mansion. On the following day she conducted them to her uncle's plantation, where they had a fine opportunity to observe the process of raising the cane and manufacturing sugar. On the following days they visited all the objects of interest in Cienfuegos, which is quite a modern and progressive city compared with Santiago. With the aid of the lady's business man the gentlemen of the company obtained admission to one of the Spanish clubs and to the Chinese club, which is an unique establishment, highly creditable to the civilization and taste of the Orientals of the city.

Two weeks were very pleasantly passed away at Cienfuegos, and the ship was ready to sail for Havana, where the voyagers intended to spend at least a month, especially as the principals of the party were now delivered from the persecution of John Scoble. During this time the Maud had lain at her anchor in the port, and no disposition had been made of her. On the morning of the day the Guardian-Mother was to sail, Louis Belgrave was surprised to receive a visit from Wilson Frinks, who had been the second officer of the Maud.

"Ah, my blooming bantam, I am very glad to see you again," said he, as he rushed up to Louis with extended hand, which the young millionaire did not accept. "You have not been very friendly or neighborly of late, for you have never taken the trouble to call upon me on board of the Viking, and I was not permitted to put my feet on the deck of this steamer."

"What do you call your steamer?" asked Louis indifferently.

"The Viking; that is her lawful and proper name, and the word 'Maud' was put upon it," replied the mate. "Now the steamer has come into the possession of Captain Scoble's wife, as she turns out to be, and she insists that the true name shall be restored to her."

"It was a piece of impudence on the part of Scoble to change her name; but he never made anything by it," added Louis.

"You have come out at the head of the heap, my jolly bantam, and I congratulate you, for you have beaten Captain Scoble at every point."

"Why should you congratulate me when you did everything you could to aid him in carrying out his plans?" demanded Louis, rather sternly for him.

"I worked for my money, and I got it."

"Then, I suppose you are quite satisfied."

"No, I am not. They say that you and your mother are very thick with Mrs. Scoble, and I have come to ask a little help of you," continued Frinks, suddenly assuming a more humble attitude. "When the Viking came out to Bermuda, Scarbury expected to be captain of her; but Scoble took that place himself, and made him first officer. I was made second officer when I expected to be the first, though I have been chief mate since Scarbury deserted."

"I should say you would answer Scoble's purpose better than Scarbury, for he is an honest man," said Louis.

"Which is as much as to say that I am not an honest man," added Frinks with a smile.

"I do not so regard you," replied the young man bluntly.   "But what is your business with me?"

"I wish you and your worthy mother to speak a word to Mrs. Scoble in favor of her giving me the command of the Viking, for she purposes to discharge me."

"A wise proceeding on her part."

"Then, I have nothing to hope for on your part or your mother's?" demanded Frinks.

"Certainly not; you have cheek enough to fit out a herd of elephants. You have been Scoble's right-hand man, and it was you who deceived and enticed me on board of the schooner, and helped him to retain my mother as a prisoner. Aside from all personal feeling, neither my mother nor myself could recom-mend such a person as you are for any position."

"Just as you like, little bantam," replied the late mate, shrugging his shoulders.

"You can take your leave with all possible haste," said Captain Ringgold, stepping out of the boudoir, where he had heard most of the conversation. for he distrusted the visitor quite as much as did the owner.

Frinks went over the side to the shore boat in which he had come off.

"That man is the counterpart of Scoble, for he does not appear to understand that he is accountable for his misdeeds, and asks you and your mother to assist him to a position for which he is not qualified at all, just as though he had never done you an ill turn," said the commander as soon as Frinks had departed. "Perhaps I know something more about this matter than he does."

"Mrs. Scoble seems to trust you as a friend, Captain," added Louis.

"She is almost alone in a strange land, and she has called upon me for advice. Her business man has caused it to be settled that she has the best right to the steam-yacht of her husband, though he failed to do anything to dispose of her. I recommended her to discharge this Frinks at once, and she will do so."

"Does she mean to keep the Viking here?"

"Not at all; she desires to visit her friend Mrs. Bondleigh at Crooked Island, and Mr. Crandall at Nassau, in her."

"It will be difficult for her to find a commander out here," suggested Louis.

"She has found one already," replied the commander with a smile: "one whom I recommended to her."

"One of your officers?" asked Louis, opening his eyes. "Surely, you would not part with Mr. Boulong?"

"By no means. When I engaged Mr. Sharp as a quartermaster, I did so because he had been a detective for twenty years, and I needed his services in that capacity to work up this case of Mrs. Scoble; and he has done it in a most admirable manner. When I made him third officer, it was to give him more time and opportunity to manage his case, for I had no real need of such an officer. For the last two weeks he has been quite intimate with Mrs. Scoble, and her husband may thank him more than any one else that she would have nothing more to do with him. In a word, Louis, I recommended Mr. Sharp as the commander of the Viking, and he has already received and accepted the appointment. He is a competent seaman and navigator."

"What will she do with her plantation?"

"Her business man will continue to manage it as he has for several years; but her city residence will be sold. I believe we have finished up all our business in Cienfuegos, and we will sail for Havana this afternoon," said Captain Ringgold.

"We don't seem to be seeing much of the interior of the island," suggested Louis, as he looked towards the wharves of the city.

"Even so magnificent a steamer as the Guardian-Mother is not exactly adapted to travelling on shore; but you can visit as much of the interior as you wish from Havana," replied the commander.

"You have noticed that white steamer yonder. I learned on shore that she leaves for Batabano to-night, and connects with a train across the island to Havana. I should like to go in her just for a change, and to see how the Cubans manage things," continued Louis.

"Now that Scoble is off the track, engine and cars, there is nothing in the world to prevent you from doing so, if your mother consents; and perhaps she will desire to go with you," replied the captain.

Mrs. Belgrave preferred the steamer, and consented that Louis should take the trip with Felix McGavonty. None of the others of the party wished to join him, and he went on shore when the Guardian-Mother was ready to depart.

CHAPTER XXXVI

HAVANA AND THE NORTH COAST

Mrs. Scoble and Signor Fonseca, her business man, had gone on board of the Guardian-Mother to take leave of the party in a boat from the Viking, and she invited Louis and Felix to visit her yacht, and return to the shore with them. The Cuban gentleman informed them that it was not necessary to secure staterooms or buy tickets for the trip on the José Garcias, and they went to her residence to dinner. Captain Sharp was present, and he seemed to be on excellent terms with the lady.

When the young travellers went on board of the steamboat they found she was precisely like a New York craft of the same class, in the interior as well as the exterior, only there was not a word of English spoken on board of her. A steward showed them to their stateroom; but the berths and bedding did not compare with those of the steamers in the United States. It was late in the evening, and there was nothing to be seen, and they turned in at once.

The next morning, when they went on deck, they found that the José Garcias was threading her way

among reefs, shoals, and islands. The bottom could
be seen all the time, and the water was almost as
clear as at Nassau. The course was inside of the
Isle of Pines, which lies about fifty miles off the
coast. In the middle of the forenoon the table was
prepared for "el almuerzo," or the breakfast, and the
young Americans took their places with the rest of
the passengers, all of whom appeared to be Cubans,
including a few very pretty ladies. The meal was a
very elaborate affair, with roasts of various meats, as
well as a great assortment of made dishes; and there
the incense of garlic rising from the board.

"Is that *olla podrida?*" asked Louis in Spanish of
gentleman next to him who was serving himself
a side dish of pottery ware.

"*calao,*" replied the Cuban with a smile.

"*alao,*" repeated Felix, who had heard the reply.

"hat mean pork and beans, or praties in a

"It means neither. The word is the Spanish for
salt fish; of the cooking I know nothing; but I will
try it."

The dish contained salt fish in hard squares rather
thick, with a sauce in which were potatoes, tomatoes,
cubes of bread, and other ingredients which the travellers could not make out. Louis thought it was not
bad, but Felix was of the contrary opinion. With
the roasts and fruits in great variety they made a
very good meal. No one came to collect a *peso,* or
dollar, for it, and Louis learned that the meals were

included in the fare, as was also the price of the "tipples " for those who ordered them.

One of the stewards had come to the Americans, and conducted them to a table at which the purser was seated. A pile of gold pieces in front of him indicated that his business was the collection of the fares. The sum required was nine dollars, or nearly double the price from New York to Boston.

" Faix, my darlint, ye's know the money of this haythen raygion," said Felix when his companion had paid the two passages.

" Don't you know it yet ? "

" Not a bit of it. I bought an orange in Fergus, and I let the woman take what she loiked. She gave me back a lot of tin-cint pieces wid holes punched in them, and some dirty rags of paper."

" Probably they punch the ten-cent pieces to keep them here. The paper money is at a big discount. A cent here is a *centavo*, and there are silver pieces corresponding in nominal value to our quarter and half dollar."

At Batabano, which Louis took pains to inform his companion was pronounced with the accent on the last syllable, the passengers were landed, and each purchased his own railroad ticket for Havana. The young Americans secured good places, and for the next two hours they were hurried across the island at very good speed. The conductor came to them with a cigar in his mouth, for everybody smokes in Cuba. They passed no towns of any importance, but

the view was delightful to them from the window of
the car, for they were going through fields of sugar-
cane, pineapples, and other tropical crops, as well as
through groves of cocoanuts, oranges, lemons, sapodil-
las, and many other plants and trees of which they
did not even know the names as they looked at them.

"I should say that we were getting near Havana
by the looks," said Louis. "The country is more
hickly settled, and the houses are finer."

He had hardly made the remark before the train
ıpped, and was boarded by several runners for the
els in the city. They spoke English enough
lischarge their duties. They addressed all the
ıngers, but they were not importunate, and said
ıre when any one indicated where he wished to

ıel Pasaje," said Louis when the right man
presented himself, and the runner took possession of
the baggage.

The Bay of Havana, with a rather narrow entrance
from the Gulf of Mexico, separates the city from
Regla, the terminus of the railroad. The boys followed the guide who carried the valises, and when
they stepped from the car, they could readily have
believed that they were on a Brooklyn wharf ready
to cross the ferry to New York, the surroundings
were so much like those at home. The steamer was
the counterpart of those seen in all the large cities
where ferries are used.

They crossed the bay, and were landed at the

Muelle de Luz. The guide put them into a carriage, a sort of victoria, and they were driven through narrow streets to the hotel. They did not see any costumes of Spain, as the pictures led them to suppose they might, but everything in the vicinity of the hotel looked very much like any large city at home. They were shown to a room by a servant who spoke a little English, but when the guests went beyond his *rôle*, he could do nothing. The hotel was well filled with Americans, for a boat from Tampa had just arrived.

"When will the Guardian-Mother arrive, Louis ? " asked Felix, when they reached their room.

"The captain said the voyage would require forty-eight hours ; and she will be here about four to-morrow afternoon."

" Then we have time enough to see the city before she arrives," added Felix, as he proceeded to take a survey of the apartment, which was hardly different from similar ones at home.

Leaving the hotel, they crossed the street to the narrow park in front of it and walked till they came to Central Park, which is quite a different affair from the one of that name in New York, for it is comparatively a very small enclosure ; but it is adorned with fountains and statues, and is handsomely laid out with trees and flowers. The various structures were like those to which the observers were accustomed. All the principal hotels were near Central Park, and they all looked very comfortable without being very attractive in architecture.

They went to dinner at six o'clock. The tables
were all in the grand apartment which occupies the
lower floor, and which also contains the office and
bureau of information, at both of which English was
spoken for all practical purposes. The bill of fare
was varied enough, and the first word Felix saw was
"bacalao;" but there was a great variety of fresh
ish, which was fresh in truth, for the finny tribes are
ıld in the market only when they are "alive and
 ıking." The dinner, as a whole, was very good.

The young Americans were on their feet at an
y hour, and, calling a carriage, drove to the Tacon
ret. They examined the food on sale there,
ially the fish and the fruit; but it was largely
ved by stalls for the sale of dry goods, fancy
wares, boots and shoes, hats, and almost everything
that could be thought of. The sidewalk that surrounded it was occupied by stands for pedlers' wares,
as they might be called.

At breakfast Louis declared that the *tortillas* were
the best he ever found at a hotel, and were almost as
good as the omelettes his mother made. The forenoon was occupied in a ride through the streets,
which are so narrow that *volantes* had been superseded;
and in some places in the oldest parts of the city
carriages were compelled to go down one street and
up another. They had seen just one *volante* at Santiago; but they were to see more of them before they
left the island.

Louis had some conversation with the runner who

had brought them from the train, though he spoke very little English. He told him that the Guardian-Mother would arrive that afternoon, and that a party from her would come to the Hotel Pasaje. He proposed to go on board of the ship, and asked the boys to go with him. On their arrival at the mole, they found a large collection of boats used in embarking and landing passengers.

The guide called for one of them, and they went on board of it. Over the after part of the boat three or four hoops, like those of a baggage wagon, were placed, upon which an awning was drawn to protect the passengers from the sun or the rain. It was provided with a sail which the boatman set as soon as he had rowed out from the wharf. It was hardly four o'clock, but the ship was immediately identified as she passed the Morro Castle which guards the entrance to the harbor. The port physician soon passed her, for she was from a Cuban port, and she came to anchor off the Muelle Caballeria.

As soon as the boat came near her there was a waving of handkerchiefs on the lookout when the party recognized the owner of the steamer. The gangway was immediately rigged out. As the seamen discovered Louis in the shore boat, they broke out in three cheers, which Louis acknowledged by lifting his hat.

"*Huesped distinguido !*" exclaimed Manuel, the runner, as he gazed with astonishment and admiration at the young gentleman he had conducted from the hotel.

"No, I am not a distinguished guest at all," replied Louis, laughing. "I am the owner of the ship."

As he spoke in Spanish, the guide understood him, and was still more astonished, and manifested still greater admiration. Louis led the way to the deck, which the party from the lookout had descended meet and welcome him. The voyage from Cien- had been a very pleasant one, and everybody was happy. Felix was as kindly greeted as nion, and they proceeded to give an account o p, and to comment upon what they had see.

"1 ged rooms for the party at the Hotel Pasaje, Ringgold, and Señor Linares, the propriete ve you a cordial welcome," said Louis.

"I suppos e does that to all his guests," suggested the commander.

"I think he puts some heart into his welcome, and I was told that he had been an author, and perhaps is still; at any rate, he makes you feel at home in his house," added Louis.

For the novelty of the thing the party decided to land in the shore boat, and in another hour they were at the hotel, and for a week they visited the sights of the city. At the end of this time they took the train for Matanzas in order to see more of the country than they could obtain by making the excursion in the steamer. Mr. Woolridge, who had been compelled to return to New York as a witness in Scoble's case, had given the commander a letter of introduction to a wealthy merchant in Matanzas, which is the next city in commercial importance to Havana in the island.

It is only fifty-two miles from the capital, and the view from the windows of the car was very interesting to the travellers, for the scenery ranks with the finest in the island. They were greatly pleased with the first view of the city, for its buildings are mostly of stone, which gives them a very solid appearance. They went to a hotel, and the commander found the residence of Mr. Gardner, the gentleman to whom his letter was addressed, and delivered it.

He was an American merchant, and he took the party in charge at once, inviting them all to his house. On their arrival at his residence the captain informed them that the house was built after the prevailing fashion in Spain. The visitors were ushered into a drawing-room, elegantly furnished, which opened into a large court, occupying the centre of the structure. The day was warm, and the host and his wife attended the guests to the *patio*, as the court is called.

The court was about twice as long as it was wide, and in one of the squares was a circular piece of ground, enclosed with a low wall of stone, from the middle of which grew a lofty palm, reaching above the roof of the mansion. It also contained other plants and flowers in bloom. In the centre of the other square was a marble fountain, from which the water was gushing from many openings.

A gallery extended entirely around the court on a
level with the second floor, from which opened the
doors to the chambers. Over the court, held by lines
reaching to the roof on both sides, was a canvas shade,
which could be moved about by the aid of cords passing through pulleys to the court. The ground was
vered with marble tiles. The space was provided
h easy-chairs, small tables, and other furniture to
it to its use as a place of resort in the cooler
f the day.

s the first Spanish house the party had ever
s least, the first they had entered, and they
reg with great interest. A luncheon was
serve ests in the *patio*, who were delighted
with t d with the peculiar Spanish refresh-
ments. cial mission of the company at
Matanzas it the caves of Bellamar; and
Mr. Gardner ly provided for this excursion.

At the door mansion were three *volantas*.
This vehicle is chaise with two wheels, and
a hood, or cover, and it is said to be the easiest riding
carriage in the world, though the ladies of the party
did not fully confirm this statement. The body is
hung on thorough-braces, like the old-fashioned chaise
of the Northern States; the shafts are extremely long,
and made of elastic wood. One horse is harnessed in
the shafts, and the animal is sometimes ridden by the
driver; but for longer courses than the streets of a
city an extra horse is harnessed at the side of the
other, which the driver rides.

The horses attached to the *volantas* of the party started off at a high rate of speed, and kept it up till their destination was reached. The first part was through the streets of the city and by the valley of the Yumuri. On their arrival at the caves, they were advised to remove wraps and all superfluous clothing, for the caves are extremely warm. Guides with torches conducted them through the several apartments, though the whole of this subterranean region has not yet been explored.

From the tops of the caves glittering *stalactites* hung down, some slender and attenuated, and others weighing a ton or more. They had assumed a variety of shapes, and names had been given to some of them, as "The Mantle of Columbus," "The Guardian Spirit." A sort of piano had been constructed of several of the slender *stalactites*, which gave forth a harmonious sound when struck with a stick. Some of the party who had been to the Mammoth Cave, and the caves of Luray, thought that these might be compared to them. The heat drove the visitors out before they desired to leave; and, taking the *volantas*, they returned to Matanzas, varying the route so as to take in more of the city.

The visitors were profuse in their expressions of gratitude to Mr. Gardner for his hospitality and kindness, and an excursion party was arranged for him and his family and friends on the steamer for the next day. The attentions of the Gardners were handsomely reciprocated, and they parted the best of friends.

The Guardian-Mother remained two weeks longer in the harbor of Havana, and then followed the northern shore of Cuba, passing several weeks in Cardenas, Sagua la Grande, and other ports, and reached Cape Maysa about the first of April. The steamer had been around the island, and the weather was becoming too warm to remain in the tropics. Louis had attended very closely to his studies, the doctor and the professor had fully recovered their health, and Mrs. Belgrave enjoyed every day of her life during the voyage.

The party had already voted upon the question of the future destination of the steamer, and it had been decided that the summer should be passed in the waters of Europe. The story of the cruising of the Guardian-Mother in the West Indies was finished with the end of the career of John Scoble; but the commander insisted that Sir Louis could not keep out of a story if he tried, for he was very much of the opinion of Uncle Moses that the millionaire at sixteen was very fond of adventure.

"I am inclined to think, Sir Louis, that Captain Ringgold did you an ill turn when he bunted into the Maud and gave you a chance to escape from her," said Squire Scarburn, shaking his fat sides with one of his jelly-like chuckles.

"Why so, Uncle Moses?" asked Louis.

"If you had been retained as a prisoner for a year or so, you would have been in a constant battle with Scoble, and only think what a field for adventures it might have afforded you!"

"You might have escaped to some desolate island, such as we have seen in the Bahamas, and lived a Robinson Crusoe life for a term of months or years," suggested Dr. Hawkes, with a repetition of the squire's fat chuckle.

"I am very glad Captain Ringgold rescued him from the power of that man, and I think he can get along without the adventures," added Mrs. Belgrave.

"But I have no doubt there will be plenty more adventures in the future, especially as we are going to Europe," said Louis.

"But take me wid ye's whin ye's have any more advintures, and Oi'll kape you out of hot wather," added Felix.

Louis Belgrave did not know what kind of a hero he would prove to be in the next story; but it will be revealed in "STRANGE SIGHTS ABROAD; or, A Voyage in European Waters."

YOUNG AMERICA ABROAD.

FIRST SERIES.

**A Library of Travel and Adventure in Foreign Lands. 16mo.
Illustrated by Nast, Stevens, Perkins, and others.
Per volume, $1.50.**

1. **OUTWARD BOUND;**
    Or, Young America Afloat.

2. **SHAMROCK AND THISTLE;**
    Or, Young America in Ireland and Scotland.

3. **RED CROSS;**
    Or. Young America in England and Wales.

4. **DIKES AND DITCHES;**
    Or, Young America in Holland and Belgium.

5. **PALACE AND COTTAGE;**
    Or, Young America in France and Switzerland.

6. **DOWN THE RHINE;**
    Or, Young America in Germany.

The story from its inception and through the twelve vol
ames (see *Second Series*), is a bewitching one, while the information imparted, concerning the countries of Europe and
the isles of the sea, is not only correct in every particular, but
is told in a captivating style. "Oliver Optic" will continue
to be the boy's friend, and his pleasant books will continue to
be read by thousands of American boys. What a fine holiday
present either or both series of "Young America Abroad"
would be for a young friend! It would make a little library
highly prized by the recipient, and would not be an expensive
one. — *Providence Press.*

YOUNG AMERICA ABROAD.

SECOND SERIES.

**A Library of Travel and Adventure in Foreign Lands. 16mo.
Illustrated by Nast, Stevens, Perkins, and others.
Per volume, $1.50.**

1. UP THE BALTIC;

Or, Young America in Norway, Sweden, and Denmark.

2. NORTHERN LANDS;

Or, Young America in Russia and Prussia.

3. CROSS AND CRESCENT;

Or, Young America in Turkey and Greece.

4. SUNNY SHORES;

Or, Young America in Italy and Austria.

5. VINE AND OLIVE;

Or, Young America in Spain and Portugal.

6. ISLES OF THE SEA;

Or, Young America Homeward Bound.

" Oliver Optic " is a *nom de plume* that is known and loved by almost every boy of intelligence in the land. We have seen a highly intellectual and world-weary man, a cynic whose heart was somewhat imbittered by its large experience of human nature, take up one of Oliver Optic's books and read it at a sitting, neglecting his work in yielding to the fascination of the pages. When a mature and exceedingly well-informed mind, long despoiled of all its freshness, can thus find pleasure in a book for boys, no additional words of recommendation are needed. — *Sunday Times.*

ARMY AND NAVY STORIES.

Six Volumes. Illustrated. Per vol., $1.50.

1. THE SOLDIER BOY;
> Or, Tom Somers in the Army.

2. THE SAILOR BOY;
> Or, Jack Somers in the Navy.

3. THE YOUNG LIEUTENANT;
> Or, Adventures of an Army Officer.

4. THE YANKEE MIDDY;
> Or, Adventures of a Navy Officer.

5. FIGHTING JOE;
> Or, The Fortunes of a Staff Officer.

6. BRAVE OLD SALT;
> Or, Life on the Quarter-Deck.

This series of six volumes recounts the adventures of two brothers, Tom and Jack Somers, one in the army, the other in the navy, in the great civil war. The romantic narratives of the fortunes and exploits of the brothers are thrilling in the extreme. Historical accuracy in the recital of the great events of that period is strictly followed, and the result is not only a library of entertaining volumes, but also the best history of the civil war for young people ever written.

THE TIDE-MILL STORIES

Six Volumes. Handsomely Illustrated. Per Vol., $1.25.

THE TINKHAM BROTHERS' TIDE-MILL
PHIL AND HIS FRIENDS
THE SATIN-WOOD BOX
THE LITTLE MASTER
HIS ONE FAULT
PETER BUDSTONE

"The more stories Mr. Trowbridge can write, the better for the boys of this generation. Flooded as our country is with literature of a dime-novel order, we have need of just such safe and interesting books as 'The Little Master,' 'Phil and His Friends,' 'Bound in Honor,' etc., to put into the hands of our growing boys."--*Living Church.*

"Mr. Trowbridge's humor, his fidelity to nature and story-telling power, lose nothing with years, and he stands at the head of those who are furnishing a literature for the young, clean and sweet in tone, and always of interest and value."—*The Continent.*

LEE AND SHEPARD Publishers Boston

LEE AND SHEPARD'S
☆ STAR JUVENILES

SOPHIE MAY'S "GROWN-UP" BOOKS.

Uniform Binding. All Handsomely Illustrated. $1.50.

IN OLD QUINNEBASSET.

"It does not seem an exaggerated statement to say that there is no living author of books for and about girls who portrays with more fidelity the mischievous, sparkling, winsome girl of the hearth and home in all the freshness and sweetness of early youth than does Sophie May.' In 'In Old Quinnebasset' the author sustains her reputation by taking her readers back one hundred years and introducing them to the equally charming ancestresses of this sweet type." —*Public Opinion.*

JANET, A POOR HEIRESS.

"The heroine of this story is a true girl. An imperious, fault-finding, unappreciative father alienates her love, and nearly ruins her temper. The mother knows the father is at fault, but does not dare to say so. Then comes a discovery, that she is only an adopted daughter; a forsaking of the old home; a life of strange vicissitudes; a return; a marriage under difficulties; and a discovery, that, after all, she is an heiress. The story is certainly a very attractive one." — *Chicago Interior.*

THE DOCTOR'S DAUGHTER.

"Sophie May, author of the renowned Prudy and Dotty books, has achieved another triumph in the new book with this title just issued. She has taken 'a new departure' this time, and written a new story for grown-up folks. If we are not much mistaken, the young folks will want to read it, as much as the old folks want to read the books written for the young ones. It is a splendid story for all ages." — *Lynn Semi-Weekly Recorder.*

THE ASBURY TWINS.

"The announcement of another work by this charming and popular writer will be heartily welcomed by the public. And in this sensible, fascinating story of the twin-sisters, 'Vic' and 'Van,' they have before them a genuine treat. Vic writes her story in one chapter, and Van in the next, and so on through the book. Van is frank, honest, and practical; Vic wild, venturesome, and witty; and both of them natural and winning. At home or abroad, they are true to their individuality, and see things with their own eyes. It is a fresh, delightful volume, well worthy of its gifted author." — *Boston Contributor.*

OUR HELEN.

"'Our Helen' is Sophie May's latest creation; and she is a bright, brave girl, that the young people will all like. We are pleased to meet with some old friends in the book. It is a good companion-book for the 'Doctor's Daughter,' and the two should go together. Our Helen' is a noble and unselfish girl, but with a mind and will of her own; and the contrast between her and pretty, fascinating, selfish little Sharley, is very finely drawn. Lee & Shepard publish it." — *Holyoke Transcript.*

QUINNEBASSET GIRLS.

"The story is a very attractive one, as free from the sensational and impossible as could be desired, and at the same time full of interest, and pervaded by the same bright, cheery sunshine that we find in the author's earlier books. She is to be congratulated on the success of her essay in a new field of literature, to which she will be warmly welcomed by those who know and admire her 'Prudy Books.'"

Sold by all booksellers and newsdealers, and sent by mail, postpaid on receipt of price.

LEE & SHEPARD, Publishers, Boston.